THE
GROUP

THE GROUP

SIGGE EKLUND

ITHAKA

First published in the UK by Ithaka Press
An imprint of Black & White Publishing Group
A Bonnier Books UK company

4th Floor, Victoria House,
Bloomsbury Square,
London, WC1B 4DA

Owned by Bonnier Books
Sveavägen 56, Stockholm, Sweden

Hardback – 978-1-80418-651-0
Trade Paperback – 978-1-80418-652-7
Ebook – 978-1-18041-653-4

A CIP catalogue of this book is available from the British Library.

Typeset by IDSUK (Data Connection) Ltd
Printed and bound by Clays Ltd, Elcograf S.p.A.

1 3 5 7 9 10 8 6 4 2

Every reasonable effort has been made to trace copyright holders of material
reproduced in this book, but if any have been inadvertently overlooked
the publishers would be glad to hear from them.

Ithaka Press is an imprint of Bonnier Books UK
www.bonnierbooks.co.uk

APRIL

1

Hanna is sitting at a pavement cafe amid throngs of people when she sees the group for the first time.

The digital sign on the front of the train station reads 26 degrees Celsius even though it's seven in the evening. The sun is low above the rooftops but still blazing bright.

There is a certain stillness on the square. Even the clusters of teenagers stroll around sleepily. Maybe it's the heat slowing everything down. The air is so still that the odours of cooking food, car exhaust and perfume linger in clouds.

The coffee tastes richer than in Sweden. The façades around the square are stately and richly detailed, with Arabic and Roman borders framing the tall windows. Beyond the rooftops rise tall church spires and cupolas. The buildings are so grand that she feels meaningless in their presence. It would be simple to vanish here, get lost in the alleys, dissolve into the swarms.

She has just raised a hand to order more coffee when she sees them approaching from across the square. She lowers her arm.

The first thing she notices is their faces.

One of the guys has a long, blond mane, an oval face and substantial eyebrows. The shorter guy is beautiful too, but in a more boyish way, with honey-coloured curls and narrow shoulders. The girl has dark hair in a messy bun, a high forehead; she looks like a fairy-tale creature with her large eyes and mouth.

Hanna observes them as they cross the square. Their shadows are fallen pillars across the open area.

The tall guy moves languidly, his long hair swinging back and forth over his face. He's so tanned you can't tell his lips from the rest of his skin. His arms move through the air as he speaks to the others. She studies his light-coloured clothing, which amplifies the impression of cool, clean freshness: his unbuttoned white shirt, his beige trousers and canvas shoes. The cigarette balancing between his fingers as he gesticulates.

The short guy walks beside him, listening. He seems more restless than the tall guy, a bouncing gait, a changeable face: now smiling, now serious.

The girl walks a few steps behind them, her brown legs gleaming in the sun. The way she walks is unusual but captivating; she seems to concentrate and stare down at her feet as though she's walking a tightrope.

As the group passes her table, they're so close that Hanna could reach out and touch them.

2

The next morning, she wakes early in the tiny flat she's renting, which consists of no more than one room with a kitchenette. She changes clothes several times. She doesn't quite know what the museum's dress code is.

At last she decides to play it safe with a plain white shirt and conservative black skirt.

When she arrives at the museum campus, she realises she's early. She sits down on a bench in the shade to wait. The sun is hot even though it's only eight thirty.

Everything around her is lush and green; the cherry trees are in bloom. The rain of the irrigation sprinklers glitters in the sunlight, and beyond the trees rises the huge museum.

When it's time, she stands up, crosses the great gravel courtyard, and walks through the tall glass doors.

The archivist is standing in the right-hand corner of the lobby just as they'd agreed. He is short and bearded and gives her a big smile as he offers his hand: 'Andrés.'

He praises her choice of outfit and adds that he's been wearing black since 1980. He laughs. Hanna had expected an interview but soon realises he's not interested in her background, which she appreciates. After a long monologue about the history of the archives, he spreads a map of the museum across the desk and launches into an explanation of all the functions of the various departments. He speaks rapidly, eagerly, as he points at the map. It's hard to follow his Spanish, but he's in a good mood and his eyes are bright behind his thick glasses.

When he's finished, he finally asks her a question: 'What got you interested in art?'

She apologises for her bad Spanish and tells him how she discovered Goya, and later, as a teenager, began to dream of working at the Prado one day. How she spent an entire year on her research paper and the attempt to understand the background behind the Black Paintings. He listens attentively but doesn't ask any follow-up questions. Maybe he's heard so many hypotheses about Goya that he's not particularly receptive to more.

He suggests a tour of the museum.

As soon as they step into the first gallery his manner changes; he lowers his voice, cupping his hand around his mouth, as if he were telling secrets.

She nods the whole time to show that she's listening.

He slowly leads her through the large rooms. The parquet creaks faintly as they go. Above them, the shadowless light enters through skylights. She tries to follow his anecdotes, but finds it harder and harder to concentrate because she knows they're approaching Room 67.

When they finally reach the wide entrance, they both stop.

He shows her the way with his hand and says: 'After you.'

She looks at him, hesitant. She would prefer to do this alone, but she can hardly ask him to go away.

He smiles and says: 'Now you can see if your thesis is correct.'

She smiles back – and steps inside.

The room is dim. The spotlights on the ceiling are surprisingly weak.

The artworks are larger than she had imagined, the reds and browns more intense. She stops in the centre of the room. It's hard to grasp that these are the originals.

He looks at her and says: 'It's really something, isn't it?'

She doesn't respond. She has spotted *Witches' Sabbath*.

She approaches it slowly – and stands close enough to see the brushstrokes. The lacquer gleams in the spotlight. She gazes up at the big, black devil. His horns are curved and sharp. Around him kneel the witches, their faces contorted. His yellow eyes stare into theirs. They await his instructions. Soon he will free them, soon the spell will be broken, but they must promise him something first. Hanna takes a step closer. She wants him to see her too, but he is turned away. The women bow before him, begging him to hurry. There isn't much time. Their bodies and faces are melting, and soon they will dissolve completely. But now he lifts his hand to them and tells them of the contract. They need only say the words, and they will become human.

Hanna's cheeks burn as though the painting were a bonfire. She takes another step forward so that he will feel the presence of the creature, the creature that wants to take shape, that squirms and twists inside her, that wants out, that has led her here. She takes one last step forward until her face is mere centimetres from the painting.

Then the silence is broken.

It's Andrés: 'I'm jealous.'

She opens her eyes and turns round.

He says: 'Of what you're experiencing right now. Your first time at the museum. You only get to do it once.'

6

3

She leaves through the museum's employee entrance that evening and sits down on a bench to digest all these impressions, drained and fulfilled all at once.

The crowns of the trees in the park are so large they swallow the streetlights; the narrow gravel paths branch off in the dim light. A group of teenagers goes by. She hears the crunch of the gravel and their laughter.

She would like to walk up to them, tell them about her first day of work and how it felt to see those paintings for the first time, but she stays put.

A young couple approaches in the dim light, tightly intertwined. She hears their tender whispers as they pass her bench.

She checks her reflection in her phone and wonders what she looks like in the eyes of others, what kind of signals she broadcasts. She has mixed feelings about what she sees. While she dislikes her body, her face retains more of its girlish roundness than others in their mid-twenties. She just has to dare to make use of it.

On the way home, she tries to catch the gazes of men but they're too drunk to notice anything but one another.

4

She spends six hours a day in the archive. Dark hallways, dynamited tunnels, five storeys down in the granite. Her arms ache from the repetitive motions. The white cotton gloves make her skin itch.

As an archival intern, her job is to make sure all the old illustrations, etchings and handwritten letters in the archive drawers are correctly categorised. She must be careful. Some of the old pages are brittle and look like they might crumble at the slightest provocation.

On her first day, she made it through ten drawers per hour, but after just a few days she's doubled that. Still, she's afraid of making a mistake. In the locker room she's heard horror stories of the fate of interns who accidentally harmed or mislabelled a work.

On her fifth day of work, she makes it through a seemingly endless number of drawers.

The same motion, over and over again. Andrés' favourite saying is 'Don't get *too* good' because he doesn't want her to become sloppy. This kind of meticulousness takes time. Over and over, hour after hour, the same procedure: unlock box after box and examine its contents.

It's not enough to zap each inventory number with the scanner; she must also manually check that the motif of the works matches the catalogue photographs on the iPad.

By the time she leaves work on Friday evening, she has examined hundreds of boxes without finding a single error. Everything appears to be in order. She feels very competent.

5

During her first few weeks of work, she develops a number of routines. On her way to work she buys a baguette at the neighbourhood shop and eats it on a bench in the Botanical Gardens near the museum. It's dry and hard but tastes good; she eats only half of it. At lunch she sits in a corner of the cafeteria, sneaking glances at the other interns' tables and wondering why she has such a tough time talking to them. Conversations with them turn out forced and choppy, no matter how hard she tries.

After work she always has a coffee at the café by the train station, trying to spot the group she saw that first night in Madrid. She guesses she's unlikely to run into them again, but it's still exciting to sit there and wait. For some reason she can't stop thinking about them, their beauty, their clothes, what it would be like to walk along beside them, laughing with them the way they laughed with each other.

In the evenings she tries to make her tiny flat look nice. She buys a cheap easel at an antique shop and sets it up by the window. She tries to paint, but she's too scattered. She rearranges furniture, and weeds out the ugly décor, stashing it in the cupboard. She buys two Goya posters at the museum gift shop and tacks them to the wall above her bed. She decides to buy a rug and some curtains as soon as she gets her first pay cheque. Maybe that will make this feel like a home.

6

Sometimes she stops mid-task at work, suddenly unable to breathe as she realises how far underground she is. She has to go to the staff toilets and run cold water over her wrists.

Everyone's saying this is the hottest April in a century and a half. It's extra stuffy down in the archives. Andrés has promised the air conditioning will be fixed eventually but says the budget is strained on account of the upcoming anniversary celebrations.

Even the nights are hot. The sun swells above the rooftops. On her way home from work she walks slowly to keep from sweating. Birds circle low over the square, as though they don't quite have the strength to soar high in this heat.

Everywhere she goes, she seeks out eye contact – on the street, at the grocer's – but it seems she is invisible.

She waits for a breakthrough, the moment she'll meet someone, anyone, at work or on the street, someone who will show up and be interested in her.

The loneliness is most palpable when she comes home at the end of the workday. She sits in her silent room rubbing lotion on her hands, which are dry and chapped from wearing gloves all day. The air is thick and warm. She sinks onto the sofa to have a cigarette in the close air, allowing herself a moment of self-pity as she is enveloped by the room's dullness, but then she opens the window. She does this every evening. The smoke mixes with the scent of wood the sunshine has baked out of the walls.

At last, when she's finished smoking, she throws open the balcony doors, goes to the railing, and gazes out at the rooftops.

She wants to tell someone about her longing. She's ready to throw herself into the abyss of another person. She wants to fall asleep next to a warm body, wake in the middle of the night to watch him sleeping, lean over and press an ear to his lips to hear him breathe, like the ocean breeze in a snail's shell.

7

One evening, the weather changes and a warm rain falls over the buildings, wild and unending. The streets are washed clean. People dash through the alleys, seeking shelter. But as soon as the rain abates, after a whole day's downpour, the heat is back and even more stifling, now that it's heavy with humidity.

She passes the crowds outside the clubs but doesn't go in. It's too painful to see such close groups of friends laughing and dancing. She doesn't want to hang around a bar trying to make eye contact with someone, even if perhaps she should.

Sometimes she doubts she did the right thing, running away from Sweden, but she reminds herself that she didn't have a choice.

8

She gets to know two other interns – Rosa, who's Dutch, and an American called Meredith – and they drag her out with them one night.

They get ready in the staff room together and head out on the town. They've planned to meet up with two German guys and three French girls who work at the Reina Sofia Museum, and Meredith excitedly informs them that a hot guy from the Norwegian embassy might show up too.

It's Friday, and the streets are unusually crowded. Everyone's talking about the heatwave. It's twenty-nine degrees Celsius. They go to a nightclub Rosa recommends. Blue light, a window-less room. Rosa and Meredith run straight for the dance floor while Hanna orders a beer. She sits down on a tall stool and looks around, but the eyes she meets are either swimmily distant or alarmingly lit and too intense.

Suddenly she feels a hand on her shoulder. She turns round. From the next stool over a man is smiling at her. He says something in Norwegian. The music is deafening. It sounds like he's saying she looks Swedish and the two of them are the only blond people in this whole place.

She looks at him, trying to understand.

He says he used to be blond, before he lost his hair. She nods. He switches to English and tells her he has a VIP table over by the dancefloor and can't drink everything himself.

Then he takes her firmly by the hand, without asking, and leads her through the crowd, across the dance floor, over to his table. She lets him do it. When they reach the table, he gestures proudly at the buckets of ice and bottles. They sit down.

The vinyl of the booth sticks to her bare thighs. The Norwegian mixes a drink for her, handing her a large glass full of ice and something red. It tastes like iron and sugar. It's like drinking blood. He's not unattractive, but his facial features are so symmetrical that the result is flattened. She searches his face for some detail, something a little off, that might be a key, but her effort is in vain.

They clink glasses.

He places his mouth to her ear as he presses his finger firmly to the outside of her ear canal and tells her about his job. He says it's like being on a paid holiday. She nods again. There's something black stuck between his front teeth, but she doesn't mention it. The strobe light blinks, flashing on his bald scalp.

After a while he stops talking and smiles.

Then he says: 'You're really too young for me.'

She does her best to smile.

He smiles too and then goes back to talking about his job.

She doesn't like the way he's pressing his finger to her ear. She doesn't like hearing about his job as the ambassador's right-hand man. He tells her that in his free time he rents out sports cars. Soon he won't have to worry about money, he says. His goal is to be able to stop working. 'It's time to hand power over to the women,' he says: 'but you have to actually *take* it.' Then he laughs. She tries to figure out how old he might be. She wonders how it feels to lose your hair. She wonders what the point is of pressing your finger into someone's ear like this. Why not just speak more quietly?

Suddenly Rosa is in front of them, reaching for the Norwegian. She says: 'Rosa.'

Under the table, Hanna places her hand on the Norwegian's leg.

9

Fifteen minutes later, they're standing in front of a huge wooden door in the diplomat district. The Norwegian beeps his card, enters a code, and lets her in.

He says: 'We shouldn't be doing this,' and smiles.

'I won't tell anyone,' she says.

He leads her up a narrow staircase to a dim, musty-smelling room. Along one wall is a small bar, and in the centre of the room is a pool table.

He explains that this is where the Norwegian embassy holds social gatherings; it's just a few blocks from the embassy.

The wall-to-wall carpet has a tartan pattern. On the wall is a framed photo of the Norwegian king and queen.

The Norwegian points at the bar and asks what she wants to drink. She replies, 'Surprise me.'

He takes out two glasses and fills them with ice. 'Listen to this!' he says. Then he pours liquor over the ice cubes. They crackle and snap as they break. He smiles proudly.

Hanna says: 'Is this really okay?'

The Norwegian stops mid-mix and looks at her.

'What do you mean?' he says.

'Bringing girls here after working hours.'

He grins. 'What are they going to do if they catch me? Call the ambassador?'

Then he laughs again. She tries to follow suit and almost succeeds.

He takes a large swig of his drink and says, his eyes fixed firmly on hers: 'Besides, it wouldn't be as exciting if it were okay.'

She smiles as seductively as she can. They toast. The drink is white and cloudy, like dishwater. She takes a sip. It tastes bitter and strong. She wonders what exactly she's drinking but doesn't ask. She takes another sip and it takes effort to keep from making a face.

As she sets her glass on the bar, she catches sight of something. There, on a wooden plinth, is a small statue. She approaches it.

Perhaps the Norwegian has realised what a strong impact the statue is having on her, because he says: 'He knew what he was doing, that Munch.'

Hanna stares at it. It makes her feel pensive and yearning all at once.

She leans closer to study the details. The statue is of a little girl, maybe eleven or twelve, whose body is still halfway inside the stone she's sculpted from. She is naked and it looks like she's trying to break free from the block of stone. She's pushing backwards with her hands, but it's no use.

Hanna rests a hand on the statue. She gazes into the girl's eyes, which are full of panic. She strokes the cool stone; it's like touching skin.

She hears herself say, almost in a whisper: 'It's wonderful.'

When the Norwegian answers, she is startled. She had forgotten about him. He says: '*You* are wonderful.'

She turns round and says: 'Thanks.'

He points at the statue and says: 'Isn't it annoying how us Norwegians are so good at everything?'

She sips her drink and says: '*Are* you though?'

He puts his drink down on the windowsill, takes a step towards her, and says: 'Yes.'

He places his hand on her hip and she lets him. Then he places his other hand under her breast, and she lets him do that too. Next he moves his hand up until it's cupping her breast. She reaches for his belt. He turns her round.

She ends up bending forward with her face close to the statue, her gaze fixed on the little girl's.

10

The same routines every morning: the small lift descends into the archive, creaking and shaking. She greets the guard and picks up her checklist and starts the day's run-through. Sometimes she runs into a colleague and stops to chat for a bit. A popular topic of conversation is the flies, which buzz around the tunnels. At first they didn't bother her much, but they've increased in number and each time she brings it up with Andrés, he just laughs and says: 'Welcome to Spain!'

At ten o'clock the order list is delivered. The guard prints it out and Hanna begins to gather the listed artworks from their flat filing cabinets and place them on a trolley. It takes anywhere from ten minutes to half an hour.

Then she rolls the trolley to the security portal.

Once the guard has let her in, she hears an audible 'click' as the door behind her locks. Then the guard reads the large plastic envelopes with the scanner to double check that the items she's gathered match the list. He unlocks the second door and she pushes the trolley into the lift. Then she rides up to the fourth floor, where the research rooms are.

The journey up through the museum takes only a few minutes, but she looks forward to it all morning. It's freeing to reach the upper floors of the building, get away from the flies and the heat, breathe some fresh air.

She studies the researchers' faces as they sit at their desks and wait for the artworks. She turns her face up to the big skylights, as if to get her fill of light ahead of the afternoon. As soon as her trolley has been turned over, the guard waves her off and she has to go back down to the darkness.

11

Meredith and Rosa have got tickets to a flamenco exhibition. After work they put on make-up in the staff toilets as they drink wine from plastic cups. Hanna tells them about the Norwegian and her visit to the Norwegian embassy's party venue. The other girls want to hear *details, details, details.*

They leave the museum and take Gran Via north, heading for the square where the theatre is located, and Hanna enjoys the feeling of walking down the street in a group, the strength in clacking their way through the Friday crowds in high heels, seeing the gazes of men, feeling the wine take hold in her blood.

They present their tickets at the door and are shown to a table near the stage. Meredith orders a pitcher of sangria for the table, full of ice and fruit slices. 'You *have* to drink sangria when you're watching flamenco,' she says.

After a while, the curtain goes up and the room falls silent. A woman in a black dress and black scarf slowly approaches the edge of the stage, gazes at the audience and squints into the spotlight. A hairy man in a suit strums a guitar aggressively as the woman claps her hands in rhythm.

Slowly but surely, the tempo increases, and a minute or so into the song the woman begins to stomp her metal soles on the floor, taka-ka-ka-taka-ka-ka, and Meredith starts to giggle. Rosa looks at her phone.

Hanna is hypnotised. There's something violent about the music, a gravity to the performance that appeals to her. She turns round to see if she's the only one so enraptured.

That's when she sees them, farther back in the room: the group from the square.

They're only a few tables away.

They're even more beautiful than she remembered.

The tall guy is clapping to the rhythm and smiling. Hanna thinks he has the sort of appearance that attracts both men and women, a disarming expression, a sensitive gaze, even as he's strikingly masculine with his strong nose and pronounced jaw.

The shorter guy is swaying so much to the music that his curly hair falls into his face.

The girl radiates a nonchalant sort of elegance as she snaps her fingers, smiling.

Hanna wonders if they're siblings, or if maybe the guys are gay, because they're so physical. They touch one another again and again, stroking each other's arms, ruffling each other's hair.

All through the performance she keeps glancing in their direction. She can't resist the temptation. She wonders what country they're from – they don't look Spanish, at least the guys don't.

When the curtain falls and the audience has finished applauding and the house lights come on, she finally sees them in the light. The guy with the long blond hair reminds her of an elf with those high cheekbones and narrow eyes. The short guy has such feminine features, with his small nose and dark eyes, and those dangling corkscrews. The girl turns round and her gaze is so penetrating that Hanna instinctively looks away.

Meredith and Rosa call to her: it's time to pay, and Hanna takes out her purse to hand them a few euros.

When she turns round again, the group is gone.

She is struck by panic and shoves her way through the crowd to reach the street – but they've disappeared.

She dashes round the corner to find them, then turns back to the small square outside the theatre, but it's no use.

12

The next Monday begins like every other workday. She changes in the locker room and takes the lift down to the archive, greets the guard, who hands her the scanner and the iPad, and then she picks up where she left off before the weekend.

As usual, she opens box after box, and as always, the work is repetitive and mechanical.

But suddenly, something happens.

In one of the plastic envelopes she finds not one but two sheets. A red chalk drawing by Jusepe de Ribera and a charcoal sketch by Francisco de Zurbarán.

She's confused. She turns them over to figure out what happened and discovers that the Zurbarán sketch is correctly numbered, while the number on the de Ribera piece doesn't match that on the box.

She tries to understand how this could have happened. Maybe the misplaced one was simply loaned out to the research room and then returned to the wrong box by mistake.

She locates the drawer where the misnumbered Ribera piece ought to be and unlocks it.

There is already a different work by Ribera inside, with the same number as the misplaced one. So two different pieces have been assigned identical numbers.

Once the shock has passed, she feels exhilarated.

This is the sort of mistake she has been hired to discover. The moment feels almost solemn. She tries to remember the protocol for what to do now, but she's too worked up to recall it. She takes out her phone to call Andrés, but there's no service down in the archives. She jots down the number of the doubles and goes to the security portal and presses the button to summon the guard.

The lift ride up feels unusually slow. She's restless and on edge, looking forward to Andrés' praise for her discovery.

She reaches street level and walks into his office, but he's not there. His secretary says he's in the Jerónimos wing, working on preparations for the anniversary exhibit.

It takes effort for Hanna not to run, she's so excited. She takes the shortcut through the Velázquez galleries and crosses the rotunda, turning left after the cafeteria.

When she reaches the Bosch gallery she spots him, but he's in the middle of a conversation, so she stops.

As soon as she realises who he's talking to, she ducks behind the big triptych in the middle of the room.

After a moment she peers out tentatively. Yes, that's them. Andrés is talking to the group she saw on the square and at the flamenco club.

She glances in their direction.

This is the third time she's seen them. She must not fail again.

She watches as Andrés shakes hands with them and leaves the room, while they stay behind.

The tall guy is wearing a light-coloured linen suit cut in an eighties style – loose trousers and shoulder pads – with a white t-shirt underneath. The short guy is wearing an oversized dark grey t-shirt with a deep crew neck. His dark chest is hairless. The girl is in a short dress and a matching headband. Around her neck is a strand of pearls that glows white against her dark skin.

Slowly they wander through the room, gazing up at the paintings. Step by step they approach her hiding spot.

The way they walk, the way they move away from each other and back again, it is as if it's a dance. The long-haired guy shakes his head with a smile as the short guy grabs his arm. Then they laugh aloud and the girl throws her arms around their shoulders.

When they're finally right up next to her, they stop in front of *The Garden of Earthly Delights*. They lean close to study the details.

That's when she hears that they're speaking Swedish.

At first she can't believe her ears. It's too good to be true.

Then she gets hold of herself and stops to think. Maybe it's not so strange. After all, she saw something familiar in them, that first night on the square, and she'd had the same gut feeling at the flamenco club.

Now her brain is working overtime to think of something to say, an opening. Then she can shove a foot in the gap and walk right in.

13

The group leaves the museum and walks into the park. Hanna comes behind, tentatively.

When they stop to light a cigarette each, she stops as well; when they begin to walk again, so does she.

At the intersection behind the big oak tree, they choose the gravel path that leads up the hill and Hanna realises she had better act fast, before they jump into a taxi or a bus up on the road.

She walks faster until she catches up with them.

'Excuse me,' she says.

They stop and turn to look at her.

Green shadows from the trees above.

The tall guy says: 'Yes?'

'I heard you speaking Swedish.'

Now the group exchanges glances.

Then the girl turns to her and says: 'Okay?'

Hanna has to say something else, and fast.

At last she manages: 'I work at the museum.'

They gaze at her, puzzled.

The only sound is the rustle of the vast treetop above. The tall guy turns away from her and glances up at the street.

The short guy says: 'You don't happen to have anything to do with the two hundredth anniversary, do you?'

The tall one says: 'We were hoping to get tickets. It didn't go so well.'

The girl adds: 'We don't have a way in.'

Hanna: 'Who did you talk to?'

'Some guy from the archives.'

Hanna: 'You should have talked to me instead.'

They look at her. She goes on: 'I work on the anniversary committee.'

The girl says: 'Really?'

Hanna nods: 'Yes.'

She watches the tall one take a step her way. Maybe he does it unconsciously.

Hanna goes on: 'A ton of fun stuff will be happening.'

The short guy says: 'We like fun stuff.'

At that, Hanna can't help but laugh. It bubbles up before she can stop it. Maybe because this is all happening so smoothly, because she can see in their eyes that they're curious about her, and maybe there's something disarming about her laughter, because soon the short guy starts laughing too, and after him it's the girl, and the tall guy, and soon enough all four of them are laughing together as though they've known each other for years.

MAY

1

They're sitting at one of the big outdoor cafés on Plaza Mayor, and Hanna observes her new friends from across the table. Once again, Tom has been teasing Samuel about his 'posh Spanish' and now they're all laughing. Samuel can take it and Tom knows Samuel's limits; he won't go too far.

Their banter is like a tennis match. Quick lines, looks, smiles, back and forth.

Leah lights a cigarette, takes a deep drag, and shapes her red lips into an o, blowing three smoke rings that float across the table. Samuel and Tom applaud.

They've enjoyed a casserole of bacon, chorizo and chickpeas. Samuel informed them that this was a working-class dish originally, but now it's made its way to the gastropubs. They're drinking cognac. Hanna asks lots of questions, they answer eagerly, often talking over one another. It's twilight. The lights have come on around the square. Hanna listens to Samuel and Leah, who are bickering about some party they might go to. She's still in a state of shock after everything that has happened over the past week. A rising wave of consciousness. A recurring thought these past few days: *What if she had never met them.* It would have been as simple as going through the gift shop instead of taking the shortcut through the Bosch gallery. That way she might not have seen them standing with Andrés, and she wouldn't be sitting here today. Now Tom and Samuel are discussing a Márquez book Samuel thinks is overrated, and she loves the way they draw out every topic, how they never settle. They even say it out loud, all the time: *You can do better, we can do better,* and they challenge each other. She likes the way they have high expectations, as though conversation is a sport.

It's the same with the way they dress. Nothing is left to chance. Hanna is fascinated to see how they urge one another on, when they're offering praise or critiques of their fashion choices, every evening.

But above all, she loves Samuel's words, which steer the conversation. Samuel's meandering monologues, always changing direction and leading to unexpected places. He's never tongue-tied. When Leah or Tom challenges him, he's not afraid to rethink his position. And his choice of words is odd, drastic. There's something precocious about him, those old-fashioned idioms and turns of phrase. But it's not so much what he says as how he says it. His mouth, his words, one leg crossed over the other, an easygoing atmosphere.

It's getting dark on the square and they order more wine. She can tell Samuel is genuinely interested in her job. He asks questions about the anniversary festivities and the organisation, saying he has a *romantic relationship to the entire building*, and they talk about Goya and Hanna tells him about the thesis of her research paper, that the Black Paintings weren't a result of mental illness at all, that they were an attempt at a rawer, truer sort of style.

'He wanted to break free from the more polished style he was known for as a court painter.'

Samuel protests: 'But he painted them on the walls of his own house.'

'Also a way to become free.'

'But he didn't show them to a single person.'

'He knew he was ahead of his time.'

'But the paintings are of goats and witches and trolls.'

'As a contrast to all the high society portraits he painted earlier.'

And on and on. At first Samuel is sceptical and poses counter-questions, but then something happens. He softens as she presents her arguments, and near the end of the evening he leans forward, so close she can smell his cologne, and says: 'Now I see why you have a position like that.'

'Position?'

'At the museum.'

And he flashes a big smile.

She stands up and heads for the toilet, so no one will see her blush.

2

All of a sudden she doesn't want to forget anything that happens. As soon as she gets home to her flat, she takes out her sketchbook and sketches from memory, writes down things said, looks, misunderstandings, laughter, all manner of loaded moments. She writes about Samuel's inquisitive gaze, his strange trains of thought, his smile, his eyes when he's impressed by her knowledge of Goya. She writes about the changeable natures of their faces, about Tom's habit of always trying to figure out where they'll go next, about Leah's colouring: her dark eyebrows, her deep brown eyes. In comparison, Hanna feels transparent with her pale complexion and colourless blonde hair, an ebbing appearance with no edges. But she knows she can change, if she just pays attention. The work has begun, she has become observant, ready to learn. They won't suspect a thing; they will assume that she is like them.

3

One evening, as she and Leah are sitting at the pavement seating at La Torre del Oro and waiting for Samuel to join them, Leah tells her he's considered a star of sorts in the diplomatic circles of Madrid, even though he's only thirty, that he was 'cut out for those environments', that he lives in a large flat on Plaza de la Villa de Paris, that the reason he's found such success is that he became interested in a single issue early on and has devoted all his energy to it since he was a teenager. To Hanna, it sounds poetic, how he organised demonstrations at the age of sixteen, wrote impassioned articles, always felt that he wanted to change the world. Leah calls him 'obsessed' and says that he sets his alarm for five every morning, to have time to read 'everything'. Hanna pictures him up at dawn, hunched over his laptop, absorbing research and news like a sponge, all to stay one step ahead.

Tom, too, is a soul obsessed, Leah tells her, spending all his waking hours writing his debut novel. 'He comes off as a little pretentious sometimes, always quoting authors and carrying collections of poetry under his arm, but at least he's consistent.' When Hanna asks how he can afford not to have a job, Leah smiles and lowers her voice and says: 'His parents can afford it.'

4

One evening, Hanna finds them at a pavement café on Plaza de Santa Ana, and they start talking about the Black Paintings again. Samuel asks what she thinks of the theory that their wild style can be attributed to lead poisoning.

He says: 'Look at the motifs. Those are hallucinations.'

'No they're not,' says Hanna.

'He was obviously poisoned by the paints he used.'

'There's no evidence of that.'

'But he painted them over the walls of his house. No one in their right mind would do that.'

'He did it to escape his own vanity. Because they were part of the wall, he knew he could never sell them. It was a way for him to find his true voice.'

'A crazy voice,' Samuel says.

Hanna loves it when they end up in these kinds of arguments, challenging one another back and forth but smiling all the while.

Hanna: 'Come to the museum sometime, and I'll show you.'

Him: 'A private tour?'

'Yes.'

Samuel smiles: 'Okay, you promised.'

Then he raises his glass for a toast.

Now she can see how lost she was when she first came to Madrid. She wishes she could travel a month back in time and tell herself that it will be okay. She also wishes she had dared to approach them that very first night on the square, so no time would have been wasted.

She's almost embarrassed to think of her fears during the weeks before she met the group. She didn't understand the city back then. She made the mistake of staring at its constituent parts, shop windows, and paintings to seek answers. Now she can see that Madrid is an organism, a massive, complex being, where all the cells fit together. She can hear the notes of the city now, the gigantic tuning fork vibrating through bodies and buildings, a note that is different from that of other big cities; it's more secret and subtle. Now, thanks to the group, she has discovered it. They have the key to places and parts of the city she's never heard of, food she's never tried.

One night, Samuel orders *calçot* for them, a kind of leek that is char-grilled and served with romesco sauce made of nuts and peppers. Another night, Tom orders patatas bravas for her. On a third night, Leah takes her to the alleys of Malasaña and the fruit markets in La Latina, where they buy fresh peaches and burnt almonds. And one Sunday afternoon, Samuel takes them to the best paella spot in town, far from the tourist traps, and they order a huge pan that sits in the centre of the table; they scoop the food out of it into earthenware bowls. After dinner they compete to see who can name the most paella ingredients. Hanna is out first. She only manages to say tomatoes, shrimp, mussels, and white beans. Samuel wins, and when the competition is over he keeps going, talking to himself: 'Rabbit, saffron, chicken, pepper, blue mussels.'

5

She sometimes looks at Leah from across the table and muses that such a beautiful face has an almost violent effect on the world, because it reveals all the ugliness surrounding it. Those deep brown eyes gleaming in the sun, that striking nose, those dimples. Everything she radiates bursts outward, strikes violently, and nothing around it can remain in balance. It's funny, really, how she subjects other people to this without comment. She and everyone around her pretend like it's no big deal. The elephant in the room remains unnamed. Sometimes Hanna consoles herself with the thought that being a model is tough, a difficult industry. Anyone who looks like that must also be subjected to constant exposure.

At the same time, Leah is so shamelessly languid as she sits there sucking on her cigarettes, as if she were totally clueless what associations that sort of gesture sparks in both women and men. Hanna wonders how different her own life would be if she were that beautiful.

Hanna sees how Tom looks at Leah and wonders if he's secretly in love with her.

Now and then he rests a hand on Leah's leg or arm, and she gently but pointedly pulls away. He radiates loneliness; he's not as easy to engage with as the others. Sometimes he seems to vanish inside himself. Sometimes, in the middle of a conversation, he will pick up a book and start reading.

There is something melancholic about him. The only time he genuinely lights up is when he's talking about his writing. He's been working on his novel for a few years now, he says, but without any support from home – aside from the financial. His parents are always getting after him to get a 'real job', but he refuses because he has such faith in his novel. And he clearly likes it when Hanna asks questions about it.

One evening, as he and Hanna are on their own at a pavement café waiting for the others, she asks if she can read some of it.

Tom: 'Now?'

'Why not?'

He looks nervous but nods: 'Okay.'

Then he looks at her intently, as if trying to figure out if she really means it. At last he hands over his phone.

She is moved to see how expectant he looks as she takes the phone from him, but it's hard to concentrate on reading because she can feel him on the periphery, studying her the whole time.

This chapter is about a couple who decide to switch identities when they have sex. To make the roleplay convincing, they exchange clothes and wear each other's perfume and cologne. Hanna figures the story is about Tom himself and his attraction to Leah, and that makes it exciting.

When she's finished reading, she says it's one of the best things she's ever read. At that, he smiles self-consciously and shakes his head.

She's become aware that he sometimes uses drugs, has heard little snippets of things to suggest as much. One time when he was visiting an ATM, Leah whispered to Hanna, 'blow time', and one night, when they were in line for Discogaga, Samuel said, 'You hid the stuff, I hope.' Those sorts of hints. But he's discreet about it, and it doesn't seem to affect his work.

She tells him about her painting, even though there's no comparing it with his disciplined writing practice.

Early on she wondered why none of them were in a relationship, but now she's starting to understand. Tom is full of unrequited love for Leah, Leah is in an unhappy relationship with an attaché, and Samuel lives for his work.

6

She's standing on Samuel's balcony, gazing out at the rooftops and feeling like this night constitutes a turning point. Now she's not just an acquaintance they hang out with at restaurants; now she's been invited to one of their homes.

She hears Samuel and Leah laughing and rattling around in the kitchen. She smells garlic and something being fried. She's touched. They're cooking for her, they want her here, they like her, she has been invited into their daily lives, and when she arrived, Samuel handed her a drink.

This is the start of a new chapter in their relationship. Because what is a flat if not a window into someone's soul? The furniture, art, books, all the choices Samuel made when he was decorating these rooms. The clutter. Soon he'll be serving food he prepared. And then they'll eat together, and after that they'll go out, and no strangers will be allowed to sit down at their table. She takes a big sip of wine. She already feels tipsy. She likes it. She takes another sip. From down on the street she hears the laughter and rumblings of a group of young people on their way downtown. She leans out to see them. They're tanned and beautiful and dressed in white. They catch sight of her and wave. She waves back. She smiles at them. They smile back. Just a few weeks ago, she wouldn't have waved back, and they wouldn't have waved to her in the first place.

7

They're sitting in a booth at DCorazon. Tom is wearing a checked Gucci suit with nothing underneath but a pearl necklace. Samuel is wearing a pair of high-waisted beige trousers with pressed creases and a tucked-in polo shirt. His skin is brown as leather. Leah's black dress has large cut-outs, showing off some side-boob and her dark stomach. They're eating grilled potatoes with red pepper-corn sauce. Hanna notices that Samuel is eating with his hands, so she does the same. Takes a potato from the basket and dips it in the sauce. The chilli burns her mouth, but she doesn't let it show. The air is thick with smoke from the grill.

Leah has been complaining once more about her attaché's ambivalence. His wife is on her way to Madrid with the children to stay with him for the summer. That means he and Leah have to take a break again.

Hanna notices that Tom finds the topic annoying.

Samuel, too, looks upset as he explains to Leah why the relationship is doomed.

Hanna is impressed by his uncompromising manner. When Samuel describes the attaché's spinelessness, he does it with a level of consideration that shows he truly cares about Leah.

Hanna watches him as he speaks. There's something about his gestures that reminds her of an actor; they're precise, grand-iloquent, direct. She wonders if it's possible to learn how to own a room, or if that's a skill you have to be born with.

Maybe his power to draw people in has to do with the fact that he allows himself to make mistakes. Sometimes when he waves a waiter over at a restaurant and converses with them in Spanish, then turns back to the group again to toss off a few quick lines, he gets his grammar wrong and starts to stammer – but in the end he always laughs at himself. The result is that he doesn't have far to fall, because he's transparent when it comes to his shortcomings. To Hanna it seems like the group radiates youth, because they want so deeply, are so greedy. A bottomless well of youth. Now Hanna is standing at its edge and staring right down into it.

8

Her only problem is worrying about money. When she's with the group, poverty is a growing pressure in her chest; she is ashamed that she can't dress like them or pay her way at restaurants. To be sure, Samuel always insists on picking up the bill, but she hates that she can't return the favour. She wishes she could show them how much she appreciates their generosity, but she can't even afford actual presents. One evening, she buys three white roses to give to them, but it pains her to hand them something so simple. They assure her that they appreciate the gesture very much, but later, when they leave, she notices that they leave the flowers on the table.

She considers getting a second job at a shop or something, but then she would miss their dinners. Besides, the wages wouldn't go far. Some of Leah's dresses cost as much as a whole month's salary from the museum. Hanna is tired of digging through second-hand shops and then sitting in her room at night, mending holes with needle and thread.

It feels like both Samuel and Leah appreciate her presence within the group, but she's not quite sure what Tom thinks. Sometimes she notices his eyes lingering on her when she's said something, as if he's trying to work out who she really is. And sometimes he asks questions that feel more prying than genuine.

One evening, at a salsa place, he suddenly leans across the table and says: 'Must be a lot to handle right now, huh?'

Hanna. 'What do you mean?'

'Ahead of the anniversary celebrations.'

'Yes, we're working hard.'

He gives her a searching look. 'Can we come visit sometime?'

She doesn't hesitate: 'I'd love that.'

'It would be exciting to meet the rest of the anniversary committee.'

'For sure.'

He won't stop looking at her: 'When can we come by?'

'Anytime.'

Tom is also the only one who needles her about money. Once he talked about the 'parasites from Sweden' who come to the city, old friends who expect him to pay for everything. Then he turned to Hanna and said: 'You know the type?'

It's hard to tell if he's joking around with her or if he's actually annoyed. Either way, the uncertainty makes her nervous, and she hates holding her breath every time the bill arrives.

Sometimes, when she's trying to fall asleep at night, a forbidden thought comes to her.

Maybe there is a solution to her problem, but each time the thought pops up she pushes it away. She would never dare to do something so risky.

9

Their nights always follow the same five acts.

First, a pre-dinner drink at some pavement café.

Then dinner, sometimes at a trendy place Samuel has found, but equally often at a random tourist trap among the throngs.

Then a walk through the neighbourhood. They might stop for a refreshing gelato at an ice-cream bar, ordering it in a cup so they can eat it while wandering around. Sometimes Hanna orders sorbet instead, because Samuel has mentioned it's healthier.

Next they visit a bar or two or three, and then they go to Samuel's flat to round off the night on his balcony.

Accordingly, their nights follow a perfect dramaturgy.

When she finally gets home to her flat, dizzy from the wine and conversation, she sometimes stops short in the front hall and recoils at how tiny it is, compared to Samuel's. It's like it shrinks more each time she hangs out with the group, as though the furniture gets ever more rustic. Nothing matches. The furnishings are a mishmash of impressions left by all the previous renters. It's like being at a flea market. A chest of drawers made of dark wood, a white IKEA bed, a threadbare sofa in green corduroy, a plastic wardrobe.

Sometimes she goes straight from the front door to the bed without turning on the lights, then lies down and closes her eyes and makes believe she's still at Samuel's and that the tiny back courtyard of her building is his lush garden.

Another recurring fantasy involves ending up at some rowdy afterparty with the group, and they decide to get out of there. They find a fire escape on the balcony and climb up to the roof together, and they find a mattress there, under the stars, and in this fantasy they lie down together and gaze at the night sky, and it's a hot night, so hot that Samuel suggests they strip down to their underwear. Then they cuddle close, whispering. In this fantasy, Tom and Leah kiss first, while she and Samuel watch, but soon she feels Samuel's hand on her hip, his warm hand moving up along her stomach. Then she turns to him and parts her lips.

10

One evening when Samuel is working late, Hanna, Leah, and Tom go to the cinema to watch a superhero movie.

She sometimes likes to spend time with just them because they are more open when Samuel isn't there. She puts together the puzzle piece by piece. She learns that Leah lived in India and London as a child with parents who worked for SIDA, Sweden's ministry for development assistance; that Tom grew up on posh Karlaplan in Stockholm, went to the Stockholm School of Economics for a year but quit, that while his parents finance his life in Madrid they're trying to convince him to move back to Sweden.

The lobby of the cinema is crowded.

Hanna appreciates the everyday nature of this activity: standing in line to buy popcorn, chatting in their seats before the movie starts, whispering and giggling during the film. This, too, is a way to be close.

When they leave the cinema afterwards, Hanna is over-whelmed by the heat in a way she hasn't been since she first got to Madrid. She feels cool drops of sweat trickling down her spine. Leah pulls off her shirt. Underneath is nothing but a cami.

As they walk down the street, Hanna notices people staring at Leah and Tom. She enjoys walking next to two such attractive people. Leah's wearing a beige skirt that moves freely in the breeze, and Hanna regrets her own choice of clothing: a thick black skirt that hangs heavily against her thighs and would never be caught by the wind in that elegant way.

After a while they come to a large intersection that's full of teenagers leaning against the buildings. The odour of marijuana is heavy in the air. The pavement cafes have opened all their windows and people are sitting on the sills and drinking beer.

At some point, Tom places a hand on Leah's back, but Leah doesn't reciprocate the gesture.

They take a seat at the big bodega outside the embassy and Tom orders something called *salmorejo*, a soup with croutons and chopped hard-boiled egg. Hanna doesn't understand the love Tom and the Spanish feel for eggs, their bad habit of sprinkling hard-boiled egg all over tapas and soups, but she doesn't say anything, because she knows Tom loves everything that's classic Spain. Along with their food they finish a large pitcher of sangria.

After a while, Samuel comes walking down the other side of the square.

He's looking for them.

Hanna sees him, but he doesn't see her.

He turns round, scouting for them. She doesn't wave and doesn't say anything to the others. She wants to have this moment to herself. He's so fragile, walking along looking for them, looking so lost.

At last he spots her and lights up with a big smile. She has to stop herself from getting up and rushing over to him.

11

One night, she finally gets to sleep with Samuel. She throws her leg over his hips and her arm over his back. At first she almost manages to believe it. But when she presses her face to his neck, the illusion breaks. She's at home on her own sofa, and its cushions smell not like Samuel but like musty stuffing.

She shoves the pillow away and tries to go back to sleep. But it doesn't work. She stares out the window. The sky is violet and cloudless. She thinks of how little the group has actually told her about their pasts – and how much she appreciates that. They look forward and only forward. What happened in the past is uninteresting because they are moving away from it. She understands them, she is like them.

Maybe that's why she dares to think more and more often about the forbidden idea. The future can be shaped like a lump of clay, can become whatever you make of it. Besides, maybe it's not even all that risky. The more she thinks about how it might be done, the less scary it seems.

The duplicate is just lying there in its flat file, without being listed in the inventory. No one would notice if it went missing. The only challenge would be getting it out of the building.

Now she's lying in her bed and toying with the thought. She closes her eyes, wonders how, hypothetically, she would go about it. She would never seriously do it, but the fantasy warms her in the dark.

12

One night, on Samuel's balcony, Leah and Tom head home around two and Hanna stays behind. She says she has the next day off, even though she doesn't.

When the other two leave, the mood in the room changes. Hanna goes to the bathroom, fixes her hair, brushes her teeth, and curls up beside him on the sofa, where he's watching CNN.

After a while, he suddenly puts his hand on her foot. She holds her breath, her temples pounding. His hand is warm against her bare foot. She stares at the TV without blinking.

At last she turns to face him, to meet his gaze, but his eyes are closed. His head has fallen to the side and his lips are moist. She sits up to observe his face. She leans right up close to him, can smell the red wine and cigarette smoke on his breath. She leans even closer. Eventually she's so close that his humid breath is in her mouth. She is struck by a wave of dizziness. She closes her eyes and breathes back, into his mouth. Their hot breath mingles: out, then in, in silence.

He opens his eyes. She jumps with the shock of it. He looks at her.

She stands up, stretches, yawns, and says: 'I'm tired.'

He says: 'Me too.'

Then he gets up and goes into his bedroom.

She is left behind, in the silence.

She thinks about what she should do next. She muses: why didn't he say goodnight? Should that be taken as an invitation? Maybe he's lying there waiting for her. She reaches for the remote and turns down the volume of the TV. She looks at his door, listening for a sound. Why did he leave the door open? She wishes she had showered after work. She wonders if he's naked in there, if he's lying on his stomach, baring his bum to the ceiling, or maybe he's on his back. She feels her heart pounding in the quiet room.

She tiptoes across the room, in case the parquet is squeaky.

When she reaches the door to his room, she stops. It's dark in there, but after a moment a car passes outside and casts pale light through the curtains. Then she sees the outline of his body under the covers.

Slowly she walks inside. Each time the floor creaks, she stops. When she finally reaches the bed, she can tell from his heavy breathing that he's asleep. Or pretending to be asleep.

She sits on the edge of the bed. The mattress squeaks.

She looks at him. She has never seen his face so bare. She thinks: *this is what he would look like if he were dead.* It feels like a gift. She wonders what would happen if she were to touch his face right now, if she woke him up to tell him about her fantasies? Would he take her hand? Ask her to crawl in bed with him?

But she sits still. She doesn't want to risk that the moment might end.

13

Spending time with the group prompts Hanna to look at her colleagues in a new light. She sees how lonely they are. How they use their workdays to flee their husbands, their wives, their boyfriends. As though work is a breather from the life they live outside it. Meanwhile, Hanna feels the opposite. She can't wait for the workday to be over.

Every day at lunch the gang of interns drinks wine, and she watches their cheeks turn red and she hears their conversations grow loud. She doesn't understand how they can stand to drink so much during the day. Sickly warm red wine in plastic cups. That sour aftertaste. Wine tastes different during the day than it does at night; it's sharper, more vulgar. She never has more than a glass.

She turns round in the huge cafeteria and thinks: they're all ants in an anthill. The hierarchy in this building is strict; if you're at the bottom, you can quickly be chewed up by the vast machinery. Nine thousand artworks, seven hundred employees, three million visitors per year. The power structure blaring from capital letters on copper nametags worn on the left side of the chest. Her work takes place below ground, under the radar.

Sometimes Andrés pops up out of nowhere to tap her on the shoulder and take her aside; he lowers his voice and says she's meticulous and reliable and he has plans for her. Perhaps she'd like to start putting in some overtime in the evenings? She flashes as genuine a smile as she can muster and shakes her head: 'I can't.' He leans down, bringing his face close to hers. He smells like garlic and saliva. He says she is a good worker and she shouldn't say no. He says this is an exciting time to be working in this building, since the whole world will be watching them in August. Then he urges her to be more social with her workgroup, maybe start going out with them a little more often after their shift.

'I don't want you to feel lonely,' he says. 'Thank you,' she says. 'I don't feel lonely.'

She hates the way he treats her as if she's transparent. If only he knew about the creature inside her, which she feeds with content every night, which she carefully fills with Leah's beauty,

Tom's artistic dreams, Samuel's engagement. The creature that grows with every moment she spends with the group, and will soon be ready to greet the world.

14

They're at a pavement café in the Chueca neighbourhood, drinking chilled Tinto de Verano to cool off.

For once, Hanna is having a hard time concentrating on the conversation. She nods and smiles and pretends to be listening, but all she can think about is her recent ATM withdrawal. She's used to being poor, but she's in dire straits now.

She takes a deep drink of her wine.

The first few times Hanna tried Verano, she thought it was too sweet, but in the evening heat it seems fresh and acidic.

They eat shrimp dipped in olive oil and garlic while Samuel tells them about a failure of a meeting with a delegation from China.

Now and then, ashes drift to the table. Samuel waves them away and catches them in his hand like snowflakes. The sky is a deep shade of red. Samuel tells them how they saw the distant fires from the conference room window, and how he pointed at the flames in an attempt to forge a connection with the other participants, but even so the discussion ended in a deadlock.

'Why do I even try?' he says.

For their main course they have *huevos a la Flamenca*. Tom orders sangria and Hanna drinks it quickly and soon her money worries fade a bit.

The meeting with the Chinese has clearly had an impact on Samuel. He's upset and says he sometimes doubts his career choice.

He says: 'Today I had an aha moment.'

Hanna: 'What was it?'

42

'That maybe I should find some other kind of work.'

Leah's wearing wide-leg trousers and a transparent blouse with puffed sleeves. Samuel's wearing a baggy, sand-coloured linen suit with a black t-shirt. He has one leg crossed over the other.

He makes a sweeping gesture at the crowds. 'It's all fucked anyway.'

Hanna: 'What is?'

'Everyone has given up, and they don't even know it.'

'But *you* know it?' Tom says.

'Yes.'

Tom laughs and takes a drink of his beer. His pupils are awfully large. He shakes his head. 'You want a revolution? Is that what you want?'

Samuel lights a cigarette.

Then he says: 'I don't know.'

He takes a thoughtful drag and shakes his head. 'Maybe it's too late anyway.'

Hanna takes in his look of concern. She wants to offer some encouragement but can't think of anything to say. She wants him to keep talking to them about the downfall. She likes it when his tone turns dramatic.

But Tom and Leah don't seem to be taking him seriously. They always make it sound like he's exaggerating when he gets in these moods, as if they think he's only putting on an act. But Hanna knows him, she realised it that very first night, that his words are grounded in passion. He's the kind of person who would never simply give lip service. She loves the way he sets his sights high. It's physical, the way he always brings his emotions into it. It's clear that it wears on him, always putting forth this effort, always wanting to be understood: the dark spread of sweat on his back and under his arms, his red cheeks, his hair, damp at his temples.

It's as if it's impossible for him to look dirty, no matter how unbrushed his hair is or how sweaty he gets, while she herself never feels presentable. It's like there's something inside her that can never be washed away, no matter how hard she tries, as though it's written on her forehead that she's damaged goods.

15

One Saturday morning, the Norwegian texts her to ask if she wants to get together. At first, she plans to say no. But then he sends another text and suggests they meet at a department store, and she takes this to mean that he wants to buy clothes for her.

Her guess was right.

When they meet up at the store, he says he wants to take her to an event at the German embassy that night, and the dress code is evening wear. He gestures at the store as if to say she can choose whatever she likes.

As she starts to browse, he moves away to take a phone call.

Since he's not looking, she also grabs a bracelet and some skirts and blouses, along with the evening gown and shoes.

When she's finished she goes to the till but holds off on getting in line, since the Norwegian is still on the call. Soon he spots her and comes dashing in, his phone still pressed to his ear, and hands her a leather card wallet. Then he returns to the street.

She opens the wallet. Inside is a credit card and two access badges. The creature whispers to her to take out one of the badges, so she does and puts it in her pocket. Then she uses the credit card to pay.

16

They go to the Norwegian's hotel room to change clothes. He wants them to have sex on top of the made bed. Her skirt is rucked up and her blouse stays on. The bedspread is slippery beneath her back. He stares into her eyes and she wonders if it would be rude to close hers, but she does it anyway.

Afterwards she showers and changes clothes in the large bathroom.

Sitting in the back seat on the way to the party, Hanna feels fancy in her new clothes and bracelet. The Norwegian is wearing a tux and looks a little younger than he had. He asks if she wants some cocaine but she shakes her head.

'Your loss,' he says, taking out a key and dipping it in a tiny metal cylinder.

The sound as he snorts it is like a backwards sneeze.

Hanna meets the driver's gaze in the rearview mirror.

The Norwegian puts the key away and says: 'What do you think?'

'About what?'

He laughs. 'The car.'

'Nice.'

'You could say I've got two lives. The embassy and the cars.' It seems as though he expects praise for this. She nods and smiles.

He says: 'Do you have two lives?'

'No.'

He smiles. 'Nothing wrong with that.'

'As long as you manage to keep them separate.'

He laughs.

When they arrive, he instructs the driver: 'Don't go too far.'

It's crowded outside the entrance. All over, people are calling out to the guards, trying to get their attention by waving tickets. The women are wearing evening gowns and the men are in tuxedos. The Norwegian seems to know the guards, because when they see him they lift the red velvet rope and wave him in. He grips Hanna's hand firmly as he leads her in between the pillars.

Soon they're on a roof terrace with a view of the city. She wishes the group were here, that they could see her now, how good she looks in this bracelet, this dress.

As the Norwegian walks around shaking hands and kissing cheeks, she leans against the railing and gazes out at the rooftops.

The sky is deep, city lights glittering. She touches the bracelet and the forbidden idea returns to her. The one that usually comes like a dream in the dark. In this evening light, it seems doable. Maybe she's been entertaining it for so long that she's simply grown used to it.

17

Being close to Samuel is discovering a landscape, one that constantly expands. She pricks her ears. Each day, she sees fresh depths in him.

One time, the two of them are on their way home from a bar when he suddenly stops in front of a bush to pee, and she takes this as a sign of how close they've become. The moment is almost erotic: she stands close to him, listening to the rustle of his stream landing on the grass, hears his sigh of relief as he turns his face up to the starry sky.

Another night, they're brushing their teeth in his bathroom, side by side, quietly so as not to wake Tom and Leah, who have fallen asleep on the sofa in front of a movie.

Hanna watches Samuel in the bathroom mirror, and he smiles at her with his white, foamy lips. Then they rinse their mouths in the same sink and she watches the strands of their slime and froth mix against the porcelain and swirl down the drain. After he leaves, she lingers in the bathroom and puts his wet toothbrush in her mouth, letting it slide around in there, sucking it clean.

SIGGE EKLUND

Another night – when she comes to his place – Leah opens the door and says, her voice full of worry, 'Samuel has a fever.'

Apparently he ate a bad paella and has been throwing up.

Hanna rushes to him in the bedroom, where he's curled up on his side, eyes closed, his hand under the pillow like a child. She doesn't understand how Leah can just watch TV in the living room and leave him here. His lips are pale and cracked. Hanna dabs his forehead and face with a towel until he falls back to sleep.

She wants to curl up next to him and hold him, lie close to his warm body.

Around midnight, Leah says she has to take off. She's going to go see her attaché. She asks Hanna to take care of Samuel while she's gone.

Hanna sits by his side all night long. One time he wakes up with the chills. She gives him water and pulls off his wet shirt.

At dawn he wakes at last with a bit of colour in his face, feeling better. He sits up and thanks her for her help and offers an apology. She opens the windows. The air is already thick and humid. She wraps him in a blanket.

His voice is weak but unusually present. Maybe it's the illness. He leans back against the many pillows and says that he's never really felt at home anywhere, not even in his own family.

He says he's sick of it.

Then he pulls the blanket tight and closes his eyes. She wants to tell him that she feels the same way, but she doesn't want to bother him when he's so sick.

Once he's asleep again, she lingers for a while, watching him.

Then she strips down to her underwear and crawls in next to him.

The sheets smell like puke, but they also smell like him.

She shifts tentatively until she's right next to him. She can feel the heat and moisture of his body. She can see his hair

47

and his face in the dawn light. She lies so close she can hear him breathing. Falling asleep is like slipping into soft, warm water.

18

The museum feels more exciting now that she knows Samuel, because she's aware of how much he loves it.

Sometimes she stays in the archive after her shift is over, at the computer, looking up works he's mentioned. The images become like windows to his soul when she makes copies of them with the scanner, takes the printouts home and tries to paint imitations.

Later, she can bring all of this into her conversations with Samuel. The works become more profound, taking on new meaning because she has him to debate them with.

When she finally gets paid, she buys two copies of a book on Goya's satirical works and gives one to Samuel so they can discuss the book together.

His words are in her body. At night she often wakes up having dreamed of him. Startling images and fantasies keep showing up out of nowhere. She might stop before a statue just because she sees his eyes or his hands in it, and her gaze traces the shape of the body: arms, back, stomach, groin.

One evening, undressing after she returns home from yet another night out with the group, she discovers a strand of his hair on her shirt. She sits down on the edge of the bed, gently pulls it loose from the fabric and holds it up to the bedside lamp. She loves its colour, that flaxen lustre. She opens her mouth and catches the hair with the tip of her tongue, gathers it into a ball against the roof of her mouth, closes her eyes. He is inside her, surrounded by the muscle of her tongue and the softness of her cheeks. Soon her mouth is so full of saliva that she can swallow him with no problem at all.

19

It's after closing time. She has just changed clothes and is on her way home through the empty museum when she gets an idea.

She goes to the unstaffed gift shop and selects a sketchpad, a set of watercolours and a coffee mug. She fills the mug with water in the bathroom and goes to Room 67.

It's a relief to find no one else in the room for once. She sits on the bench in the centre and opens the sketchpad.

She wants to see if she can do better in person. She has painted copies of the Black Paintings many times, but always using reproductions in art books. Maybe something different will happen when she's face to face with them.

She starts with the painting of Saturn since the motif is relatively simple.

First, she sketches the outline in lead, with light strokes. She stops now and then to compare. Erases. Starts over. The lines are thin as spider's silk. With each new layer, the outlines become clearer and clearer, but it's difficult.

She gives up more than once, turning the page and starting over.

She gazes into Saturn's eyes, making an effort to go more on feeling than on technique. She tries to make her hand relax so the forms will be softer.

After a while, she's sufficiently satisfied with the contours to switch to watercolours. She dips the brush in the mug and colours in the red face. She rinses the brush and changes colours. She paints the knuckles, gleaming white, the sinewy muscles, the torn flesh, the protruding bones.

But her depiction lacks nerve. Unlike Goya's painting, it's thoroughly unthreatening. She goes back to pencil, trying to bring out an uneasiness in the shape, and presses the point so hard to the paper that tiny holes appear.

Her disappointment is so great that she wants to cry. She hates herself for not being able to recreate what she loves.

She takes a piece of rag and runs it across the paper, smearing the colour.

That done, she stands up.

In the dirty stain left behind, a face appears.

It's not Saturn gazing at her from the paper but the creature. Its eyes are the black holes of a skull and the crooked mouth is a grimace. Its lips are brown and its teeth yellow. The creature laughs at her for thinking that she could do this on her own, for having the gall to try at all.

She crumples the paper, shoves it in her pocket, and leaves the room.

20

She appreciates Samuel's love of old objects, loves to accompany him to antique shops on Sunday afternoons. He's unusually gentle and empathetic then, as his fingers run along leather backs and stroke yellowed pages.

It doesn't seem to be the money that spurs him to buy and sell, but the kick he gets out of being part of a cycle. He might buy an old etching at one antique shop for 500 euros, then spend the rest of the day in a great mood after selling it at another for 550.

As they wander from shop to shop, he talks about the cultural heritage of Spain, of future generations' responsibility to be good stewards of it. He says he wants to build bridges between what

will soon disappear and what will soon come to be. He tells
Hanna she ought to make her dream of writing a book on Goya
a reality, that he can help her. She says she doubts the world
needs another book about Goya. He replies, 'The world always
needs another book about Goya.' They laugh.

One Sunday, he's showing her an antique shop that he says
sells stolen goods. It's an exciting place, dim and cramped, full
of books and framed art floor to ceiling. Samuel whispers that
the reason the prices are so low is because so much of it was
lifted.

They cautiously sneak around among the shelves, as though
they were committing a crime simply by being there.

She appreciates the secrecy of this moment, how he tenderly
pulls a book from the shelves and leans in to her and opens it
and invents stories about how and where it was stolen.

After they leave they take a seat at a pavement café, under
a large red sailcloth that shades them from the sun.

Once their coffee has arrived, he says: 'How are things going
with that meeting, by the way?'

She pretends to study the menu.

'You said you could introduce me to your boss.'

'Yeah.'

He says: 'The anniversary celebrations are coming up.'

'That's right.'

'I'd really like to make it happen before the holiday.'

She replies: 'He's in London for a week, but he'll be back
soon. On Monday, I think, or Tuesday.'

Samuel nods. 'Okay.'

He says: 'And when are you going to let me see some of
your paintings?'

To sidestep his questions, she asks one back: 'Have you ever
painted anything?'

He looks at her: 'No, but I suppose the dream is to live that
way even so.'

'What do you mean?'

'Seeing your life as a work of art.'

He lights a cigarette, blows out the match, and says: 'But it takes a certain kind of bravery.'

Then a shadow seems to cross his face. He's suddenly serious. She tries to figure out what's going on inside him.

He says: 'I need to shed my skin soon.'

She wants to ask about his childhood, but she knows he doesn't want to talk about that stuff, so she says nothing.

21

One evening, she shows them around the museum.

For once, she's the leader of the group, and it's an intoxicating feeling to hang the badges around their necks and lead them through the galleries.

She planned out the route they would take ahead of time, but once she's talking she gets too excited and has trouble keeping herself under control, pulling them from painting to painting. Her knowledge buoys her on. There's so much to show them and tell them about.

It's clear that Leah and Tom aren't really listening, but Samuel walks beside her, attentively hanging on her every word, gazing up at the art with wide eyes, pointing and asking questions, so eventually Hanna stops caring that Leah and Tom are mostly looking at their phones.

At last they reach Room 67.

Now even Leah and Tom are moved and put down their phones.

They sit down in the centre of the gallery.

'Now I understand why they're called the Black Paintings,' Leah says. 'This is the scariest shit I've ever seen.'

Hanna waits for a moment, to allow the group to settle into their impressions, then tells them how the paintings came to be, when in his later years Goya withdrew to his villa outside Madrid.

'The house was called "House of the Deaf One", because he had lost his hearing by then.'

She sees that they're all listening closely, so she tells them how the murals were discovered after his death, and how experts from the Prado cut out the plaster walls and relocated the paintings to this mythical room, number sixty-seven.

'It's like being inside his head,' Samuel says.

'Is that a good thing?' Leah asks.

Hanna: 'Sometimes people faint in here.'

'It's not sane,' Tom says, pointing at the Saturn painting. 'A father killing and eating his own son!'

'It's a symbol,' says Hanna.

Samuel stands up and approaches Saturn.

He doesn't move for a moment, but then he turns to Hanna: 'A symbol of what?'

She goes to stand next to him, so they're standing side by side and gazing up at the painting.

'Goya had to kill his own history so he could paint freely.'

'He thought about suicide?'

'No, like a mental suicide. He wanted to kill everything he had learned. Kill his style, which was so rich in detail. He felt trapped by it. That was why he retreated to his house and switched techniques, motifs, colour palettes.'

Samuel looks up at the painting. Then he begins to nod and turns to her with a smile: '*Bueno, eres la experta.*'

Hanna nods and smiles back. She thinks she has noticed a shift in his eyes. They stand like that for a long time, gazing at one another under the great painting. For an instant, it feels like the two of them are the only ones in the room.

22

She's already an expert on the group's daily lives. She knows their favourite restaurants and bars. She's familiar with their traditions. She knows that on the way home from the bars they always stop at a churro stand to get a doughy, sugared treat, and when their fingers get sticky they find a square where they can rinse their hands in a fountain. She knows Samuel plays tennis with a group of English diplomats on Mondays, that he keeps a diary, writing it by hand in a red Moleskine notebook. She knows he hates social media and has a private Instagram account where he's posted just three pictures but has 708 followers. She's also starting to understand Leah better. She knows her neuroses and secrets. She knows all about those lonely years in Paris, where she spent her teens sitting in various hotel rooms and waiting for a call from her agent. She knows most of the details of her relationship with the attaché, their sneaking around, his empty promises. And she knows Tom, his writing, his focus, his darting gaze when he's high on something, his secret crush on Leah, his complicated relationship with Samuel, whom he seems to idolise but also has some sort of little-brother complex about. She knows all three of them grew up in a world that's totally foreign to her. Sometimes she gathers her courage and asks about it, and slowly but surely an image of their families' positions emerges. Now she's learning how that sort of wealth is deployed, how the relatives regularly pay out money based on the yields of various family funds, how they will someday inherit so much that they become financially independent. She realises what a one-dimensional view of the rich she had before. She feels that there's an aspect of liquidity to upper-class life, a root-lessness, and it fascinates her. Because they have the financial ability to choose whatever life they'd like, they're always worried they haven't chosen correctly. In some ways, this makes her feel an affinity with them. She, too, lives outside established structures.

23

One Sunday, they get coffee to go from Carlito's and walk down to El Retiro Park. Hanna keeps a few steps behind the group, observing them. Samuel is wearing a thin white shirt and red shorts, brown Italian leather shoes without socks; Tom is in a loose silk Versace shirt. Leah is wearing a blue shirt of Samuel's, dressy white linen shorts and platform trainers. Hanna doesn't understand why she herself is incapable of attaining that casual sexiness: low-key but still eye-catching.

The sun is blazing. A few creamy white clouds stand still in the deep blue sky. The park is full of people. Hanna visited it once in April, back when she was still curious about the city's tourist spots, but she found it deserted and boring. Now she realises she only saw a fraction of the park that time.

They show her the rose garden, a labyrinth of gravel paths among giant bushes. She has never seen such huge roses, has never smelled such an intensely floral scent. It's like being in a perfume shop. In the middle of the garden is a small fountain. Curled rose petals float on the surface of the water. A cherry tree bows down over the water, heavy with pink and white flowers.

Hanna stops and looks at Samuel, who's sticking his nose in a rosebush. Then she observes Tom, who has lain down on a concrete bench with his headphones on, and she watches Leah walk along the fountain with her hand trailing in the water, and it's like something bursts inside her.

She cautiously sneaks off among the rosebushes to catch her breath. She leaves the fountain and walks further into the garden until she finds a park bench on a small rise, under a big oak. There she sits down in the cool shade and closes her eyes.

Just a short time ago, she was alone in her small flat, in the quiet halls of the museum archive. Now every day is full of promise.

She is filled with gratitude so vast that it overflows.

She wants to express it, but she doesn't know how.

When she opens her eyes again, she sees Samuel, Tom and Leah walking along the path. When they see her, they wave. She waves back.

24

The museum park is beautiful in the blue light of dusk when she leaves through the staff entrance. The streetlamps have come on under the trees. People move along the gravel paths like shadows.

Once she has passed the crowd of museumgoers outside the entrance and is on the path up the hill, she hears a familiar voice calling her name. She stops and turns round.

Nearby is a woman around her age. At first she doesn't know who it is. Or she *knows*, but it takes a moment to process it. It's just *wrong* for Vera to be standing there, it doesn't make sense.

Hanna knows she should say something, but instead she remains silent and doesn't move.

At last she manages to raise her hand. Vera waves back and comes up to her.

The crown of the tree is like a roof above them. Vera's face is half illuminated by the lamp.

She says: 'I thought I might run into you.'

Hanna looks at her in silence. She thinks about leaving, just turning round and disappearing into the trees.

Vera: 'How are you?'

Hanna: 'Good.'

Vera: 'Why haven't you called?'

Hanna: 'What is there to say?'

No one says anything for a moment. When Vera starts talking again, she suddenly sounds annoyed: 'I don't get why you just disappeared.'

Silence again.

Vera continues: 'You just took off.'

'I've been busy.'

'With what?'

'Work. And friends.'

Vera nods. Hanna doesn't understand why Vera wants to subject them both to this. Vera: 'Where do you work?'

Hanna is annoyed by the suspicion in her voice. She replies: 'The museum is turning two hundred. I'm in charge of the anniversary celebrations.'

Vera stares at her without blinking.

'I have to go,' Hanna says. 'It was nice to see you.'

She raises her hand in farewell, but Vera quickly says: 'Look, hold on. Hold on,' and sticks out her hand. Hanna stares at it, hanging between them like a question.

Vera says: 'Can't we go somewhere to talk?'

'I can't.'

'We could just sit right here on a bench.'

'I don't have time.'

'What about tomorrow?'

'I can't, I have work.'

It's dark where they're standing, but Hanna thinks she can see tears in Vera's eyes.

Vera says: 'Don't you ever think about me?'

'I have to go now.'

Vera takes a step towards her and says her name.

Hanna says: 'Stop.'

'Please.'

Vera puts out her hand again.

This time, her fingertips brush Hanna's hand, and Hanna starts, looking down at her skin as though she's been burned.

Vera looks down at her hand too.

And for an instant, Hanna sees this scene from the outside.

She and Vera, facing each other on a gravel path in a park. She and Vera, their similarities and differences. Their hands almost meeting in the glow of the streetlight. And she's not sure she can handle the strain. Grief presses into her. The fragile bubble that could burst at any moment. The growing weight.

At last Hanna turns round and hurries up the hill.

She expects Vera to call out to her, but everything is quiet.

All she can hear is the crunch of the gravel and her own loud breathing.

25

When Hanna wakes up, it's night-time and her work clothes are damp with sweat. She fell asleep sitting up on the sofa. She doesn't know what city she's in. She doesn't know her name. She doesn't know what she did wrong. She stands up. She's dizzy. She goes to the balcony. The night is so black it has neither beginning nor end. Time is stuck. She has no protection. She thinks about things she doesn't want to think about. Everything that was, everything that went wrong, that she left behind. Mom's panic-stricken eyes. Vera's face in the park. Her escape from Sweden. She goes back inside and turns on all the lights to get rid of the images, but it doesn't work. It's as if the walls are closing in, bringing with them all the bad stuff she can usually block out. Now it's flooding over her. The dry heat underground, the smell of cement and disinfectant, the flies that settle around her lips and move so fast they can't be killed. She thinks of how fragile the thread is, how easily she could lose the group. She thinks about the duplicate again, a potential gift, a possible solution, and she wonders why she can't bring herself to take that step. She doesn't want to be ruled by fear. She doesn't want to be like Vera. She thinks about all of this until she manages to stop thinking about it.

26

They're at a pavement café in Paraíso Park, next to the little lake. It's eleven at night. The table is full of food. Silver candle-holders with tealights. Platters of Iberico ham and fuet sausage, porcelain bowls of burrata and Manchego to dip in honey before placing them on the fresh bread. Samuel tears off a piece of bread and Hanna watches as the insides release steam. Then he dips it in olive oil and places a few fried sausage rounds on top. He's wearing a white shirt buttoned all the way up. For once his hair is slicked back, revealing his entire face. Hanna is so used to his long hair being in the way that to her it almost feels like he's naked right in front of her. And she has a hard time meeting his gaze. When they finish eating, he asks them what they want to do with their lives.

Leah laughs. But Samuel is serious.

He repeats the question. There's a note of gravity in his voice. It's as though they must decide here and now.

Tom turns to Hanna: 'What do *you* want to do?'

It sounds like an accusation.

Tom: 'You haven't told us much about yourself.'

'All you have to do is ask.'

'I just did. What do you want to do with your life?'

Luck is on her side and there's no time to respond, because Samuel takes over and launches into a description of recent conflicts at his job. He's drunk. He's slurring a little. He says that most of the diplomats are 'losers', that he was stupid to romanticise the career, that he had painted a picture for himself of a universe of well-read people who went from one important meeting to the next. Today, he says, relationships between countries are determined not by diplomats but by a handful of people at just a few companies and the leaders of just a few countries.

Hanna notices that his eyes are moist.

He says: 'I don't want to become bitter.'

Then he opens his mouth as if to say more, but nothing comes out.

The tealights flicker between them and make his face and eyes look almost hollow.

He continues: 'It's time for a change.'

She wants to take his hand and say that she hears him.

And later that night, once they've moved on to a different pavement café on Gran Via, around one-thirty, he returns to the topic. Won't let it go. They're drinking cortados and nibbling on dark chocolate and Samuel says he feels invisible at work, that no one listens to him.

Leah's looking at her phone. Tom puffs on his cigarette and practises blowing rings. It's not going well.

Samuel keeps talking: 'I'm finally ready to face the facts – I have no influence whatsoever.' He looks serious as he continues: 'You, for instance,' and he points at Hanna, 'presumably have more power than I do. Right?'

Hanna: 'I don't know.'

'Or—what is it you actually do?'

She has to force herself to smile: 'What?'

Tom looks up from his phone and fixes his eyes on her. 'Yeah, what do you actually do?'

Leah looks down at her phone and laughs. She's received a text from the attaché, she says.

SIGGE EKLUND

Samuel is still facing Hanna: 'Is your boss back yet?'

Hanna. 'Huh?'

'You told me you could arrange a meeting. So I told the embassy it was happening. And now it's been two weeks.'

He nails her with an accusatory gaze she doesn't recognise.

He continues: 'Wasn't he in London?'

'Yeah, he ended up having to stay.'

At this, Samuel raises his voice: 'I need to meet him!'

Hanna is so taken aback that she can't say a word.

Suddenly, Leah lets out a screech: 'Fuck!' and smacks Samuel.

He turns to her: 'What?'

She says: 'What is wrong with you?' and holds up her hand.

Hanna sees a red spot near her wrist.

Leah shouts: 'You burned me with your cigarette!'

Samuel's eyes are unusually narrow as he smiles at her: 'Okay.'

She nudges him: 'What is with you tonight?'

He raises his palms in the air: 'Guilty!'

Leah: 'Yeah, guilty as fuck.'

Samuel says: 'Yeah, yeah, yeah. You all hate me, fine.'

'You're just stressed out.'

'Yes, I'm very sorry, that can happen when you work at a job. You should try it sometime.'

Tom: 'Stop it.'

Samuel points at Tom: 'You should try it too.'

Then he leans back in his chair and lights another cigarette.

He looks sad. Hanna watches him. A drop of sweat trickles down his cheek and falls from his chin.

The bill arrives. The waiter places the little silver tray on the table between them.

Hanna stiffens. Tom and Leah take no notice of it, and Samuel has retreated inside himself, his gaze blank. Typically, Samuel would grab it, but this time he's sitting still, not making any move to pay. Either he's lost in thought or he wants to make a point that it's about time for someone else to pick up the tab.

61

Hanna looks at the bill and realises she has no choice. She gets out her wallet and takes out her Visa card, reaches across the table to place it on the tray. Suddenly she feels Samuel's warm hand on her own. Without a word he pushes her hand away, shakes his head and puts down his own card instead.

27

Once Samuel and Tom have left, Leah and Hanna linger at the noisy pavement café and split a bottle of chilled Verdejo that smells like melon and mint. Leah says she thinks she's going crazy, that she deserves better. She says she's thinking about calling the attaché's wife and telling her everything. She says she's tired of Samuel always urging her to break it off, without ever asking her how she *feels*. She says: 'Just leave? Easy for him to say. He has no ties to anyone.'

Hanna: 'Exactly.'

Leah turns to face the throngs on the square. Nearby, a fire-eater has gathered a small crowd, and when he blows out a cloud of flame, Leah's face lights up.

Leah says: 'Something is up with Samuel. He's changed.'

'How so?'

'He's taking everything so seriously. He hardly ever laughs any more. He should be a little more like his dad.'

Hanna: 'What's his dad like?'

Leah smiles: 'Charming. Old school. You have to meet him.'

'Does he live in Madrid?'

'No, outside Alicante. And in Dubai. And, like, Saudi Arabia.'

'Are they similar?'

Leah smiles at her: 'No. Ivan is always so positive. Tons of positive energy.'

'But Samuel has energy, doesn't he?'

Leah says, with a laugh, 'Sure, dark energy.'

'Are they close?'

'I'd say their relationship is complicated. Ivan likes living in his big house, with all his money, his job. Samuel is never satisfied. He's always on the run. Always wanting to move forward.'

Hanna nods. Leah's right.

Samuel seems close to a breaking point. That's how she interprets his behaviour. He has found himself at some sort of dead end, and he wants to start over. She knows all about that feeling. Maybe that's why she's drawn to him. Leah doesn't understand that it's a survival strategy.

Leah says: 'I miss the old Samuel.' Then she stubs out her cigarette and goes to the toilets.

Hanna, left behind alone, catches sight of Samuel's abandoned wine glass.

His lips have left smudges along the rim.

She reaches for the glass, looking around. Then she brings it to her mouth and allows her lips to meet his. She drinks the wine, and when she swallows it down in big gulps, it is his sweet blood filling her mouth, but she still isn't satisfied once she's emptied it, she wants more, has the urge to take a bite of the glass, let the shards crunch in her mouth until her blood mingles with his.

28

One night, when they're drunk at Bar Palestine, Hanna asks them if they want to come with her to a 'forbidden place'.

Tom grins. Clearly the phrase gets him revved up.

Soon they're standing under a streetlight, smoking and waiting for their Uber, and Samuel suddenly turns his face up to the yellow glow and says that this is an underappreciated sort of moment.

'What?' Tom says.

Samuel: 'The moment before the moment. I think this is one of those times you'll look back on when you're older and think, "Why didn't I appreciate it more? That time we were standing at an intersection in Madrid in the middle of the night, waiting for a taxi, with no clue how privileged we were."'

Hanna can't help but smile at his romantic view of the world, while Tom merely shakes his head.

Samuel points at Tom: 'You should write about this.'

Tom says: 'Should I though?' and flashes a crooked smile.

Samuel rests a hand on his shoulder: 'We're young and smart and pretty hot too. Can't we try to be happy about it?'

Leah: '*Pretty* hot?'

At last Tom laughs too.

And Hanna wants to tell Samuel she feels the same way, even though she maybe can't put it into words like he can.

When the Uber arrives, Samuel flicks his cigarette away with his index finger. Then he blows the last of the smoke up at the streetlight and Hanna watches it rise and swirl above them.

The driver is reaching dangerous speeds, as though he's being chased, but Hanna is too tipsy to worry. On the contrary, she enjoys the sensation of speeding. Each time he hits the gas, she gets butterflies in her stomach. She turns round and notices that Leah's eyes are closed; she's smiling in the glow of oncoming lights.

'Where are we going?' Leah calls.

'Soon, soon,' Hanna replies.

Tom turns up the volume and the music of the car stereo fills the compartment, a voice singing about secret love, about a bond that only gets deeper. Samuel and Tom sing along and Hanna mouths the words, even though she doesn't know the lyrics.

They get out of the Uber and cross the street. Tom and Leah are still singing the song aloud, and Hanna brings her index finger to her mouth: 'Shhh . . . I don't know if anyone is here.'

Then she walks up to the wooden door, presses the badge to the pad and enters the code. She's worried she might not remember it, but soon there's a click from the heavy wooden door and she pushes it open.

Then she leads them up the steep staircase.

Upstairs, she turns on the lights.

They're silent for a moment, gazing around the room.

'Where the fuck are we?' Tom asks. Then he sees the big Norwegian flag and starts laughing.

Hanna turns on the radio and music fills the room.

It's clear that the group is impressed, although this place is basically just a pool hall that smells like cigarettes. She says she has 'Norwegian contacts' that gave her access to the venue.

Leah says: 'I want Norwegian contacts!' and takes a cue stick from the wall on her way to the pool table. Samuel stands behind the bar, under the portrait of the Norwegian king and queen, in the same spot where the Norwegian stood, and asks:

'What do you want?'

Hanna says the same thing now as she did then: 'Surprise me.'

They hear a bang outside. It sounds like a gunshot, and Hanna freezes.

Samuel, too, stops what he's doing: 'What was that?'

Tom opens the balcony doors and goes out.

Soon they hear a cry of joy from out there: 'Fireworks!'

Samuel and Leah dash out to join him, but Hanna lingers in the room. She wants to look at the statue again.

It's still in the same spot, on its wooden plinth in the corner.

Hanna rests a hand on it.

Outside, the fireworks burst.

The girl so badly wants to get out, but her little hands are cemented into the stone. She can't get loose.

Hanna gazes into the girl's eyes.

She's been so happy in recent days, but it's not enough. She wants to be free, as free as the others. When they're talking about art she feels confident, but the rest of the time, her words get caught halfway out; come out wrong. She knows how she wants it to sound, she can hear it as clear as music, but it's like she's hitting the wrong keys on a piano. She wants to be as free as Leah on the dance floor or Samuel in their conversations or Tom when he's writing. They have extended a hand, yet she won't quite give them her own.

She looks at the statue. It's taunting her. Why can't she just rip her hands free? Maybe it has to do with money. As long as she's poor, she'll be stuck in the underworld.

Which means she has to be brave and do the thing she knows she should do.

She promises herself she'll make a decision soon. She has put it off for way too long.

She strokes the girl's back one last time. Then she joins the others.

The exploding fireworks light up the rooftops and chimneys. Leah shrieks with joy and the fireworks are reflected in her eyes. Tom shouts something in Spanish and raises a champagne glass to the sky, his face blue from the falling sparks, and down on the street they hear some teenagers cheer. In the distance, horns honk and people whoop.

'What is going *on?*' Leah yelps jubilantly. 'It just keeps *going!*'

'Must be celebrating some saint,' Tom says.

'Gotta love 'em for believing all those fairy tales,' Samuel says.

'Yeah, for real,' Hanna says.

Then Tom shoots the champagne cork across the rooftops and they take swigs straight from the bottle as they pass it around and the bubbles tickle Hanna's nose, and Tom raises the bottle to the showering sparks and says this is going to be the best summer of their lives.

29

When Hanna wakes up, the room is dark. The balcony doors are still open and the air is damp and hot. Her mouth is dry and her head is pounding. Leah's asleep on the couch beside her.

Hanna realises where they are and leaps up. 'What time is it?'

Leah: 'What's the matter?'

Hanna says in a panic, 'We fell asleep!'

Hanna looks at the Norwegian flag and the crystal chandeliers, trying to remember why they decided to fall asleep on the sofas.

Leah says: 'What time is it?'

Hanna takes out her phone. 'Five in the morning.'

Leah: 'It's fine. As long as we're gone before anyone arrives.'

'When will people arrive?'

'Around nine, maybe. Or eight.'

'How do you know that?'

'Where are Samuel and Tom?'

'They left after you fell asleep.'

Leah stands up. She's wearing nothing but pants yet she doesn't make any attempt to hide her body. Hanna looks away. Leah goes to the bathroom without closing the door. Hanna can hear the pee burbling into the toilet.

She looks over at the statue of the little girl. From this angle it looks like she's drowning.

Leah calls from the bathroom: 'By the way, where were you yesterday?'

'At work.'

'Weird.'

'What?'

'We went by the museum and asked for you.'

'What?'

'It was Tom's idea. We were in the neighborhood and he thought we should surprise you.'

Leah comes out of the bathroom: 'We went to the counter and asked if we could visit the anniversary committee, but they said no.'

Hanna: 'Security is pretty tight.'

'We snuck up anyway.'

Hanna looks at her.

Hanna: 'Snuck up where?'

'They said it was on the second floor. So we took the stairs.'

'Okay?'

'But there was some guy there who said he didn't know who you were.'

'What did he look like?'

'I don't know. Spanish. But we said, "We know Hanna!"'

'And?'

'He was all, "Who?"'

'Must have been one of the interns. I haven't had a chance to get to know them.'

'That's too bad. It would have been fun to see you at work.'

'Yeah.'

'Watch you bossing people around!'

Hanna turns to the open balcony doors. It's getting light over the rooftops. She says: 'Shall we go?'

Leah points at the half-empty bottles on the bar: 'Shouldn't we finish the champagne first?'

'I don't know if I can drink before work.'

Leah says: 'I've got gum,' and grabs a bottle and two glasses.

Then they curl up on the sofa, under the same blanket, and Leah gives her the latest on the attaché. She says their relationship has had a fresh spark ever since his wife came to Madrid, because now they have to sneak around again just like back when it was all brand new, and it's romantic.

Hanna: 'Do you think he's going to leave her?'

'He says he will.'

Hanna notices a mole on Leah's breast that she's never seen before; it's perfectly placed to draw the eye. What Hanna envies most about Leah's appearance is that it must save her so much energy. She never has to put in any effort to draw attention, because she already dominates the room, just by looking the way she does.

Leah pours more champagne: 'Here's to bad relationships.'

Hanna smiles and raises her glass.

She can tell Leah is getting tipsy. So she jumps at the opportunity: 'Have you ever had sex with Samuel or Tom?'

Leah peers at her over her glass. 'Have you?'

'No.'

She smiles: 'I have with Tom, obviously, but it's just a bad idea.'

'Why?'

'He gets ideas.'

'Like what?'

'He just gets weird.'

'How so?'

'No comment.'

Leah pours more champagne.

Hanna asks, 'What about Samuel?'

'He's more like a brother. I have trouble seeing him that way.'

Hanna: 'Yeah.'

'I feel embarrassed just thinking about it,' she says.

'For real,' says Hanna.

'It's just wrong.'

'No, yikes. But what if you had to?'

Leah looks at her. She says: 'What do you mean?'

Hanna reaches for a cigarette. She turns to the window, feigning disinterest, lights a cigarette, and says: 'I mean . . . if you were forced to have sex with him.'

'What?!'

Hanna turns to her and says: 'Would you like it?'

Leah doesn't respond. She looks at Hanna and tucks her knees in close to her body. Then she says: 'I don't think you should fall for Samuel.'

Hanna gives a shrill laugh. 'What?'

Leah takes a drag of her cigarette and smiles at her.

Hanna: 'Why would you say that?'

Leah blows out smoke and says: 'There's something wounded about him. I think it has to do with Rakel.'

'Rakel?'

'His mother.'

'What's her deal?'

'She was sick when he was little.'

Hanna feels her temples pounding. She takes a drag of her cigarette to calm down.

Then she says: 'Sick, how?'

'Mentally ill.'

'Depressed, you mean?'

'And five years ago, she had a stroke on top of it. It's awful. She just lies there.'

'Oh my god, that's terrible.'

'Samuel doesn't like to talk about it.'

'Oh.'

'I guess we'll see when we meet her.'

Hanna: 'Is she coming to Madrid?'

Leah: 'No, we're going there on holiday.'

'Where?'

'To his parents' place.'

Hanna stares at her, trying to absorb what she's saying. Then she says: 'Holiday?'

'Yeah, me and Samuel and Tom. Didn't you know? It was Samuel's Christmas present to us. We're heading down to Alicante, we'll stay with his parents for a bit and then travel around the coast. I can't fucking wait.'

The words are like a kick to the stomach.

30

When Hanna arrives home, she plops down on the edge of the bed, but she's too shaken to sit still and quickly gets back up.

She goes out to the balcony. The sky is leaden. She tries to remember everything Leah said. In the moment, she was so shocked that her ears were ringing. She didn't even dare to ask any questions, too worried that her voice would tremble. She just sat there in silence, staring as Leah went on and on about all the places they're going to visit on their trip and all the clothes she's going to buy, and how exciting it's going to be to see Samuel's parents again.

All Hanna could manage to say was, 'How can you afford it?'

At that, Leah looked at her in surprise and said, as though it could not possibly be more obvious, 'I'll just ask Mum.'

'What about Tom?' Hanna asked.

Leah laughed: 'He can afford it. Trust me, he's got the money.'

And now Hanna realises she was an idiot to think she could ever be an equal member of the group. She's been a visitor in their world for a little while, but that dream will soon be over. Samuel, Tom and Leah are made of different stuff, and soon they will leave her behind.

31

When she arrives in the archive, she notices right away that the flies have increased in number. It's especially obvious around the fluorescent tubes in the ceiling. But when she points it out to the guard, he just laughs and hands her a flyswatter. She takes her trolley and heads down the corridor, but soon she stops because she can't stand it any more. They're going for her eyes. They're trying to get in the corners of her lips.

She turns round and goes back to the guard and asks to use the phone.

She calls Andrés and tells him she has realised she might have some kind of fly phobia. She asks if she can work upstairs in the museum, just for this week, or at least for today, but he sighs in annoyance and says he grew up on a farm: 'Talk about flies. They were the size of bumblebees.' Then he laughs and tells her she'll simply have to deal with it until the exterminator can come to investigate the issue.

After she hangs up, she stares down the dim corridor and thinks of all the eggs just waiting to hatch in there. She thinks about how she doesn't want to be there, of the group's trip, their nights on the coast, far from these culverts; she thinks of what Leah told her about Samuel's mother's illness, of what would happen if Hanna could meet her, if Samuel could see Hanna with his mother. She desperately tries to wave the flies away from her neck and ears, but new ones just keep landing on her. A wave of nausea washes over her and she realises she needs some fresh air.

When she emerges into the park, it feels like she's running out of a burning building.

32

Samuel is beating eggs in the kitchen. There's a heavy scent of sautéed butter and garlic. When he's finished, he places three plates of fluffy potato omelettes on the balcony table, as well as two bowls of sausages and tomato sauce. He also hands a special bowl of fried anchovies to Leah, who doesn't eat omelettes.

They sit down on the large balcony to eat. Hanna tries to smile and nod during dinner, pretending to follow the conversation, but she has trouble listening. All she can think about is their trip.

After dinner, they drink coffee and calvados. Beyond the rooftops she can see the lights on the hills of Moratalaz flickering in the distance. Samuel puts on some music. They're lounging on beanbag chairs. Leah's texting the attaché, Tom crawls down to lie on his back on the Indian carpet and lights a joint. The sweet smell spreads over the balcony. Hanna tries to figure out what to say. After a while, she turns to Samuel: 'I talked to my boss.'

Samuel: 'And?'

'He'd be happy to meet you.'

'Are you kidding?'

'No. It's just, he has a lot going on right now, before the holidays. But I'll get back to you when I have a date.'

Samuel: 'Thanks.'

Hanna: 'Of course.'

He gets up to refill her wine. She takes her chance: 'Leah told me, by the way.'

'What about?'

'Your trip.'

He settles back into his chair. 'Okay?'

'You're going away?'

'Yeah, it's going to be so nice.'

'Where are you going?'

And Samuel describes their plan, and Hanna soon realises it was a mistake to ask, because he gets so excited when he talks about how much fun they're going to have and what beautiful places they're going to visit, and about his mother and father's house, and how large it is, and how close to the sea it is. Hanna wants to ask him to stop, she wants to say enough is enough, that she doesn't understand why they haven't invited her, even if they planned the trip before she came on the scene, but she sits quietly, nodding and listening, with mental images flickering by of Samuel, Tom and Leah together on beaches, enjoying long lunches at different pavement cafés, in various villages and harbours.

At last she can't take it any longer. She says she has to go home because she has to be at work early the next day. Blames it on a headache. The others are so engrossed in their travel planning that they hardly seem to notice when she leaves.

33

The Norwegian sounds surprised when she calls from the hotel lobby, but he says she can come up.

In the lift she checks the mirror, fixes her hair and make-up.

The Norwegian answers the door dressed in a suit and lets her in. On the floor is a packed suitcase. He says he's just returned from Barcelona, where he has his car dealership.

She asks him to help her with her dress. When that's done, he takes out a hanger and stashes it in the wardrobe.

She feels oddly blank. Maybe it has to do with the fact that she has no choice.

She sits down in the easy chair, wearing only her bra and pants, while he goes to the minibar and mixes a drink, which he then hands to her.

Then he sits down on the edge of the bed and says: 'Touch yourself.'

She takes a sip of her drink. It's lukewarm and tastes like vodka and grapefruit. She says: 'I want to talk about your cars first.'

At that, he smiles. 'Oh really?'

'I need to borrow one.'

He takes a sip of his whisky and smiles: 'Borrow?'

'In July.'

'I don't lend them out.'

'Why not?'

He sips his drink, leans towards her and says it again: 'Touch yourself.'

She pretends not to hear. She says: 'Not even to a friend?'

'I have so many friends that I would go broke if I operated that way.'

He stands up and goes to the wardrobe. It takes time for him to undress, he does it so meticulously. Each garment must be folded and hung carefully.

Then he sits back down on the edge of the bed, wearing only his briefs: 'Didn't you realise that what I sell is a dream?'

'What do you mean?'

'It's not the cars people pay for, it's the image of themselves in the cars.'

They regard one another.

'That's why it's important that they pay. For the experience of it.'

'The experience of it.'

As he drinks, he stares at her body. She watches his gaze move up her legs and stop where they're spread.

He sips his whisky and says: 'What image do *you* see?'

She takes a drink and says: 'I see myself in a convertible.'

He laughs. 'Do you now?'

'Do you have a car like that?'

'Do I have a car like that?'

'Yes.'

He smiles: 'A Bentley, for instance?'

'Tell me.'

'I do have a Bentley. Hold on!'

He holds up a finger. Then he continues: 'Now I can picture you in it too.'

'Describe it.'

'You're driving by the sea.'

She can feel the drink now. She takes another sip.

She says: 'Tell me more.'

And he describes what she'll look like as she drives the car and how happy and free she'll feel. He describes how the landscape and the sea will look around her. And when he's finished, he pauses for a moment. Then he says: 'I'll give you the friends and family discount.'

She laughs, which makes him laugh too.

Then he tells her once more to touch herself – and this time, she does as he says.

34

She's sitting at Café Gijón with Leah and Tom and sees Samuel walking their way, taller than everyone else, blonder, more beautiful. Do people on the street see what she sees? Now he's raising his hand to wave at her. She waves back. The two of them smile. This is how it happens, apparently. She's spent all her life wondering. Somebody shows up out of nowhere and sheds a new light on the world and it turns out it's bigger than you thought. She pulls out the chair beside her own. He takes a seat. She pours him a glass of red wine.

He's all wound up because he just talked to his dad about their upcoming visit.

Hanna says she's curious and asks Samuel to tell her about his father, and Samuel is reluctant at first but then he describes what he looks like, his personality. Soon she can picture him clearly. She likes what she sees, even though Samuel tells her their relationship is complicated. She even likes his name. *Ivan.*

Samuel tells her: 'His job is all about making connections between big oil companies and countries all over the world.'

Hanna: 'Are you close?'

He considers this, puffing on his cigarette.

'He's a hard man to get close to.'

After a while he goes on: 'I'm a different person around him.'

Hanna wonders what that looks like in practice, for Samuel to become a different person. She would love to see Samuel and Ivan in the same room, see Samuel acting subordinate to his father. She, too, wants to be subordinate to him, alongside Samuel.

She pictures an older Samuel, a venerable, white-haired version of him. She thinks Ivan will like her. She doesn't know why, but her gut feeling tells her they'll get along very well.

On the way home, they walk through a small park. The sky is full of stars and the air is balmy.

She and Leah are walking side by side. The gravel crunches beneath their feet. Leah's wearing woven sandals, black Frame jeans and a lightweight white jumper. Hanna wonders if she's ever seen Leah in the same clothes twice.

Samuel and Tom have found two abandoned badminton rackets on a bench and they launch into an improvised game on the lawn nearby.

Hanna and Leah sit down on a bench to share a cigarette. They are quiet in the dusky light for a bit. Then Leah says: 'I'm thinking about sending an anonymous email to his wife.'

Hanna: 'What?'

'I want to hurt him the way he's hurt me.'

Hanna looks at her.

Leah takes a drag of the cigarette: 'Yesterday I was standing outside their building, in the park and I watched them when they came home. And I realised I'm prepared to do anything now.'

Hanna: 'Maybe it's a good thing you'll be away on your trip soon.'

'I don't want to leave without figuring this out first.'

'What do Samuel and Tom say?'

'They just get annoyed. They think I should break it off.'

Hanna turns to her: 'You can always talk to me.'

Leah nods and says: 'Thanks.'

Hanna says: 'I'm actually going to the coast too.'

Leah turns to her and says: 'I didn't know that.'

Hanna: 'My holiday starts the first of July, so I'll be heading down right away. I have friends who are renting a house in Alicante.'

'Oh.'

Tom and Samuel wave in the distance.

She stands up and waves back, while Leah remains perched on the edge of the bench.

Hanna turns to her: 'Come on.'

Leah doesn't move; she gazes down at her hands. 'I feel old. I don't usually feel like this.'

Hanna looks at her.

Leah says: 'Like an old woman.'

'You're young.'

'In my industry, twenty-eight is old.'

Hanna takes her hand and pulls her up so they're face to face. Hanna says: 'You are young.'

'What does it matter, when I can't enjoy it?'

Then they hear music in the distance and turn round.

Across the park they see a café where a band is entertaining the packed patio seating.

Tom and Samuel have already found a table, and they're waving Hanna and Leah over.

They take a seat. The music envelops them like a scene in a movie.

The air is thick with the scent of stone pine and lavender. Above them are strings of little lightbulbs that run between the trees and the café roof.

Samuel orders a carafe of red wine.

Now the band is playing a tango. A man with an accordion joins in. Leah hums along. Tom reaches for Leah and pulls her up. They embrace under the lights. Tom says something in her ear and she nods. She looks serious. He strokes her cheek. Hanna wonders what he's saying. She wonders if he knows the latest twists and turns with the attaché or if that's something Leah has only confided in Hanna. It looks like he's comforting her. They stand still as he speaks to her, and she nods. It looks like she's saying, 'I know, I know.'

At last he kisses her on the cheek and they start to dance, slowly, between the great stone statues.

Beyond them loom the high-rises of Pacifico, and beyond that they can see the quiet mountains in the darkness. The sky is lofty and midnight blue. Here and there, an aeroplane blinks in the dark. Tom and Leah are dancing more tenderly than the other couples. Samuel and Hanna sit side by side, watching them.

Hanna says: 'What day are you going to the coast?'

Samuel: 'We're heading off on the first of July.'

'Seems like everyone has holiday at the same time.'

He doesn't respond.

She continues: 'It'll be nice.'

He says: 'What are you going to do?'

'Visit friends in the south.'

Now Tom and Leah rejoin them at the table. Tom's forehead is glistening with sweat. Leah looks more animated now.

Hanna goes on: 'In Alicante.'

Samuel: 'Us too.'

'How are you getting there?'

'By train.'

Hanna: 'I'm a little scared, because I'm going to be driving a Bentley.'

Then she pauses for a few seconds, her eyes on the dancing couples, before she goes on. 'I've never driven such a fast car.'

Tom: 'A Bentley?'

'Yeah, a convertible.'

Tom: 'A Bentley *convertible?*'

'Yeah.'

Tom looks stern: 'How can you afford that?'

Samuel turns to Tom: 'What kind of question is that?'

But Tom doesn't take his eyes off Hanna.

Hanna: 'I know this Spanish art collector who's a little bit interested in me. Or . . . kind of a lot interested. And he said I could borrow it, and I accepted the offer, but now I'm not so sure.'

Leah: 'Might as well take advantage.'

Hanna: 'Maybe.'

Samuel: 'When do you leave?'

Hanna: 'My holiday starts on the last day of June. So I'm getting the train to Barcelona on the first of July, and I'll pick up the car there.'

She lights a cigarette.

Samuel: 'We were planning on starting in Barcelona too.'

Leah: 'But we're taking the train the whole way, I'm afraid.'

Samuel: 'Then we'll travel down to Alicante.'

Leah: 'We should ride with Hanna instead. If that's okay, I mean?'

Hanna: 'Of course.'

Leah: 'I love convertibles.'

Samuel turns to Hanna: 'Are you sure?'

'Yes.'

'Are you really sure?'

'I'm sure.'

Tom, smiling, turns to Samuel: 'What happened to always taking the train?'

Samuel: 'We're taking the train to Barcelona.'

Leah: 'Will all four of us fit in the car, though?'

Tom points at Leah: 'If we don't, you have to stay home.'

Leah throws a napkin at Tom.

Samuel: 'Can you drop us off at my dad's house? It's right outside Alicante.'

Hanna takes a drag of her cigarette. 'Sure.'

Samuel: 'On the way to meet up with your friends. Or, where do they live?'

Hanna braces herself. Then she says: 'I wasn't exactly being honest.'

They stare at her.

Hanna: 'I lied.'

Tom: 'What?'

'I'm not meeting up with friends. I'm travelling by myself – to get away.'

She stubs out her cigarette. Then she continues: 'I always go away somewhere on the first of July because it's the anniversary of my mother's death.'

They watch her.

Samuel says: 'My condolences.'

She replies: 'Thank you.'

Samuel: 'I didn't know.'

'It's not something I talk about very often.'

'You don't have to.'

'It's okay.'

Leah: 'How old were you?'

Hanna: 'Fifteen.'

Leah: 'Shit.'

'She drowned.'

Leah: 'Whoa.'

Tom: 'Jesus.'

They're all looking at her. She's never had the undivided attention of the group this way.

Hanna: 'I actually have no problem talking about it.'

The waiter arrives. Hanna says: 'A margarita, please.'

Tom adds, 'Four, please.'

When the waiter walks off, no one speaks for a moment. Then Hanna says: 'I was there on the boat.'

Then she pauses and lights a cigarette.

She goes on: 'It was a sailboat. And I always thought it was so boring to go out in that boat. I always wanted to stay home. It was no different that time. But Dad kept nagging me, saying we'd only be out for a few hours.'

She looks into Samuel's eyes, which shine in the glow of the streetlights.

She continues: 'We almost didn't set sail, that day, because the people on the pier said we should stay in port, the wind was blowing so hard. Mum wasn't sure about it, but Dad insisted, and finally we set out. And after a while, once we got quite far out, I was so scared, because I realised how strong the storm was. Like, the waves were several metres high, and the boat was making sounds I'd never heard and soon it was hard to steer. And Mum said we should turn back to the harbour, and they started pulling on the ropes to come about. But by now the waves were so high they were coming over the deck and somehow Mum slipped and fell in. And I ran to the edge. At first I wasn't all that worried, because I knew she was a good swimmer, but when I leaned over the railing I couldn't see her.'

As she speaks, she watches the group's faces change. They're sitting perfectly still, turned to face her.

'We could see her arms now and then. And Dad was shouting over and over that she should stay put while he tried to turn the boat round. And I started shouting at Mum too, but she was so far away she couldn't hear me, I don't think.'

Tom: 'You remember the whole thing?'

Hanna nods softly.

'Every second.'

Leah: 'Go on.'

Hanna: 'She got farther away from the boat, farther and farther away, and sometimes she disappeared behind a wave, and sometimes she popped up again. And Dad was trying to turn the boat, but the wind was so strong, and I could see him pulling on ropes and trying, but it seemed really hard, and I don't know why, but I went, like, totally—'

Hanna's voice breaks.

She starts again, and her voice breaks again.

She sees Leah bring her hand to her lips.

At last she goes on: 'I was paralysed. I just stood there, not saying a word, holding on to the mast. And Mum must have panicked or something, because she was swimming so clumsily, moving her arms but not getting anywhere. It wasn't like her. She just splashed around in the foam. At some point I saw her eyes, and sometimes I saw her open her mouth like she was going to shout, but she didn't make a sound. And finally I started screaming, 'Mum! Mum!' . . . and I didn't recognise my own voice. 'Mum! Mum!' And sometimes it was 'Dad! Dad!' But neither of them answered me.'

She takes a sip of her drink.

Then she resumes her tale: 'When the boat finally reached her, we had to work together. Or, I mean, I wasn't that strong, she was floating face-down, but Dad hauled her up on deck and I remember how he . . . I mean . . . how he . . .'

Her voice breaks again, and in the silence she looks at Samuel and sees that he is rapt. Tom's mouth is half open. Leah's eyes are brimming with tears.

Hanna goes on: 'And her body is cold and white. Dad turns her over, onto her back, on the floor of the boat, and I feel a ray of hope because I think he's going to give Mum mouth-to-mouth and she'll wake up, and Dad starts doing CPR, here, on her chest, and he presses his mouth to hers, and it seems like . . . It seems like he's crying while he does it. And finally he gives up and aims for land instead . . . and it takes a long time . . . because the storm is so fierce . . . and when we reach the pier he screams, in a panic, screams for help, I mean, and two women help us moor at the pier, and those same women

come onboard and give her CPR and mouth-to-mouth too . . .
but . . . after a while they give up . . . and I don't understand
why . . . why are they giving up? . . . so I go over and try to
breathe air into Mum, and maybe I'm . . . I do it too hard . . .
because her teeth hit my mouth and cut my lip . . . and I start
bleeding here . . . and then someone suddenly grabs me, pulls
me away . . . and someone is holding me . . . and someone
else puts a towel over her body . . . and I don't understand
why they're in such a rush . . . and then Dad comes and holds
me . . . and says he'll take care of me . . . or something like
that . . . He says he's going to protect me . . . He will always
protect me. He says a bunch of stuff, but I still can't cry. He
holds me. And then that's the last thing I remember.'

When she's finished, she turns to the group and sees, through
her tears, that they're all crying too, all three of them.

35

On the walk home, she replays the scene in her mind, over
and over: how Samuel stood up when her story was over,
embraced her and held her; how Tom offered his condolences
and said something about how she should have told them sooner;
how Leah kissed her cheek and hair and shoulder, how Samuel
said: 'Maybe you should come to my dad's house for a few days
too. You shouldn't be alone.'

Leah chimed in: 'You should come along for the whole trip!'

Hanna replied: 'We'll see.'

Now she's walking homeward and smiling at how silly she
had been, imagining that they didn't want her along.

She looks at the people walking by and meets their eyes and
smiles and people smile back. The bass thumping from the clubs
is like a heartbeat. Everything is pulsing and alive. She has to

stop doubting herself. Things usually do work out in the end, as long as you put in the effort.

All of a sudden she even feels calm as she accepts what she has to do in order to afford the trip. The solution has been there in front of her for a long time. Coincidence opened a gap in the weft of reality and all she needs to do is reach inside.

JUNE

1

She searches through the old neighbourhoods around the Almudena cathedral. She knows what she's looking for, but she doesn't remember the address and is too scared to google it. She doesn't want to leave any traces.

She starts at Plaza de Oriente. A group of tourists is taking selfies around the statue of Felipe IV. She inspects the shop windows and signs, moves on to the grungier neighbourhoods north of Malasaña. The bells of the cathedral chime six; the sound is ominous. She's on the verge of giving up and going home.

That's when she finally locates it, the antique shop Samuel showed her. It's half-hidden on a small square, under the stone bridge that leads down from the cathedral square, its window full of old maps and leather-bound books.

She turns round to make sure there are no security cameras in the shops next door and is reassured. The only businesses on the square are a fruit shop, a butcher and a fabric store, shops she would guess don't have modern security measures.

Later, as she walks home through the hot, dark streets, the voices in her head are so loud it feels like her thoughts can be heard from the outside.

2

At work the next day, she continues her reconnaissance. She studies how the guards work and finds that security is actually quite lax. The guard at the lift checks the numbers on the envelopes without opening them. There are only a few cameras, all of them located by the lifts.

At ten o'clock she walks up to the guard, as usual, to get the day's list. Then she goes on her rounds, taking out envelopes and placing them in the trolley. Now she will pay meticulous attention to the routines.

She goes to the security portal and presses the button. The guard comes out of the break room and zaps the bar codes on the plastic envelopes, compares them to the list, and lets her through to the lift.

On the ride up, she's exhilarated. She realises her suspicion was correct. Since the guard doesn't check the contents of the envelopes, only the bar codes, her plan will work.

The lift stops on the fourth floor and she gets out. As she pushes the trolley ahead of her towards the research room, she looks around in search of a good hiding spot. At the end of the corridor she discovers a tall black glassed-in cabinet that's full of brochures. She realises that all she has to do is switch the duplicate to a different envelope while she's riding up in the lift, and then she can stash it in this cabinet. The plan feels watertight.

3

She's walking hand in hand with Leah, behind Tom and Samuel, and all four of them are laughing aloud, and maybe it's just her imagination, but something has changed since it was decided that she would come along on the trip. A new sense of ease, a new closeness. It's been raining and the cobblestones are slick and shiny, but that doesn't matter. They're on their way to the next bar together, and Hanna knows how it works now: it's the seeking that's the point. At first she didn't understand the restlessness, why Tom or Leah always had to text someone to find out which spot might be better than the one they were already at, why they were always switching clubs, but now she knows: the hunt has intrinsic value, the search is an adventure in itself. Tom gets a text about some new place. They hop into yet another taxi. She observes the others in the back seat while the car sails on, and she swells with love for them, because she's thinking of the trip, of everything they will get to experience together. She closes her eyes and gives in to the speed. Everything that happens now happens because it must. It's preordained, that's how it feels.

She muses: would Samuel, Tom, and Leah have it in them to take the sort of risk she's about to take? Presumably not. They've never needed to. But just like her, they carry this sense of yearning, and that's why she fits in with them. She has seen their dreams, she has seen the way Samuel longs for a new life, Leah's need for arms to hold her tight, Tom's obsession with his writing. Now they're singing along to the music as the car hurtles through the night.

Dawn has come before they give up and decide to go home.

By the time they leave, Samuel is so drunk that Hanna has to lead him to the taxi. As soon as he sits down in the back seat, he passes out. It's up to her to give the name of his street.

As the taxi slews through the city, she looks out the window and wonders if the time is right.

She reminds herself that she has to be cool about it, not act too eager, if it happens.

When they arrive at his flat, Samuel goes to the living room and she goes to the bathroom.

She puts on make-up, brushes her teeth and washes up. By the time she returns, he's fallen asleep in the big leather chair, the cigarette still glowing between his fingers; he's shrouded in smoke. It's almost full daylight outside. She pulls the curtains and tries to think clearly. She's supposed to be at work in an hour and a half. She needs to drink some water. She can't miss work now; she has to act normal.

She gently takes the cigarette from his hand, pulls a blanket over him and goes to the kitchen, where she drinks two glasses of orange juice. She discovers that the coffeemaker is half full of old coffee and heats a mug in the microwave. She bolts it down, then starts doing laps of the flat to sober up.

The morning light forces its way through the curtains. Once again she's struck by how large the flat is. Each room on its own is bigger than her whole flat. She even finds rooms she didn't know existed. A tastefully decorated guest room, a gym with an exercise bike, and a sauna.

She goes back to the living room and checks to see if Samuel is still asleep.

Then she takes the key that hangs from a hook in the front hall, opens the front door cautiously, and steps into the stairwell.

She crosses the hallway and unlocks his office.

She has never been in there, has only seen him vanish into it now and then. The room is pretty small, with a large desk by the window, giving it a view of the lush green courtyard. It's full of books and papers. She's touched to see the evidence of his hard work. All over there are open books, full of post-its. So this is where he sits and works on his articles and investigations. She wants to wake him up and tell him she understands and appreciates his dedication.

She opens one of the notebooks on the desk and runs her fingertips over the ink. It's like touching his skin. She tries to make out the words.

Then she notices a framed family photo on the desk. She picks it up to look at it.

Samuel must be about ten. Behind him is a well-dressed man in his forties, who Hanna guesses is Ivan. He doesn't look very much like Samuel but is at least as attractive. About a metre away from them stands a woman Hanna assumes is Rakel.

She looks into the woman's eyes and feels a chill spread through her body. That gaze is familiar; she knows it all too well. A different mother, a different life, but those are the same tortured eyes. She leans towards the photo to get a closer look.

Suddenly she hears a voice: 'What are you doing?'

A silhouette in the doorway, black and faceless. Hanna jumps and immediately drops the photo on the desk. She slips the key into her pocket.

She says: 'I have to go to work.'

4

She hasn't slept a wink but given the circumstances she feels okay. She stops in front of the full-length mirror in the locker room at work and discovers she's lost weight, which makes her happy. It's clear to see when she looks at her thighs and her arms, and when she turns round she notices her bum is smaller too. If she keeps on like this, maybe she can borrow Leah's bikinis on the trip. She decides she will never accept being out of shape again. The white pudge that used to well over the edge of her pants, that made her work clothes bulge, that made her dresses cling to her stomach. She will never again accept losing control. She will never again eat empty calories. She will carve away all the excess and a new form will emerge.

They will see who she is underneath all of this. She goes to the toilets and takes a toothbrush and sticks it down her throat.

When she's finished, she drinks a load of cold water straight from the tap. With that done, her system is balanced. She takes a deep breath to collect herself and takes the lift down.

At first, she has little trouble focusing on her work, but during the late morning the pressure inside her increases and her heart pounds. She tries to avoid thinking about tomorrow, but it's impossible. A hum in her ears that only gets worse, and she doubts she can actually pull it off.

When lunchtime rolls around, she begins to feel dizzy and decides to go up to the cafeteria. She needs to eat to make it through the day.

She only grabs a salad and bread, to avoid having to pay, and takes a seat in the corner.

Soon Rosa and Meredith arrive and sit down next to her. They tell her all about what they're going to do on holiday and about the different men they'll meet in various cities, and Hanna listens to their chatter, thinking that it's only a matter of time before she'll never have to see them again. If only they knew what she's planning to do.

It's afternoon before she manages to feel calm again. The flies are finally gone and she chooses to take this as a sign. She reminds herself of why she has to do what she's about to do. Soon she will be sitting in a Bentley, driving along the coast with Samuel at the wheel, with Tom's smiling face next to him, Leah's mane of hair in the breeze, on their way south.

5

On the day it's going to happen, she is careful to act exactly the same as on any other day. On her way to work she even makes sure to buy the same baguette as usual, from the same bakery, and she sits on the same bench as always. She's not usually one for superstition, but today it feels extra important to stick to her routines.

But she has no appetite. She tosses the sandwich in a rubbish bin and heads to the museum.

The morning passes slowly. She's so anxious that she's having trouble reading the inventory numbers and has to check some envelopes more than once. It's like the digits keep moving around.

At ten o'clock, it's time. She wonders if it's clear to look at her that she's a mess on the inside. She goes over to the guard and asks for the day's list. It's only a single page and it contains seven items, which is unusually low.

She starts by filling the trolley with the seven plastic envelopes. Then she stops to listen, to make sure no one is nearby. She finds the drawer that contains the duplicate. She has memorised the number.

She opens the drawer with the magnetic key and takes out the envelope. Gingerly she fishes out the sheet and quickly tucks it into a another envelope from the trolley. She locks the drawer again.

She pauses for a moment to catch her breath, wants to make sure her face isn't blazing red. Then she goes over to the security portal.

She presses the button and waits.

Maybe it's her imagination, but it feels like the guard is really taking his time.

When he shows up, he does what he always does, asks what she got up to the night before, and she does what she always does, lies and says she just stayed home. The guard says she should get out more, that a good-looking girl like her should be *living her life* before it's too late, and she says he's probably right.

They've had this conversation dozens of times, and it's always made her feel uncomfortable, but today it's unbearable.

Once the guard has zapped the bar codes, he puts the envelopes back in the trolley. Then he turns away from her and enters the code to open the lift.

She steps into the lift, and once inside she smiles at him. The instant she sees his surprised look, she realises her mistake. He takes a quick step forward and uses his foot to stop the door from closing. The door opens again.

They stand there staring at each other.

He says: 'Should we have dinner tonight?'

She curses herself for smiling; she's had this feeling that she must not do anything to stray from routine, but the fact that it was a *smile* is so annoyingly banal. Her brain revs into overdrive.

She should say yes so she can get out of here quickly, but she can't spend this particular evening with him.

She says: 'Not tonight.'

'Tomorrow, then?'

'Unfortunately, a childhood friend of mine is visiting for a week. From Sweden.'

'What's her name?'

'Vera.'

'Childhood friends are important.'

'Yep.'

'How about next week then?'

'That would be nice.'

He smiles, moves his foot, points at her, and says:

'You promised.'

She smiles in response. The lift door closes.

When she exits the lift on the fourth floor, she turns round to look up at the ceiling. She knows there aren't any security cameras here, but she does it out of old habit.

An older couple is coming down the corridor. They're paging through a museum brochure and look lost. They stop in front of her and ask her about the ceramics gallery. Hanna wants to tell them to go to hell but instead she explains how to get there and wishes them good luck.

Once they're gone, she waits for a moment until she's certain no one else is nearby. She reminds herself to breathe normally. It would be terrible to faint in the middle of all this.

She takes a deep breath and looks around one more time. Then she takes out the plastic envelope with the two sheets and wriggles out the duplicate.

She can feel how old and brittle it is. Something happens inside her when she holds it. Her crime becomes real. De Ribera's signature in the corner, the year 1640. There's no doubt about it: this piece is extremely valuable. But now it's too late to change her mind. She opens the glass cabinet, stands on tiptoe, and places the duplicate on the top shelf. Then she closes the cabinet door again and rolls her trolley to the research room.

6

She wakes up several times during the night to police sirens in the distance, to someone pounding on a neighbour's door. It feels as though her life is over. Then she falls asleep. Then she wakes up with a start. Then she falls asleep again. She hovers between sleep and wakefulness. She dreams of the moment when she went back to the glass cabinet and took out the work, placed it in a bag from the museum gift shop and headed for the exit, but in the dream she gets caught, as dozens of guards come running from all directions. She dreams that this is her last night of freedom. She dreams of a jail cell, of the trapped creature scratching at the walls with its black claws, roaring in panic. But when she finally wakes up for the last time and sits up in bed, everything is quiet and still. Just a gentle rain outside.

The drawing is on the coffee table. It depicts an acrobat walking a tightrope over a field. The paper is old and yellowed. She wonders how much it's worth.

She sits there until the sun comes up. She doesn't dare fall back to sleep.

7

The next day is an ordeal. Her stress is physical. She has stomach trouble and walks around in a cold sweat. Each time someone says her name, it's like a stab in her gut.

The underground guard is chatty; he tells her about the restaurants he's considering for their date.

She nods and smiles and does her best to act normal.

When she gets home, she leaves her phone in her jacket. For the first time since they met she doesn't text or talk to anyone in the group for several days.

8

It's a few days before she starts to relax, and on Friday evening she decides to hang out with the group again. She messages Leah, who says they're having a breakfast picnic in the park the next day.

She walks downtown the next morning, and only now does she realise how awful she's felt all week. Now she can breathe again, and the people she encounters seem less threatening. Now she understands how shaken up she's been.

When she reaches the stairs that lead down from Mirador de la Cornisa, she stops for a moment to gaze out at the city, which is still shrouded in a morning fog.

Then she continues down to the square.

When she spots them in the distance, at a table under the big oak, she feels so happy that she laughs aloud.

After having coffee at the pavement café, they go to El Paraíso Park and spread out blankets and stretch out in the sun. They talk about the trip, and now Hanna is included in their conversations. Tom pours wine from a Tetra Pak into plastic cups. It's warm and smells like vinegar, but Hanna drinks it anyway, for her nerves.

Samuel says he's spoken with Ivan: 'I told him about you. He's glad you're coming along.'

She's so moved that she doesn't know what to say.

Samuel goes on: 'He's curious about you.'

'Really?' Hanna says, unable to hide her joy. Samuel smiles at her reaction.

It's all too much to take in.

She stands up and says she's going to the toilet. Then she crosses the lawn to the café. She's having trouble keeping her balance. It's like she's back in the archive, has just placed the duplicate etching on her trolley and is heading for the lift.

She can't wait for the trip. She just wants some peace and quiet.

She goes to the café counter, buys a San Pellegrino and takes a big gulp. But the water is warm and flat and only makes her feel even more nauseated. She goes back to the blanket. Tom and Leah are playing boules nearby; Samuel is resting by himself.

She watches his chest heave up and down. She takes in his face, half-hidden under a shirt. It looks like he's sleeping. She tentatively lies down beside him. Cautiously moves closer. He is breathing heavily. She feels the heat of his body and can't resist the temptation. The past few days have been rough. She needs him, his strength. She creeps even closer, brings her thighs to the backs of his, places her hand against his back. It takes a moment, but eventually she's spooning him, her arm over his body. She feels his breath wandering into her. She feels how he is resting, how he's floating on a dream. She closes her eyes and brings her nose to the back of his neck, sinking into his depths, enveloped by his slumber. The sound of children playing in the distance. The rustle of the treetops grows softer. She is safe. She doesn't care that it's getting damp and sticky between their bodies. She wants to stay here. She closes her eyes and breathes in time with him. She thinks of how little time is left before they leave, she thinks about the trip, of everything that can happen, of what might be set free when they're on their journey, their bodies on the beach, in the sea, in the hotel rooms, of how things can happen naturally there, how simply it can happen, how his naked, tanned body can stand before her, his eyes looking at her breasts, her stomach, how she leans back, opens herself for him, how their new life begins.

9

She's sitting on the edge of her bed, smoking as it gets dark outside. She can still feel the heat of Samuel's body against her own. Her dress is still damp from their time on the blanket. She should take it off, in this heat, but she leaves it on. She wants to linger in those moments.

On the coffee table in front of her is the drawing. She is a bit taken aback, because earlier she had bought a book about Spanish art history at a bookstore and has just read about de Ribera's importance as an illustrator. She suspects this drawing is not just a sketch but a meaningful piece in and of itself.

She knows she needs sleep, but she feels too wound up to go to bed. It feels like the work might simply burst into flame. She is struck by an urge to call Samuel just to hear his voice, but she knows she shouldn't. It might seem desperate. She must not be impatient. She has to wait for the trip. Everything has its season. She looks at the time, which is moving unbearably slowly.

She sits down at her desk, opens a Goya book and starts to draw.

At five, she finally hears the first bird wake up, and it wakes the other birds, and then she sees the first red glow of dawn emerge over the rooftops. Soon it will be time. In a few hours, the hard part will be over, and she can set her sights on the future once and for all.

10

At ten o'clock, she hits the streets. It's Sunday, and there are crowds everywhere. The sun is so harsh that her clothes stick to her after just a block. The exhaust fumes from the traffic smell acrid and toxic. Now and then she feels hot gusts of air from the manholes, as if the city is gasping for breath.

She reaches the Malasaña neighbourhood and the antique shop under the bridge.

The light inside is dim, but the shop is larger than she remembers. She discovers a shelf of taxidermy animals she didn't notice when she was there with Samuel. On the walls are yellowed maps. Behind the counter, an overweight man is reading the paper. When he sees her, he puts out his cigarillo and asks how he can be of help. There are beads of sweat on his forehead. His eyebrows are bushy. She tells him she has something to sell.

He replies, 'What?'

'I bought an old drawing from a different antique shop a few days ago. And I think it might be worth more than I paid.'

'I'm listening,' he says.

'I could go back there, except I forgot the address.'

He looks at her for a long moment, his face unchanging. Then he says: 'I see.'

She takes the work from her portfolio and places it on the desk. The man leans over and inspects it in silence; then he takes out a magnifying glass.

'One moment,' he says, and he takes the sheet and vanishes into a back room.

Once he's closed the door after himself, all is quiet. Hanna listens closely to hear what's going on back there. She turns towards the entrance and spots a small security camera above the door. She stiffens. But when she recognises the model from the museum, she's relieved. She knows the light is supposed to be steady red when the camera is on. She thinks so, anyway.

When the shopkeeper comes back, he says brusquely, 'Come with me.'

At first Hanna hesitates, but then she follows him into a back room, a small office. Its walls are just as reeky as the rest of the shop. Behind a computer sits a man who has to be at least eighty, but is as fat as his colleague. His chin hangs over his collar like dough.

The old man says: 'Who are you?'

Hanna explains that she's a language student from Denmark, spending six months in Spain to study Spanish.

He says: 'How did a language student come to possess this?'

'I saw it in a shop window at an antique shop, and I liked it. So I bought it.'

'Which shop?'

'I don't remember.'

He looks at her for a long time. Then he says: 'Is there any chance this same antique shop has more artworks you could sell to me?'

'No.'

He nods. 'I see.'

Then he lights his cigar again and blows out the match.

'Here's the thing,' he says, looking at the cherry of his cigar. 'I wouldn't have been able to keep this shop running if I dealt in stolen goods. I would have gone to jail years ago. You see?'

'It's not stolen goods.'

'As luck would have it, I established a close relationship with the police many years ago, a collaboration that's been of great mutual help.'

He gestures at the door behind her, and his colleague walks over to lock it.

Hanna is struck with a wave of dizziness. She says: 'Give me it.'

The old man puts his hand on the etching and shakes his head. 'No.'

She looks at him.

He goes on: 'I'm going to call the police now. And when they arrive, you will tell them where you stole this. If I were to guess, I'd say it's from a museum. You see, papers stored in museum archives have a specific hue. It has something to do with the humidity level. What's it called?'

His colleague replies: 'Don't remember.'

Hanna turns round to see that the overweight man is still blocking the door.

The old man reaches for the phone.

Hanna wants to stop him but doesn't know how. She wants to plead with him to let her go, but she can't produce the words. Her eyes follow his hand as it picks up his cell phone and dials the number.

But suddenly he pauses.

He says: 'I just had an idea.'

He takes a deep drag on his cigar and blows out. The blueish-white smoke fills the small room. Hanna has a hard time suppressing a cough.

He says: 'Do you want me to call the police?'

Hanna gazes out the window. The square is full of tourists and families.

She says: 'No.'

'Then I have a suggestion.'

There's so much smoke in the room that her eyes sting.

He says: 'If I do you a favour and refrain from calling the police, maybe you can do me a favour in return.'

'What?'

'Let me buy this on the cheap.'

She turns round to look at the old man's colleague. His expression is hard to read; he's staring into space.

She turns to the old man again and says: 'How cheap?'

11

The first thing she does when she gets home is place the money on the bedspread, in thirty-five piles of one thousand euros each. The bills are fresh and crisp. She tries to take joy in them, but she's still too shaken up.

She feels naïve to have expected it would be a simple process. It wasn't. Her clothes smell like cigar smoke. Her skin feels hot. She thinks of the old man's face as he picked up the phone. She stood as still as if she were on a tightrope, readying herself for a fall, but somehow she made it to the other side, and now her temples are throbbing.

She looks at the bundles of cash on the bedspread and is struck by the urge to place them on top of her body. She wants to grasp the fact that the money is hers, she wants it to become part of her. She wants to talk to someone about it, in order to understand it, put words to it. She's tired of secrets. She wants to let go, feel someone catch her. She wants someone to possess her, wants to stop dreaming of possessing, herself. She picks up one bundle, weighs it in her hand. It's the same weight that drew her to the group.

It was clear to see from that very first day that they were anchored in something greater than themselves. She understands that now, and she knows it would suit her, too, to live that way, because she could get away from herself. Next to the weight on the bed, she is light. Maybe that's why she loves hearing about Ivan's fortune. His wealth is so massive that everyone and everything that comes near gravitates towards it, herself included. She looks at the weight on the bedspread and feels the walls of the room tilting in towards it. She thinks of her time in this flat. She sees the months as stops on a journey. April, when she first arrived in the city, when she met the group for the first time. May, when she was invited into their lives and their curiosity was directed her way. June, when they invited her to come along on their trip. July, when they will travel. She likes dividing her life into chapters, because that gives it weight.

12

The next day, she calls Leah to ask if they can go shopping. Leah sounds surprised, so Hanna explains: Once a year she gets a payout from her mother's life insurance, and now she's finally got cash again.

Leah: 'Cool.'

Hanna says: 'I should learn to save up, but it's the same story every year. I blow it all.'

Leah: 'Good!'

Hanna laughs.

They meet up at Puerta del Sol and walk through the throngs to the shopping streets of Chueca.

Hanna tells her what she needs: bikinis, of course, but also sandals and dresses to wear out in the evenings, and hats and tops. Leah adds: And sarongs, sunglasses, skirts.

Hanna wants to make a good impression on Samuel's dad, she says.

Leah laughs. 'I don't think you need to worry.'

'What do you mean?'

'You're a girl. He likes girls.'

Before they hit the department store they have a glass of wine in the bar near the entrance. Then Leah takes her by the arm and they head up the escalator.

'Good thing you got the money before the trip,' Leah says.

'Yeah, for real.'

They walk side by side into the boutique. Hanna enjoys making an entrance with Leah, and how people stare. They're both wearing short skirts and their high heels clack against the marble floor. For the first time, they have a common goal, in contrast to the times Hanna accompanied Leah before, when she mostly sat in a corner and watched Leah try on garment after garment, unable to purchase anything herself. They're giggly from the wine and they pick up as many items as they can carry. Soon a female shop assistant arrives to help them, and over by the dressing room a man in a suit approaches to offer them Cava, and they accept, and then they each take over a dressing room, going in and out, laughing and pointing and offering critiques of one another's choices. Hanna buys a pair of snake-skin pumps for going out to fancy restaurants, and a tight, black ribbed Balenciaga dress, and a pair of white Chloé trainers, as well as leather gladiator sandals for beach days. More clothes, bags, bikinis. By the time they're ready to head for the cash registers, they've chosen so much clothing that the man in the suit comes over and offers them membership cards. They accept. When Hanna gets home to her flat, she opens her new YSL bag on the bed and starts packing, even though there are three days left before their departure. Each time she folds a garment and puts it in the bag, she fantasises about the experiences she'll have while wearing it.

13

On the last night before they leave, Samuel books a table at a hotel outside of town.

They sit at the poolside restaurant in the twilight, each with a dry martini. Tom recites poetry by Gunnar Ekelöf.

A DJ is playing lounge music next to the bar. The tables are buzzing. Other hotels tower around the pool: tall white buildings with glass balconies, neon logos.

Hanna has never been a fan of the dry martini, but tonight she gets it. In the bite of the drink is a signal: the night to come will also have a bite, and *mean* something.

Leah asks if she can have Hanna's olive and she pops it between her red lips. Samuel is wearing a white polo shirt and striped trousers. Tom is unusually colourful, in a bright red baseball jacket and baggy blue trousers. Samuel teases him, saying: 'You look like a walking American flag.'

Tom replies: 'Thank you.'

Hanna feels great in her black minidress with its puffed sleeves. She couldn't have worn it a month ago. Moreover, Leah let her borrow a hair product that gives her a matching wet look.

Samuel says: 'You two look awfully similar tonight.'

Hanna says: 'Thank you.'

She feels like the moment is right. She takes out the envelope and turns to Samuel: 'My boss sends his apologies that he hasn't had time to meet. There's been so much to do ahead of the anniversary. But he wanted me to give you these to make up for it.'

She places the envelope on the table.

Samuel opens it and takes out the three tickets. The gold emblem gleams in the sun.

Hanna says: 'Three VIP tickets to the anniversary gala.'

Tom reaches across the table and takes the tickets from Samuel: 'What?'

Leah leans over: 'Can I see?'

Samuel turns to Hanna and says: 'Tell him I say thanks.'

Then he looks at Leah and Tom with a grin.

If they only knew what she'd had to do to get them. The Norwegian's firm grip on the back of her head, the words he hissed. Yet another memory that must be erased along with all the others.

Tom taps his fork against his wine glass and says: 'I think we've got another reason to celebrate, too.'

Leah: 'We leave tomorrow!'

107

Samuel raises his glass: 'To our trip.'

Hanna: 'Cheers!'

Then Tom leans over the table and whispers that he *scored something special* for their celebration. And he starts fiddling with his jacket pocket.

Samuel shakes his head and smiles: 'What have you done this time?'

Hanna takes another sip of her martini. It's so cold that the liquid is sluggish.

Tom says: 'I wanted to thank you for planning the trip.'

Samuel: 'Thanks for coming along.'

Hanna and Leah say, in unison: 'Thank *you.*'

Tom points at Leah and Hanna and says: 'You two really are twins tonight.'

Leah and Hanna look at one another and smile.

Tom: 'May I see your hands?'

Hanna can guess what it is, but she isn't scared. Maybe it's the martini. The sky is purple and pink. There's something in the air, too. It's humid and salty.

Tom takes her hand under the table and gives her a pill. She opens her palm and looks at it, pink and triangle shaped. She places it on her tongue. It tastes sharp and bitter. She washes it down with her drink.

Hanna: 'What's going to happen now?'

Samuel puts a hand on her thigh. A jolt travels up between her legs.

They exchange glances.

He says: 'You're gonna love it.'

14

Dusk falls. It's a loaded moment, as they anxiously await the effect. On occasion someone points at the mountains in the distance, and Hanna nods and smiles, but really she's only thinking about what's going to happen any second now.

Sometimes Leah asks, 'Do you feel anything?' and the others shake their heads. Hanna wants to stop time. It's so nice to just sit here and wait, nursing her third dry martini. She loves the fact that they have a common secret, that they're waiting for a common experience.

A little while later, they have an even bigger secret. From one second to the next, everything changes. The warm evening breeze brushes her skin like a gentle caress. Everything becomes body and flesh. Warm blood simmering. And she can tell that everything is going to be okay.

She smiles at the others in the group. And the group smiles back at her. And she appreciates that they're exactly where they are, by this pool, against the backdrop of well-dressed people. When she moves her arm, the movement itself is important, she even conducts an experiment: she unfolds her napkin and realises that the napkin has body, that it was woven with a delicate technique, touching the material is like stroking the hand of someone you like. And words, too, have body, when she speaks, they are flesh and blood. She can say whatever she wants to and it feels genuine and true. She wonders how people stand it, the rest of the time, when words are only words, carelessly written notes that can be carried off on a breeze. Now each word is body and it's the body that is the link between them and the experiences they share. The work they have done together, from the first drink at the first pavement café, all the nights on Samuel's balcony, the risks she's taken, the courage she's demonstrated, everything that has led up to this moment.

Samuel stares at the mountains, and she smiles when she notices this – because she knows that out there is their journey, their future. He turns to her and they smile at one another, and it's a new kind of smile, gentle and solemn, like children breathlessly watching a blazing sparkler on a dark Christmas Eve. Everything contracts, everything buzzes, she feels it in her shoulders, in her chest, that the summer is compressing into this point, everything leads to this, flesh compressing, muscles and tissues tightening. Someone by the bar lights a fire in a large iron pot, and the heat reaches her face, the flames reach for the sky and illuminate faces, and she looks at strangers' faces and feels tenderness towards them as well. The fire, too, is body, she hears it crackling and whistling. Maybe it's because of the fire that her face feels hot. Maybe not. She brings her fingertips to her face and feels how wet it is. Maybe it's because of the fire that Leah's face is rosy and dotted with tiny drops of sweat.

Tom tells them to drink water.

They obey. His knowledge is deep. She likes the fact that he's guiding them. She loves him for figuring all of this out for them. She drinks the cold water. It's a remarkable experience. It's like swallowing meat. It's neither delicious nor disgusting. Tom urges her to drink more. She fills another glass and drinks it too, even though it's repellent. Then Tom says they should join hands. Hanna thinks that sounds reasonable. Leah reaches over and Hanna takes her hand. Tom and Samuel join hands as well. And Hanna watches Leah's face, so open and full of dreams, and she regrets having underestimated Leah at first. Maybe she didn't understand her greatness, but now she knows Leah is the most beautiful soul in the whole group, wild and sincere, unsentimental and real, and Hanna squeezes her hand, and it's muscles and blood vessels, and it's adorned with beautiful jewellery, it's well taken care of, it has been refined and optimised at salons and anointed with creams for years, and now she looks at Leah's face, just as well cared for, just as perfected, Leah's lips, wet and pink like peeled cherries, full of shimmer and glow. Her lips that are flesh. Her tongue, behind them, that is flesh. And her flesh lips are saying, 'I'm happy,' and they're even more beautiful when they speak.

'Me too,' someone says. And Hanna turns to the right. It's Tom. Hanna looks down at his hand, which is holding her own. It's a man's hand. She has misunderstood him. She thought he was a boy. But that hand belongs to a man, full of desire, which makes him a kindred spirit. Maybe he's even the one of the group she understands best, because he is an artist, he lives a life of creation, which she would like to do too, if only she dared. She realises now how much she admires him for that. She knows what he subjects himself to and what he sacrifices, and she understands his pining for Leah because she pines for Samuel. She and Tom have a bond that no one else understands. He smiles at her, and in his smile Hanna sees a deep and wonderful sorrow. And suddenly she understands where it comes from. This must be the secret Tom has been keeping from them. Now she understands why he was forced to withhold the drugs from them. He wanted to shield them from sorrow – from how sorrowfully beautiful this is. She understands. This is a holy place. Visiting it demands great responsibility. She is willing to bear that responsibility. She looks at his hand again. It's strong. It can bear this. It has been here before. Of course his soul is bleeding, of course he is as soft as candle wax, of course he is full of sorrow, because you cannot carry this into your everyday life. Now she realises why there's always been something a little absent-minded about him, something she couldn't quite grasp. Now she understands everything. He is protecting this holy thing. It also explains how concerned he sometimes is when he talks about how hard it is to write: maybe he's actually been talking about how hard it is to capture this in words. She brings his hand to her face to show him she understands. He closes his eyes and lets her do it. His cheek is cool and soft. With his eyes, he says: *now you get it.* And she nods. *Now I get it.*

And she looks at his face, a man's and a boy's. His shirt is unbuttoned to his navel and on his hairless chest are beads of sweat, and it's a man's sweat, salty and rich, but it's also a boy's sweat, pure and clean.

'Me too,' says another voice. And Hanna turns to the left and sees that Samuel has turned to her.

Now he smiles at her, and for the first time since they met she looks into his eyes without blinking. She always has trouble meeting them. It's always been like staring into the sun. Often, she will look away, or dart her eyes, or do something weird with her face, but now she is calm and so is he. His gaze is body, and it is anchored in everything that has happened to them and everything that will happen to them. There is nothing frightening about sinking into one another's eyes. He is a riddle, but he is also the answer to that same riddle. He exists. She exists. His gaze flows into her and, at last, answers the question. And his hands. In them are all his dreams. She has never really observed them this closely.

But Leah wants them to become a group again. She says: 'Hey,' and repeats, 'HEY!' And she even says it out loud: 'Can't we be a *group?*'

And Hanna nods: 'We *are* a group.'

Tom: 'The group!'

And Samuel says: 'Just think, we're going away.' Then he gestures at the skyline. 'We're going away,' and after a moment he adds: 'Away.' And they all laugh at how high they all are, and then they laugh at themselves for laughing. And Hanna is the one who laughs hardest of all, for once, but it's a quiet laugh, for some reason. She can hear how strange it sounds, like an exhalation, a hoarse exhalation. Samuel smiles, and when the waiter comes by she orders the same thing he does, because she wants to drink *him,* and when the large, colourful glasses with umbrellas arrive she can't taste any alcohol, it's like drinking fresh, pure coconut milk, and as the sweat drips from her forehead and the tip of her nose she accepts it, or even embraces it.

She takes Samuel's hand again; she has to.

'You can't even taste the alcohol,' she says.

He chuckles. 'There's no alcohol in it.'

And there's that laugh of hers again, the silent one: 'Hhhhh . . .' and she suddenly feels a thrill low down, it buzzes up between her legs, everything there is flesh, full of wet, warm flesh, and now, as she watches Leah adjust her dress, she thinks about how astonishing it is that it's acceptable to show so much skin, it's weird that it's legal, sitting there and getting other people hot like that, in that plunging neckline, but it's so nice, too, that it's allowed, and comical, all of it, when she thinks of how many lines are crossed in every moment. And Samuel is pontificating about something now, and Hanna loves him because he never runs out of steam, because he can just keep *going*, and she looks at his hands moving in the air and thinks that the moment is close now, those hands are close to helping themselves, so boldly, grabbing what they want, pulling her body near without being ashamed, maybe later tonight, who knows, he'll shove her up against a wall and turn her round, almost violently, and thrust his hand under her skirt and feel his way forward with warm fingers, and in her fantasy he's already reached the flesh as he kisses her mouth, her chin, her ears, with coconut on his breath, with flushed cheeks, with dark sweat stains on his shirt. She takes another sip of the coconut drink and notices that Leah has tucked her umbrella behind her ear. Typical. That's cheating. How does she do it? How does Leah always manage to stay one step ahead? But it's okay. Normally Hanna might be annoyed that she didn't think of it first, but right now she accepts it and appreciates it, because Leah looks so pretty.

And then she doesn't understand what's going on, because now they're at a nightclub, even though they were just at a

113

restaurant. All of a sudden, the music is harsh and people are standing up around their table and dancing. And Tom explains: the bar turns into a club at nine o'clock. And Hanna laughs so hard she can't breathe: *It's only nine?* Haven't they been here for like five or six hours? No, no, no, Samuel says, laughing. And Tom stands up and shouts, 'You gotta get up. Time to get up! I think we have to?' and Samuel laughs and yells at Tom: 'I love you!' and Tom yells back: 'Same!' and Hanna and Leah laugh at them and Hanna loves that they're *guys,* and that she and Leah are *girls,* and Hanna and Leah get up too and are immediately surrounded by bodies, and Hanna lets go and lets herself be carried off by the bodies, enjoying the pressure in front and behind. And suddenly she's in the toilets, smiling at herself in the mirror and feeling beautiful, feeling like for once her appearance is eye-catching, is skinnier than expected. Then she's standing at the bar ordering water and drinking cold flesh. And then she's suddenly in the toilets again, finding that her face conveys something wild, something she hasn't really seen before, a gaze that has body, that speaks to her, and she thinks: maybe this is how it works, when a real change occurs, there has to be a certain amount of madness. When she comes back from the toilets she sees Leah on a sofa near the dance floor, her face blazing red, her dark hair damp with sweat, her eyes closed. Hanna asks if she's okay, and Leah says she's *never felt better.* And Hanna smiles back and says she has *also never felt better.* And then she strokes Leah's dark arms and Leah places her hands on Hanna's hips. And under her touch, Hanna's body is given weight, her weight is given body. And Leah whispers: *Now everything is perfect.* And Hanna says: *You are perfect, you are perfect.* And Tom shouts something about moving on but Hanna and Leah say they want to stay in this exact spot. And they nod at each other. They never want to leave this spot. And Samuel shouts at them that they have to drink some water. And Hanna laughs: 'Hhhhh', and Leah replies: Yeah, yeah. And Samuel sinks into the sofa as well, and says, grinning: 'What kind of material *is* this?' and soon Tom joins them too and finally all four of them are sitting there, side by side. These four people who belong together, who have a world of their own that no one else understands. And Samuel, Leah, and Tom hug each other and Hanna strokes their backs and is so happy to be close to them.

JULY

JULY

1

She wakes up in the compartment to the rhythmic sound of the wheels hitting the rails.

Leah has fallen asleep with her head in Hanna's lap. Her hair flows out to cover Hanna's legs like a blanket.

Outside the window are endless fields of wheat and a high, cloud-free sky. Now and then they pass small villages in the distance, between hills of glowing yellow citrus groves. She should be hung-over, but she feels energised and exhilarated.

She turns to her friends. If Samuel were awake he could tell her how much longer it will be. He knows that kind of thing. She hopes they don't wake up for a while because she's enjoying this moment. She looks at their sleeping faces and takes out her phone and uses it like a mirror. For once she likes what she sees. She's tanned and has lost weight. It's like their beauty has rubbed off on her.

She glances at her suitcase and thinks of the expensive black Loewe dress that fitted so well in the dressing room. She thinks about the receipt from the antiques dealer in the interior pocket, like a gem, proof of her courage. She almost threw it away while she was packing, but in the end she couldn't bring herself to.

She thinks about all the garments wrapped in delicate tissue. She looks forward to wearing the red Chanel top, the Stella McCartney dress, the gingham bikini and all her new shoes. She leans back in the seat and gazes out the train window. The Spanish countryside unfolds around her.

Tom wakes up first and gazes at her sleepily.

She smiles and stretches as though she had been asleep too.

Tom reaches for the Tetra Pak of red wine. He pours it into two white plastic cups. They toast and each takes a sip. He says he's happy to leave the city, that it will be nice to be able to concentrate more on writing. He says that his goal is to finish the novel this summer. He asks if she has any ambitions. She tells him about how hard she's been working on the anniversary celebrations but doesn't mention her painting. They speak softly so as not to wake the others. They drink more. Her thoughts grow light and free. Tom says he likes being in motion. She listens to him and decides she agrees. This past spring, her dreams were unclear, if she even had any. Now her direction is clear. There is no doubt. This was what she needed. Now she can look up at the clouds and appreciate their fluffy shapes and be satisfied with simply sitting like this, reclining in her seat, because she is doing it alongside the group.

She raises her little plastic cup in Tom's direction again, and he returns the gesture, and the two of them smile.

2

When they arrive at Barcelona's central station, Hanna takes an Uber to pick up the Bentley, while the group heads to the Mandarin Oriental Hotel to check in.

The rental place takes up a whole building, with huge picture windows facing Passeig de Gràcia. A dozen sports cars are parked on the shiny black showroom floor. She walks inside. The chill of the air conditioning hits her. It smells like tyres and new car. She goes to the counter and shows them her text from the Norwegian.

The price is higher than he'd promised. She doesn't understand all the terms, but the insurance and additional fees raise the total price to four thousand euros. She tries to act nonchalant.

She goes outside and calls the Norwegian, but he doesn't answer.

She goes back inside, pays, and signs the contract. Then she is led out the back, where the car is parked.

Once the clerk has shown her how to drive the car, and has left her on her own, she folds her copy of the contract and hides it at the bottom of her bag. Then she gets behind the wheel.

3

They're driving along the coast. The roof is down. Samuel is at the wheel. His long hair flutters in the breeze. Tom is next to him, wearing a pale blue linen shirt, selecting songs on his phone. Leah has never been more beautiful, in a shimmery yellow midi skirt, black pumps and white sunglasses.

Hanna smiles to herself as she thinks about the group's faces when she pulled up outside their hotel and honked the horn. Their cheers and shouts echoed off the building façades. Then Leah demanded to know everything about the Spanish art collector who had loaned it out. She begged Hanna to introduce her to him, and Hanna said she would make it happen as soon as they get back to Madrid.

Something is happening to them on this trip, even now, she can already tell.

She's taking up more space in the group, talking more. It's as if the words are less serious, losing meaning, the farther they get from Madrid. It started on the train. It's continuing now that they're on the road.

The cliffs look like dried mud, as if they might crack in the heat at any moment and plunge into the waves. There's hardly any traffic on the road.

Leah shouts into the breeze that it's as if they're in a car commercial. Samuel speeds up. It's as though the car is glued to the asphalt. Tom turns up the music.

They reach Tarragona around three and check in at a hotel right next to the harbour. They go down to the hotel restaurant and eat pasta vongole on the veranda in the afternoon sun. Hanna winds a mouthful onto her fork. The garlic and chilli explode in her mouth. She turns to Samuel and he smiles too, in silent understanding.

After they eat, they get changed in their rooms and go down to the pool.

The evening sun is red. They recline on loungers. It's busy both in the pool and around the bar.

Hanna sneaks glances at the women's sleek, golden bodies; the men's chests and arms. The scent of coconut oil and chlorine is thick. Samuel dives in from the edge of the pool. Leah paints her nails. Tom falls asleep. Hanna has her book propped open in her lap, but she looks at the people gathered in small groups around the pool from behind her sunglasses. She stares at the shoulders, the legs, the bums. Something has been sparked inside her; she doesn't remember ever being so easily aroused before. She regrets eating the pasta. She wonders how much weight she can lose before they get to Ivan's house. She asks herself if anyone will ever admire her body the way she admires others'.

4

Hanna has changed into her Missoni pyjamas, which she bought when she realised she and Leah would be sharing hotel rooms on occasion.

In the mirror she notices that her hair has become sun-bleached. She likes it. She brushes her teeth and applies creams. Then she goes back out to the large hotel room, which faces the sea.

Leah is leaning over her suitcase, unpacking.

The balcony doors are open and through them Hanna can see the lights of the coastline twinkling on the horizon to the south. The bed is so tall that she essentially has to climb up onto it, and the pillows are so soft that they release a sigh as she leans back against them.

She watches Leah arrange her clothes in the wardrobe.

She admires how orderly Leah is and wonders why she herself is always such a failure in that respect. In just a few minutes, Leah has placed her dresses on hangers and categorised them by colour; she has placed skirts, shirts and underwear in neat rows in the drawers. It's like watching a shop assistant at work. Hanna's clothes are still in piles on the easy chairs.

She asks: 'Do you think Ivan's going to like me?'

Leah replies: 'What would stop him?'

Hanna tries to work out if this is supposed to be a compliment.

Leah takes off her dress and stands in front of the full-length mirror in only her pants. Her breasts are white against the brown of the rest of her body. She turns round to observe her back and bum and then asks Hanna if she's gained weight. Hanna assures her she hasn't.

Leah says: 'Good.'

Hanna wonders what it's like to have a perfect body. For her part, she feels like she's always gone through life hand in hand with an appearance that doesn't match the one she actually has. It's like there are two: her actual one and the one she plans to have, soon, if only she can lose weight or find the right hairstyle or get enough money to dress better.

Hanna says: 'Have *I*?'

Leah: 'What?'

Hanna: 'Gained weight.'

123

Leah eyes her. Then she says: 'I don't think so.'

The more Hanna thinks about the pasta, the more annoyed she is at herself for eating it. She considers going to the bathroom and pretending to pee. That spaghetti had been drenched in melted butter and the memory of it makes her want to see it all floating around in the toilet bowl.

Leah sits on the floor in front of the mirror and spreads her legs. She bends forward to look at her own crotch. Then she takes out a pink razor and runs it along her bikini line.

Hanna wants to look away but can't; she sees the tense muscles where Leah's thighs meet her body, the outline of her vulva against the fabric. She wonders what it would be like to put her hand there, on those white panties. Nothing more. Just let her fingers rest there, on the white fabric, and feel the heat.

5

A slow day, a quiet day, in blinding white light. A preview of a different life. The sound of high-heeled shoes walking through a hotel lobby. The smell of fresh flowers in antique vases on dark wooden bureaus. The dull sound of the maid running a hoover over the deep pile carpet in the hallway. The silence as the waiter lifts the silver dome from the plate.

In the evening, they lie on the beach and gaze out at the sea.

Samuel has rented a cabana, and its white canvas flaps above them. The lounge chairs have nice, soft cushions covered in sheets.

Hanna and Samuel are next to each other; Tom and Leah are nearby. When Samuel changes position to light a cigarette, his leg presses against hers. He must notice, yet he doesn't move away. Their legs are lovely together. His curly blond calf; her smooth-shaven tanned one.

Leah has dozed off and Tom has his AirPods in, so it feels as though she and Samuel are alone. She likes watching him as he smokes. He looks so thoughtful. His beautiful fingers come to his mouth. She takes in the back of his neck, which is so close that she could reach out and touch it. Her days, now, are all about interpreting him, reading his signals. Does he feel the same way, is he on his way to the same destination as she is?

She says: 'Are you looking forward to seeing your parents?'

He takes a drag. Blows it out. Says: 'Every time I visit, I think, *maybe this is the time I can be myself there.* But . . .'

Then he hugs himself. Hanna recognises that gesture; she sees how he's closing himself off. She wants to say something comforting but doesn't know what that might be. He looks out at the water and bites his nails.

Suddenly music comes from the pool area behind them, and a few seconds later, the lights along the promenade come on.

It sends a current through the whole area.

Soon Leah wakes up, and Tom takes out his earbuds. It's like those two have a sixth sense for parties. Now they turn round, ears pricking and noses twitching.

Leah waves over a waiter and orders wine.

Soon the music comes on at the beach bar near them too.

Leah goes up to a speaker and starts dancing barefoot in the soft sand.

It's like they've got the beach to themselves, like the music is only for them. Leah moves to the music. Her body casts a long shadow over the sand, her transparent yellow sarong fluttering in the breeze. Around her neck is a string of enamelled beads.

After a while, Samuel's favourite song comes on, a wonderful coincidence, and Samuel and Tom get up and join in the dancing. Hanna does the same, and soon they're in a ring, all four of them, singing along, and Hanna sees how Samuel mouths the lyrics to the sky, and she wonders if the song might mean something special to him. He had a religion, but he's starting to lose it. He was part of a movement, but now he's full of doubt. Maybe something like this is what happened to her too, that at a certain point she realised that nothing is what it seems, that she can't depend on anyone, not even Vera, and on that day she began to search for a new life – eventually leaving Sweden. And now she's found a way forward, in the group. Now she and the group can find a new religion together.

Tom lights a cigarette and takes a deep drag, and he finally manages to do what he's been practising for so long: he produces a perfect smoke ring, to Samuel's delight, and the white O floats out across the beach, and Leah shouts: 'You did it! You did it!' and in front of them, beyond the shining sea, the sun swells like a giant meteorite hurtling towards the earth.

6

The next day, Samuel suggests they take off on a bike trip for a few days, to visit two nearby medieval villages, and stay at a hotel.

Hanna wonders what it will cost but doesn't ask.

She's already blown over nine thousand euros on clothes and hotels. She knows she should start keeping better track of the money.

At ten, they meet in the driveway. The hotel has set out four bicycles and filled their baskets with water bottles and sandwiches.

Samuel rides first, leading them down the avenue; it's down-hill for what has to be a kilometre, and they follow him, their legs sticking out to the sides of their pedals, and it's a wonderful feeling to glide along between small fields together. Tom hoots and Leah laughs. Samuel turns round and smiles. The wheels of their bicycles crunch on the gravel and dust billows up.

Then they ride between larger crop fields. The wheat is so high that it's like travelling through a trench. The land around them is rolling, hilly. On the slopes the lemons shine yellow in the trees, and goats stare at them from the pastures. They pass villages, farms and churches. The cut hay in the fields smells like freshly steeped tea.

On towards afternoon they see smoke in the distance, rising to the sky in black pillars. It looks dramatic. They stop on the road to take pictures. Samuel looks at his phone and tells them the fire department has called in reinforcements from the military to fight two large fires in the area.

They arrive at the little hotel just as the sun is going down. Its driveway is an avenue of cypress trees, lit from below by spotlights, that leads them to a stone building. A porter welcomes them.

They park their bikes and stretch.

The hotel looks like an old cloister, entirely built of stone, iron grates barring the windows. Insects buzz around the lanterns. Crickets chirp noisily from all directions.

At the check-in desk, she hears Tom ask Leah: 'Should we share a room?'

Leah: 'I promised Hanna.'

Hanna shakes her head. 'It's okay.'

When Tom turns round, Leah makes an annoyed face at her, and she realises her mistake.

But when she gets to her room, she's glad it turned out this way. It's nice to be able to toss her clothes on the floor and walk around naked, even though it costs more to stay by herself.

The room must be twice the size of her flat in Madrid, with high ceilings, stone arches and a large fireplace. She walks across the cool stone floor and opens the balcony doors.

Outside, the cicadas are so loud they sound like fire alarms.

Fields reach as far as the eye can see. Stars twinkle above them. She pulls the curtains and draws a bath in the tub that stands in the centre of the room. By the sink she finds a number of small bottles full of various bubble baths and oils. She empties two of them into the water, which quickly turns milky-white and foamy.

After she's had a bath, put a hair mask in, dried off on the large terrycloth towel and laid down in the enormous bed, she suddenly hears muted voices through the wall.

She sits up in bed.

She holds her breath in the dark and presses her ear to the wall. She recognises the voices. She presses her ear to the wall. It's Tom and Leah and they're talking about Samuel, but it's hard to make out the words, just his name. Then, silence. She presses her ear more firmly to the cool stone wall.

Soon she hears what sounds like muffled moaning. Fragments of sentences. She moves her ear. Silence. Then a gasp. Hanna pictures their bodies. She knows their shapes. She closes her eyes. Leah's flat stomach heaves up and down. Tom strokes her small breasts. Hanna sees his open mouth, his strong shoulders, as he supports himself with his arms. Leah spreads her legs, the dark brown hair is shaved at the sides. Hanna imagines that they took a bath just before this, that they're clean, they smell good, like her.

7

They're sitting in the morning sun, alone on the veranda with a view of the valley, eating melon and peaches for breakfast. Tom is wearing a dressing gown; Leah has on Samuel's black-and-white striped shirt. Leah laughs at how messy and sticky the fruit is. Juice trickles down her chin. Tom is no better. He gulps down wedge after wedge of watermelon, unbothered by the juice running and spraying everywhere. Hanna looks at Tom and wonders if that's what it looked like last night.

Leah looks at Hanna and says: 'Did you do something to your hair?'

Hanna: 'I trimmed it a little yesterday.'

'Where at?'

'I did it myself.'

'Nice.'

'Thanks.'

Samuel is nearby, talking to his father on the phone. Hanna tries to hear what he's saying, but no luck.

They head out around noon, to visit another village.

Samuel takes the lead and Hanna and Leah follow him. Tom brings up the rear, his cigarette in the corner of his mouth.

The road winds up the mountain, and Hanna and Leah laugh at what bad shape they're in and how slowly they're going, but soon they're too tired to laugh.

After two hours of biking, they finally spot the little medieval village on a hill in the distance.

It's a relief to turn off into shaded alleys.

They park the bikes next to a large oak in the middle of the square and collapse at a pavement café, in the shade of an awning, out of breath from their ride. They drink horchata over crushed ice.

Hanna is relieved to see that the others' faces are red too. She's not the only one who looks ugly. Under the table next to theirs, two kittens are sleeping.

The large clouds of smoke in the distance are deep purple. Samuel says: 'Say what you want about the end of the world – at least it's beautiful.'

They sit there for hours as the sun gets lower in the sky and it cools off. Sometimes they're silent, checking their phones. Hanna thinks it's nice that they can be quiet together too.

Around six, the outdoor seating starts to fill up. Samuel orders orange liqueur. A few minutes later, the waiter arrives with a whole bottle and four glasses. Tom applauds. The orange liqueur is sugary and sharp. The glasses are heavy. Hanna gets drunk after just three glasses. She doesn't usually feel so changed when she drinks, but this time she does. Maybe riding in the sun has made her more susceptible.

Samuel, too, seems drunk. At one point, he stands up and says: 'Come on.'

Tom says: 'What?'

'Come on, I said.'

Leah: 'But I ordered food.'

Yet Hanna and Leah go with Samuel, who leads them to the edge of the dining area, where he stops and points out at the valley, over at the clouds of smoke, and says he wants to recite a spell to make the fire stop spreading, and Leah laughs, but Samuel repeats himself in a sterner tone, as though he's really serious, and he asks Hanna to recite the spell too, and when she and Leah have done as he says, he embraces them and pulls them close, and he's warm and strong, and he says he's happy they're along on this trip, and they say they're so glad to be along, and Hanna can smell the alcohol on Samuel's breath, acrid and sweet, and she rests her forehead against his temple until his breath puffs into her mouth. She sees the other restaurant patrons glancing their way, but she doesn't care.

Suddenly they're interrupted.

It's Tom's voice, from over at the table: 'Now let's see if you've got a secret boyfriend.'

Hanna whirls to face him, but it's too late.

He has her phone in his hand.

'Who's Vera?' Tom asks.

She's so shocked that it takes a moment for her to react, but then she hurries over to him and reaches for her phone.

Tom is quick, though, and has time to stand up. She throws herself at him again, but he feints and dashes out to the courtyard, still holding her phone, as he calls: 'Who's Vera?'

She runs after him, chasing him down the slope, away from the building, and she grabs hold of his shirt and he slips in the grass and tumbles down, and she grabs his arm and tries to yank the phone from his hand, but he won't let go; she tries to pry his fingers away roughly, and they wrestle, next to the restaurant parking lot.

Eventually she manages to get the phone away from him, and the two of them roll onto their backs, side by side.

Hanna lies still and hears him panting beside her. She tries to think of something to say or do but can't.

Tom laboriously sits up and holds his elbows. He groans. Samuel and Leah have run after them, and now they're standing right there. Hanna sits up as well.

Tom says: 'What the fuck was that all about?'

Hanna: 'I'm sorry.'

She helps him up. He has brown and green stains on his white shorts and has skinned his knees.

He brushes the dirt off his shirt and legs.

Leah says: 'What happened?'

Tom replies: 'Want to get out of here?'

8

They bike through layers of fog at twilight. It's like inhaling cold water. The smell of hay and manure. They pedal in silence. Hanna is last in line. She's wobbly, but feels a little more sober after what happened. She's having a hard time assessing the extent of the problem. Oftentimes things go away if you don't talk about them. If you don't talk about what's inside you, and how it tries to dig its way out, it's like it doesn't even exist.

The fog is getting thicker, she's too cold, and her bum hurts on the narrow saddle.

After a while, Samuel slows down, so Hanna, Leah, and Tom do the same.

On the road before them is a group of older men, wearing sooty work clothes.

Samuel parks his bike in the ditch and approaches them.

He says: 'What's going on?'

The men urge them to turn back. The fires are closer, they say.

Samuel replies that he wants to see.

The men say it's dangerous, but Samuel insists.

The men shake their heads and walk away.

The group mount their bicycles again and keep going. In silence they aim for the red haze in the dark. The smoke gets thicker the closer they come. Soon they can see flames flickering in the distance.

When they're about fifty metres from the fire, they stop and lay their bikes down in the wet grass. There's so much smoke that it's hard to get a sense of things. The flames crackle and spit. Hanna's face feels hot. She turns to the group. The glow of the fire dances across their bodies. The scene reminds her of Goya's *Fire at Night*. Samuel is closest to it, staring gravely into the light; Leah has brought her hands to her face; Tom's head is wound in a shawl and only his squinting eyes are visible. Tiny glowing flakes of ash swirl all around them.

Hanna sees them from the outside, sees herself, sees the group encircled with smoke, and thinks about how transitory everything is, how quickly she could lose everything, how she can't take anything for granted. She thinks about how she cannot mess up again. From now on, she won't make any more mistakes.

9

The next day, they check out of the hotel and drive south. Tom is at the wheel. She sees his face in the rearview mirror. Hanna has trouble telling if he's avoiding her gaze because he's concentrating on driving or because of what happened.

Leah's wearing Prada sunglasses with white frames and an Hermès scarf around her head.

The farther south they get, the drier everything is. Along the highway are rows of half-built houses, concrete constructions that seem to have been abandoned halfway through. The mountains get ever higher.

Around two in the afternoon, they approach Valencia. The hotel is not far outside the city.

When they pull into the driveway, four hotel employees surround the car. Two to unload their luggage, one to take the key and park the car, and one hostess to welcome them with four glasses of bubbly.

The lobby is beautiful, with orchids in tall vases, mirrors in gold frames and a welcome table of sorts for new guests, with a guest book open in front of crystal carafes containing juices in every colour imaginable.

They approach the check-in desk. The clerk asks for their cards, and Hanna hands hers over. Even though she knows there's money in the account she feels nervous, out of old habit. She smiles at the clerk and nods. When the receipt finally prints out she can relax. She signs with the signature she's created for the trip.

Once they've left their luggage in their rooms, they go down to the sea.

The water is so clear they can see the rocky bottom.

Leah is wearing a polka-dot bikini with high-waisted bottoms and a big white hat with a black brim. Around her neck is a thick, heavy gold necklace.

Samuel hands a few bills to a hotel employee and they each get a lounge chair with an umbrella.

They order lunch, which is served on small wooden tables the waiters set up between the lounge chairs. Now Hanna understands why rich people are skinny. It's possible to eat delicious *and* nutritious food. She eats a salad with grilled salmon, and the fish is so tender it falls apart as soon as she pokes it, exposing the wet pink insides. Tom and Samuel have Caesar salads with chicken and anchovies.

When they've finished eating, Leah says: 'Can you get my back?'

Leah lies on her stomach and Hanna undoes her bikini top. As she rubs Leah's skin, she decides she should sunbathe more often too. Leah's skin is the colour of chocolate and it emphasises her slender body. Hanna has noticed that Leah never talks about her lack of eating, she just does it without complaining. Hanna feels muscles and bones under her thin skin.

Tom has ordered white wine and he takes the bottle from the bucket of ice and serves them. As he fills Hanna's glass he offers her a tentative smile, and that makes her happy. Maybe the phone fight is forgotten.

She gets up and walks down to the sea.

As she reaches the water's edge, Leah rushes past her and dives straight into a wave and swims off, while Hanna walks in tentatively.

When she's far enough out that the water reaches her crotch, a jolt rises from between her legs. It feels like the cold water is filling her up. She bends her knees. Soon her whole body is underwater, only her head sticking out. She feels her warm skin cooling. She takes a few strokes and glides into the sea. The water tastes salty. After a while, Leah swims up next to her. The current is strong and tugs at her legs. Slippery seaweed tickles them from the depths and Leah laughs aloud. Hanna thinks about how Leah once said that guys love to hear girls laughing together. Maybe she's aware that Samuel and Tom can hear them laughing. Hanna makes sure to laugh as well.

As they leave the water, hand in hand, Hanna notices Samuel and Tom watching them as they scamper over the hot round beach stones. Hanna thinks about the silent agreement of youth: everyone looks at everyone else and steals images of each other's shapes, encapsulating into their memories the images of arms, bellies, legs, wet and clingy swimming trunks. When Leah happens to step on a squishy jellyfish she lets out a shriek, and Hanna cries out too, and the two of them laugh, and soon she can hear Samuel and Tom laughing at them.

Hanna takes Leah by the hand again and they head back up to the lounge chairs. The grains of sand on Samuel's stomach are like stars in the sky. Tom's teeth shine white. The sun is so hot that she isn't freezing for long. She's grateful that she's lost weight, because now she can move freely across the sand without being ashamed.

Leah hands her a towel and says: 'I wish I had your breasts.'

Hanna looks down at her chest.

Leah goes on: 'Mine are so small.'

Hanna: 'Aren't mine small?'

Leah: 'Are you kidding?'

And then Leah lifts her hand and places it on Hanna's breast, cupping it, sort of weighing it in her hand.

Leah: 'I would die for these.'

Hanna feels her chilly fingers on her skin.

Then they stretch out on their lounge chairs with towels over their heads to rest. She burrows her feet into the hot sand. Deeper down it's cool and wet. She smells her burning skin, like freshly baked bread. She slips in and out of sleep. Distantly she hears Samuel's music coming from the portable speaker, mixing with the rush of the waves. She's floating. This was what she dreamed of when she first heard about the trip. Now she slips into sleep again. In her dream, Leah's hand is back on her breast. There's nothing strange about it, two girls on a beach by the sea.

10

She can't sleep, is just lying awake in the cool, clean sheets. Leah is sleeping beside her; her covers have slipped off her body, which looks black against the white fabric. Hanna wonders what effect it has on someone, to have slept in such nice sheets all their life.

She is amazed at how loud the sea is outside, even though the balcony door is closed. She lies on her back and listens to the crashing waves.

She walks out on the balcony.

It's warmer out there than inside. It's not light out yet, but it's not entirely dark either. She watches the waves break and wash way up the shore. In the distance she sees some teenagers staggering along the water's edge. Even farther off, a dog owner is walking their dog.

She thinks of Samuel, in the room next door, weaving his dreams. She thinks of the nerviness in his voice when the topic of Ivan comes up, how nice it is that he's so transparent with her about his worries. She likes that he feels able to open up to her.

She thinks probably something will happen with him when they arrive at his parents'. When he finally sees Hanna alongside them, sees how well she fits in. Maybe that's when he'll understand that she understands.

She misses him so much that she can't bear to wait until the sun comes up. She wonders what he would do if she knocked on the door of his suite. If she suddenly stood there in front of him and told him how she felt.

11

The next morning, Hanna wakes up to pounding on the door of the room she's sharing with Leah. She opens her eyes. The room is dark, but sunlight is streaming through the gaps in the blinds.

'Who is it?' Leah calls in Spanish.

'It's me,' Samuel replies.

'What is it?'

'Can I come in?'

'Hold on!' Hanna calls. 'Yes!' calls Leah.

No response for a moment, then Samuel says: 'I'm coming in!'

The door opens and Samuel sticks his head through the crack and says: 'Get yourselves ready!'

Hanna quickly pulls the covers up to hide her face so Samuel won't see her without make-up.

Leah: 'Why?'

Samuel: 'We're going on a little adventure!'

Leah pulls off her sleep mask and gets out of bed and says: 'What time is it?'

Hanna is surprised at how casually Leah will let Samuel see her in just her pants. Maybe that's one of the advantages of having a perfect body, that it doesn't reveal anything about you.

Samuel says cheerfully: 'Nine!'

Leah: 'Nine?!'

Samuel says: 'Get dressed. See you at the car,' and closes the door.

Leah goes over to the wardrobe and opens it. She picks out a white satin top and a coral-pink crocheted skirt that's half see-through, so her black bikini bottoms are visible underneath.

Hanna stays in bed, watching her and wondering what she should wear.

She's already gone through all her new dresses.

She goes over to her wardrobe and chooses the lightweight DKNY caftan even though she wore it on the train to Barcelona.

When they get to the driveway, Samuel is waiting for them, leaning on the Bentley and grinning behind his sunglasses.

Hanna and Leah climb into the back seat.

'Where are we going?' Leah asks.

'You'll see!' says Samuel, getting into the driver's seat.

Tom settles in beside him and lights a cigarette. He looks unusually elegant as he leans back and releases a smoke ring.

He says: 'It's like we're a family out for a drive with Daddy.'

Samuel laughs.

Hanna laughs too, although she doesn't quite get why it's funny.

12

The road winds along, following the coast. Hanna feels dizzy when she turns to face the sea, since the cliffs plunge straight into the waves. Samuel picks the music, and Hanna has heard these songs so many times now that she can finally sing along properly, and she is moved when she views the scene from the outside, sees them in the beautiful car, surrounded by this dramatic nature.

'How long till we get there? Where are we going?' Leah yells again, her hand on her giant white hat, but it's so windy Samuel can't hear her. She has to repeat her question twice before he turns round and shouts: 'Soon! Soon!'

Hanna has never seen him so hyper.

After about an hour in the car, Samuel turns off the highway and drives into a small village by the sea, with narrow cobblestone streets and small stone houses.

They park by the harbour.

The sea is glittering so brightly that Hanna has to squint, even though she's wearing sunglasses.

Samuel jogs onto the pier and waves to an older man next to a motorboat that's moored at the end. The man, who looks like a tiny old fisherman in his coverall and black cap, waves back. It's clear he's been waiting for them. Once Samuel has helped them into the boat, he gives the man instructions in Spanish.

The little boat putts out into the swells, and when they get farther from shore, the waves are higher. Hanna holds on to the railing to keep from losing her balance. Samuel rests a hand on her back.

'Is this tough for you?' he asks.

'What?'

'Because of your mum.'

She replies: 'Yes, of course. A little.'

After half an hour an island appears on the horizon.

Now it's Tom, asking: 'What is that?'

Samuel gives a secretive smile and says: 'Soon.'

The closer they get to the island, the more beautiful it looks. Cypress trees reaching for the sky. A small harbour full of little boats. White cliffs of lime and grey granite. Tiny sugarcube houses balancing on the slopes.

They dock at a pier in the harbour and Samuel hands the fisherman a few bills. Hanna hears them agree on a time when he'll pick them up again.

When Hanna jumps out of the boat and has firm ground beneath her feet, it's like it keeps rocking. She takes a deep breath to overcome her dizziness. The sun is already high.

Samuel stops in front of them and says: 'I have something to show you.'

Then he leads them through narrow alleys, purposefully, taking long strides.

Alongside the houses run low stone walls full of cracks, where flowers and rosebushes break through. Here and there, cats lie in the gravel, staring. Between the roofs are clothes lines full of laundry.

Leah complains that she's wearing the wrong shoes for cobble-stones, but Samuel keeps heading up the hill at a rapid pace. At one point, Tom asks to stop and catch his breath, and they take a break, breathing hard for a little while. Tom lights a cigarette and takes a few quick puffs. Then they go on.

When they reach the end of the hill, which also happens to be the edge of the village, Samuel takes a key from his pocket and walks up to a wooden gate.

'What's this?' Leah says.

Samuel opens the old gate and says: 'Welcome.'

13

The house is like a palace, with tall columns and arches. It's dusty and seems to have stood empty for a long time; the walls are bare, but the rooms are full of beautiful furniture. Corduroy sofas and Indian rugs, bureaus made of dark wood, tall bookcases. Stone mosaic floors in different patterns. Thick beams on the ceiling, stained-glass windows.

Samuel walks in first, followed by Leah and Tom.

Hanna brings up the rear, slowly, trying to figure out where they've landed.

Samuel leads them up a wide stone staircase and they emerge onto the roof. Once again it's so bright that Hanna has to shield her eyes. There's a light breeze.

Once her eyes adjust, she absorbs the breathtaking view. The azure sea surrounds them in all directions. On the horizon they can see the mainland shrouded in haze. Here and there are white sails, leaning into the sky.

Leah says: 'It's like we died and went to heaven.'

They sit down on a group of sofas under a sailcloth.

Samuel sounds solemn when he says: 'What do you think?'

Leah: 'About what?'

Samuel doesn't respond. The sailcloth flaps in the breeze above them.

Leah looks confused. Hanna turns to Tom and sees that he's as perplexed as Leah.

Samuel says: 'I haven't been exactly honest with you.'

He takes off his sunglasses and continues: 'Last Christmas when I was visiting my folks, I walked by a real estate office that had a load of ads for houses in the window, and on a whim I went in. And the agent tried to sell me on all sorts of places but they were mostly just your average boring bungalows, and various timeshares in ugly hotels, and I said I wasn't interested. But then he asked me if I wanted to see the best one he had. A property that had just come on the market, a "once in a lifetime thing".'

Leah shrieks: 'You bought this?'

Samuel shakes his head: 'No, no.'

He's silent for a moment, but then he goes on: 'So, here's the thing . . .'

Hanna loves it when his voice takes that tone, as if he's about to say something life-altering.

He takes a drag of his cigarette. Then he stubs it out, folds his hands, and says: 'The reason we're going to see my dad is because I want to buy this house.'

Hanna turns to Tom, and Tom turns to Leah.

Leah looks shocked. She takes off her sunglasses. Her eyes are wide.

Samuel: 'Something happened to me when I came here.'

Tom: 'How much?'

Samuel: 'Five hundred thousand euros. Or . . . four hundred thousand. But of course, it'll need renovating.'

Hanna hears the dull echo of a church bell in the distance.

Samuel goes on: 'I hate to beg, but I feel something special for this house.'

Tom: 'He's definitely going to say yes, once he sees it.'

Samuel nods and smiles; he looks like a proud little boy.

Hanna is glad she's wearing her sunglasses, because otherwise they would see that her eyes are full of tears.

Samuel sinks onto the sofa between them.

He says: 'What do you think? We could come here on weekends, in the summer, and in the winter when Madrid is too cold, whenever we want. The minute we get bored.'

Leah smiles: 'Are you joking?'

Samuel: 'I didn't just see a *house* when I came here. I saw a whole different life.'

He remains sunken into the sofa.

He lights a cigarette and places a hand on Tom's brown thigh. 'This could be the next step for us.'

And Hanna wants to embrace him, rest her face against his neck, stroke his hair, tell him how much she likes the idea.

Tom reaches for his pack of cigarettes and she notices that he's moving sluggishly, as though the gravity of the moment is slowing him down. He gives one to Leah, one to Hanna and sticks one into his own mouth. Then he lights all three, still slowly.

All four of them take a drag at the same time.

They look at each other and smile.

When they blow out the smoke, it's on a long exhalation, as though they all share one set of lungs.

Tom nods with a grin and says: 'I love it.'

Samuel gives a laugh.

Leah: 'Me too.'

Hanna: 'Me too.'

Tom: 'So it all comes down to Ivan?'

Samuel's smile fades. He nods gravely. 'Yes.'

'Do you think he'll say yes?'

Samuel gazes at the sea as he considers the question. 'It depends how I present it.'

Leah stands up and goes to Samuel; she sits down next to him and embraces him, saying: 'It's the most beautiful house I've ever seen.'

Samuel smiles and hugs her back.

Hanna wishes she had hugged him first. She sees Leah whispering something into Samuel's ear.

Tom mumbles, as though he's talking to himself: 'I could write here.'

Samuel says: 'We could do all of it. Everything we've been dreaming of, everything we've talked about. This is the place where we could do all of that.'

Leah says: 'This is nuts. This is just nuts.'

Then she takes Samuel's hand in her own and brings it to her cheek. Tom takes her other hand and brings it to his chest, and they sit there for a long time without saying a word, while Hanna watches them.

14

They wander slowly around the property. Olive groves, lemon trees, dates. The lawn is in bad shape, dry and burned, but Samuel says it can be restored. He shows them where the guest house will be, and where the reading corner will be built, and now she understands how carefully he's planned this and how well the plan reflects his dissatisfaction at the embassy. He's been under-stimulated for a long time. They could build their own little world here, separate from the real world. Hanna feels like she's ended up in a fairy tale, a modern fairy tale.

After their tour of the property, they return to the village at a languid pace.

As they walk, Samuel points things out and talks about them. 'Time moves more slowly here. There are hardly any TVs around.'

He smiles: 'This is a place the news doesn't reach, the real estate agent said. And in the small orchard past the church, you can pick peaches and mandarins straight from the trees. And in the morning you can wake up and walk down the hill and straight out onto the rocks in the light and dive into the clear water. There are no tourists here. And sometimes a fine red powder falls from the sky and the whole village gets covered with the dust that the North African winds carry in from the Sahara.'

Leah laughs: 'Poetry.'

Samuel continues: 'After that it's just about inviting the right people, people who can stay with us for a little while.'

Tom nods: 'We'll only invite the best.'

Leah: 'Should we really invite *anyone?*'

They laugh.

Samuel: 'If we ever get restless we can just take the boat over to the mainland and go to a restaurant or the clubs.'

They walk down the hill, back towards the sea.

Hanna wanders along slowly behind the others. The wind is balmy and feels nice in the shade. She looks at her three friends from behind. Their backs are strong and lovely.

She thinks of how natural it feels.

When she catches up with them, she can't help herself. She places a hand on Samuel's shoulder and says: 'Thank you.'

And that's when it happens.

He stops, turns to her, pulls her close and embraces her.

Her face is in his long hair, she can feel his large hand on her back and he says into her ear: 'I just hope it actually works out.'

She says: 'Of course it will work out,' and he says something about how it's not a sure thing, because his dad can be 'touchy when it comes to money', but she's not really listening because his warm body is pressed to hers, his stomach against her stomach, his chest against her chest, his breath against her ear.

When he lets go of her and starts walking again, she lingers for a moment so that no one will notice how red her face is.

15

When they get down to the harbour, they take a seat at a bar to wait for the fishing boat that will take them back.

Samuel orders a Bloody Mary, Tom a beer and Hanna and Leah café con leche.

The awning flaps in the breeze above them; gulls screech. It smells like the sea. Oil from the fishing boats makes patterns on the water's surface. She thinks of the veranda Samuel says he wants to have built, with a view of the village and the sea. Now she pictures lying there with Samuel, once the others have gone to bed, in the dense dark of night, as insects bump into the glass of the lanterns.

No one says anything.

Tom sips his beer; Samuel stirs his drink with his straw.

Leah is absorbed in her phone. Hanna guesses she's texting her attaché again. She recognises that concerned expression, her focus aimed down at the screen.

Tom turns to Samuel and says: 'When are you going to talk to him?'

'I don't know. Not on the first night, anyway. Probably after a few days, once we've reconnected a little.'

Tom places a hand on his back. 'It's going to be perfect.'

Samuel nods: 'Cross your fingers.'

Leah puts her phone on the table, screen down, and says: 'I did it.'

She takes off her sunglasses. It's clear she's been crying. She takes a napkin from the dispenser on the table and wipes her eyes.

Samuel: 'Did what?'

Leah: 'I told him it's over.'

Tom: 'What?'

Hanna can tell that Tom is searching Leah's face to see if she's serious.

Leah: 'I blocked his number. Forever.'

Leah nods at her own statement and tries to smile but can't do it.

Tom pulls her close and holds her. She cries into his shoulder.

Hanna turns to Samuel, who doesn't say anything, just gazes at the sea. He looks unusually serious.

16

Hanna and Leah are in front of the bathroom mirror in their hotel room, putting on make-up in preparation for their night out. Hanna watches Leah and is impressed by the way she can apply a perfect curve of lipstick in one motion. The bass from the DJ down by the pool thumps in the distance.

Leah is drunk. She started drinking in the bath. Hanna appreciates this, because it means she doesn't have to try as hard not to say something wrong.

'Fuck him,' Leah says.

'For real,' says Hanna.

'Fuck him!'

'Fuck him!' Hanna replies.

Leah says: 'I waited for three years,' and bursts into laughter. It's a strange kind of laugh, one Hanna doesn't recognise.

'You did the right thing,' Hanna says.

Leah turns to Hanna and says: 'Can I do your make-up?'

Hanna looks at herself in the mirror. Compared to Leah's face, her own looks crooked, as though she's been struck with facial paralysis.

'Come on,' Leah says. 'I've got an idea. Come here.'

'I don't know.'

'Please. Can't I do your make-up?'

Hanna wants to refuse, but she can't think of a good excuse. Leah is already digging through her make-up bag. She takes out a tube of mascara and leans towards Hanna's face. Hanna closes her eyes.

Leah: 'Just relax.'

She breathes through her nose, since Leah's face is so close.

Leah: 'Relax your eyes.'

Hanna nods. Leah's breath smells like wine and peppermint.

Hanna: 'Okay.'

Leah says she's going to try out a more outlandish, challenging style. She says Hanna has to learn to let go a little. Hanna wants to ask what she means by that, exactly, but she elects to give a single nod instead.

Hanna looks at her face up close. Leah's skin has no pores. It's the face of a mannequin.

Leah: 'Close your eyes.'

When Leah is finished, she takes Hanna by the shoulders and turns her to face the mirror.

Hanna is surprised at what she sees. It shakes her to the core. Her first impulse is to wash it all off immediately. Leah has brought out something she thought was a secret.

Leah: 'What do you say to that?'

Hanna can't help but smile at how happy Leah is. Leah interprets the smile to mean that Hanna is pleased: 'What did I tell you?'

Hanna turns to the mirror and takes in her make-up from different angles.

Leah says: 'Come on,' and tugs her by the hand over to the minibar. Leah crouches before it and begins to rummage. Hanna has never seen such an extensive minibar. In the fridge door alone she sees four rows of tiny bottles and on the shelf inside is a group of full-size bottles, spirits of various brands.

'You pick,' Hanna says.

Once Leah has mixed two gin and tonics, they go out to the balcony. It's dark outside now. Music is coming from multiple sources, the different rhythms rolling in and out over one another. They each light a cigarette and sit down in the wicker chairs to gaze out at the alleys and the beach.

Leah stares at Hanna.

Then she says: 'I want to go one step further.'

'What do you mean?'

'With your make-up.'

They look at one another.

Leah says: 'Wait here,' and goes to get her bag of make-up. Hanna stays put and looks out at the sea, watches the waves breaking down there, thinking of the house. The group will probably bond even more strongly now that they have a plan together. Leah has never before been so attentive with her.

Leah comes back with her make-up bag and pulls her chair over so she's sitting across from Hanna again. There are so many insects around the light that their shadows play over Leah's face.

Leah's large, soft blush brush sweeps over Hanna's cheeks. It feels like a gentle caress. It's as if Leah is taking something away instead of adding something. Like an archaeologist methodically brushing sand from an artefact.

Leah's lips are pink. Sometimes she licks them. Hanna has often thought about how Leah's mouth is always open. It's inviting. She wonders if Leah has practised that, or if it comes naturally.

'There,' Leah says, leaning back in her chair. 'Now you couldn't be any prettier.'

17

She wakes up early. The curtains are drawn, but she can see through the gap that the light is dawning blue outside. Leah is still asleep beside her in the big double bed, her hand over her eyes. It's relaxing to listen to her breathing.

Hanna gingerly gets out of bed, puts on her dressing gown, and goes over to the vanity table. She picks up her hairbrush.

After a while, she stops brushing and looks in the mirror. What was it that changed about her gaze when Leah did her make-up? It became as powerful as Leah's or Tom's or Samuel's. She was no longer hollow; she existed.

On a whim she goes to her bag to get her watercolour pad and a pencil. Then she sits down at the vanity table again.

She studies her own reflection for a while and then gets started. First she draws her hairline, then her chin and neck. The pencil rasps against the paper.

When she gets to the eyes, she stops. Studies them in the mirror. There's something missing. It's always been this way. The others in the group have a certain depth to their eyes, and it's reflected in their personalities. Her eyes are two blank holes. She looks down at the expressionless drawing. Her eyes look like Vera's, vague and meek. She sharpens the pencil and makes an attempt to bring them to life.

She draws the eyelashes, eyebrows, irises. But it's hopeless – no matter how she tries, it only reveals emptiness.

She looks down at her hands, which are talentless, which lack the gift. She is struck by the urge to punish them. She sharpens her pencil once more. She turns towards Leah to make sure she's still asleep. Then she shoves the tip of the lead under the nail of her left ring finger. It hurts so much that she hears herself whimper. But she shoves it in farther. The reddish-black drops land on the paper like melted sealing wax. She dips her finger in the puddle of blood and gets started, drawing her fingertip around the eyes of the portrait, and when the blood runs out she shoves the pencil lead under her nail again and squeezes out a few more drops. Then she uses her finger like a paintbrush. After a while, something happens. The eyes light up. The creature's eyes. She hesitates for a second but keeps painting, filling in the lips, and soon they start to move. The creature whispers that it's ready to lend a hand, and all she has to do is dare to open the cage.

18

The next day, they head further south. The sun is high in the sky. The landscape is dry and burned. Here and there they see an orange orchard or a vineyard on the slopes, but mostly it's white grass or just gravel. Dried-up riverbeds and scorched fields. There's more traffic than on the road by the sea. Little mopeds darting between cars, dangerously close, with whiny little horns. Big, dusty trucks with horns that bellow as they pass.

As they approach Alicante, Samuel puts his playlist on again and the group sings along. Hanna listens to the lyrics and it's as if every song is full of subtext about their future. Each time a key word pops up, she puts extra emphasis on it when she sings. 'Hope', 'love', 'future', 'truth', and others that describe them in some way.

They pull into the city around five. The sun is lower in the sky, but it's still blazing. Samuel takes a wrong turn at first and has to turn round at a petrol station. He's unusually touchy. Cursing and shouting at other cars.

The closer they get to the house, the more nervous Hanna feels. Time and again she takes out her compact to check her hair and make-up. It bothers her that she's sunburned from all the pool and beach visits.

Ivan and Rakel live in a village just south of the city. Samuel slows down to give the group time to admire the stately buildings, and both Leah and Tom have their phones up.

At last they reach the house, which is perched on a cliff by the sea, surrounded by leafy woods, and beyond the trees Hanna can see how tall the house is.

They drive up to the closed iron gate. Samuel slows down and stops. A security camera moves to point in their direction.

'Are you nervous?' Leah asks.

'Shhh,' says Samuel.

Then he presses the button.

A woman's voice answers in Spanish.

Samuel says his name and the large iron gate opens slowly, creakily.

19

Ivan is waiting for them in the driveway, his hands in his pockets and a big smile behind his sunglasses. He's wearing a double-breasted navy jacket with a white shirt underneath, and he looks more robust than Hanna had expected.

Behind him are two teenaged boys in pale blue shirts and white shorts, standing at attention like the bellboys she's seen at the luxury hotels recently. As soon as Samuel parks, they rush over and open the trunk and start taking out suitcases.

Ivan approaches the car and reaches out. He and Samuel embrace.

'I missed you,' Ivan says.

Samuel smiles and holds him.

Then Ivan takes off his sunglasses and turns to Leah and Tom, hugs them, asks how the trip was and praises their even tans.

Hanna stays by the car, a few metres back, observing.

He doesn't look very much like Samuel. His features are coarser, his ice-blue eyes more piercing and wilder than Samuel's narrowed, wary ones.

Above all, she immediately senses a brand of self-confidence Samuel doesn't quite possess. The way Ivan moves, his small talk, his deep, powerful voice, the way he puts a hand on the back of Tom's neck, the way he laughs – it all radiates authority and strength.

After a while he spots Hanna and says: 'This must be Hanna.'

Hanna has trouble meeting his gaze.

He offers his hand. When she takes it, he pulls her close, gently but firmly, until she is enveloped in his strong arms. He smells strongly of cologne.

'Welcome home,' he says.

'Thank you,' she says.

He lets go of her and turns to the group: 'You're actually here!'

Tom: 'Thanks for letting us *be* here!'

Ivan puts a hand on Samuel's shoulder and says: 'Your mother is glad you're here too.'

Samuel nods silently.

Ivan turns to Leah: 'She's sleeping now. But she'll be up soon.'

Then he waves to the group: 'Come on in!'

They head up the grand front stairs.

'I hope you're hungry,' Ivan says. 'There is a *horrific* amount of food.'

'Everyone's on a diet,' Samuel says.

'Guess we'll just have to puke it up later,' Tom says.

Ivan laughs aloud and says: 'Diets are banned here.'

When Samuel notices that Tom is carrying two suitcases, he says: 'Are you crazy?' and waves over one of the blue-clad boys.

'It's like a hotel,' Leah says.

'Five-star, let's hope,' says Ivan.

'If not, we're out of here,' Tom says. Another laugh from Ivan.

It feels nice to enter the cool house. The floor is black-and-white chequered, and a crystal chandelier hangs from the high ceiling.

'Come in, come in, don't be shy,' says Ivan, waving them inside.

Then a tour begins. It takes a long time. In each room there's a painting or piece of furniture with its own anecdote. Hanna walks close behind Ivan, as close as she can, because she doesn't want to miss a word, and she's starting to wonder why Samuel never mentioned how charming he is. Everything he says and does oozes worldliness. She loves his fashionable style of dress and his well-spoken manner, the posh way he says his *sj*-sounds in Swedish, his slightly backwards-leaning gait with his hands in his pockets, his slicked-back grey hair. Only his laugh departs from the elegant upper-class vibe; it's a loud, booming guffaw.

Hanna notices that the others act differently around him too. Tom is suddenly some sort of joker, always trying to make Ivan laugh, and Leah is the flirty version of herself that Hanna recognises from clubs, where she touches her hair and takes on the shrill tone of a teenager. Maybe that's how it works, people with Ivan's charisma bend energies the way black holes bend light. Hanna wonders what it's like growing up in the presence of such a person. She looks at Samuel, who is unusually quiet and shy. She has so many questions now.

Suddenly Ivan stops in a hallway and falls silent, bringing a finger to his lips.

He whispers: 'Wait here.'

Then he opens a door, vanishes inside the room and closes the door behind him.

Hanna turns to Samuel.

His shoulders are thrust forward. He looks scared.

Leah takes his hand: 'It's going to be okay.'

After a moment, the door opens and Ivan sticks his head out: 'Come in.'

20

The room is stuffy and dim. Black curtains darken the tall windows. The white wall-to-wall carpet is fluffy and soft beneath their feet. The bed is draped with mosquito netting. A nurse is leaning over the nightstand, fiddling with some pill bottles.

Ivan gestures at Samuel, urging him to approach the bed, but he shakes his head.

The group is quiet for a moment, standing in a semicircle around the sickbed, until Leah says: 'I'll start.'

She pulls the mosquito netting aside and crawls onto the bed.

Ivan, Samuel, Tom and Hanna don't say anything.

The mosquito netting is in the way, but Hanna can see the outline of Leah sitting on the foot of the bed.

She hears Leah's voice: 'Are you doing okay?'

No answer from inside.

Hanna thinks she can make out the silhouette of Rakel's head to the left. A fly is buzzing somewhere, but otherwise everything is quiet. Next to the bed, the nurse takes out a syringe and inserts the needle through the stopper of a small glass bottle. She slowly sucks up the contents.

Hanna wonders why it's so warm in the room.

Now she hears Leah's voice again, from the bed: 'It's so nice to see you.'

Silence.

Both Ivan and Samuel are staring at the floor.

Leah says: 'We arrived today. Just now.'

Hanna turns to Tom, but he's staring at his feet too.

She hears Leah again: 'How are you feeling?'

A lengthy silence.

Leah: 'There's someone new with us this time.'

Then the mosquito netting lifts and Leah peers out. She points at Hanna.

Hanna shakes her head.

Leah beckons again. Hanna turns to Samuel, but he's out of commission. Then she turns to Ivan, who nods encouragingly and points at the bed.

Hanna realises she has no choice, approaches the bed, and pulls the netting aside.

She boosts herself up onto the tall mattress. It's like crawling into a fort. It's airless and smells funny. Rakel is all tucked in, with her head on two giant pillows. Her hair is long and white, her face contorted.

'This is Hanna,' Leah says.

Rakel looks at Hanna in silence.

Hanna tries and fails to smile. Rakel's face is a question mark. But what's the question? Hanna isn't sure she wants to know.

The mattress feels like quicksand. Now she understands why Samuel didn't want to talk about his mother. Hanna thinks: it's like watching someone sink below the surface without being able to do a thing. The smell is so strange. It's sweet like beeswax but with an undertone of egg. Hanna looks at that twisted face. It should be illegal to look like that. Someone ought to do something, hammer it into the proper shape somehow. The broken symmetry, that drooping, leaking left eye, that desperate gaze, that gaping mouth, locked into an expression of surprise, like a hole in a tree, an owl's nest. But looking away is not allowed. She looks at Rakel and Rakel looks at her, and it's a chilling experience, because it's clear that Rakel is staring straight into her soul, and Hanna is struck with the sudden impulse to hit her, in order to make this all end somehow.

For lack of any other idea, Hanna points at her own chest and says: 'Hanna.'

And now Hanna sees Rakel's arms. The skin is flaking and peeling like a fresh pastry.

On the other side of the mosquito netting, Hanna can hear Ivan and Samuel arguing. Ivan sounds stern. 'Go in there and see her.'

Samuel: 'I said no.'

Ivan: 'Do you hear me?'

Samuel: 'Stop it.'

Ivan: 'She misses you.'

Hanna turns to Leah: 'Should we maybe let her rest?'

Outside, the voices get louder.

Samuel: 'What do you want me to say?'

Protracted silence.

Then the netting is pulled aside. It's Ivan: 'Let's go.'

21

Some time later, they're sitting under umbrellas by the pool while a woman in a white uniform sets out glasses and bottles. The pool is kidney-shaped and tiled in a blue-and-white chequered pattern that keeps changing shape as the surface of the water moves.

Hanna wants to say something about what just happened, but Samuel only stares at the table and doesn't seem to want to talk.

Once the woman in the white uniform has retreated, a man dressed in black appears with a carafe full of iced water with lemon slices. Hanna takes a big drink. The water is fresh and cold. She drains her glass quickly.

In the meantime, Ivan is pacing around the pool as he talks on the phone. From what little Hanna can catch, it seems to be work-related. He sounds upset.

Samuel is slouched in his chair, half lying down, his gaze absent.

Tom and Leah are googling local nightclubs on their phones, talking about what they want to do while they're here, and Hanna pretends to be engaged in their conversation although she's having trouble concentrating on it. She wants to ask Samuel how he's doing after seeing his mother in that condition, but he doesn't seem eager to talk.

After a while, Ivan wraps up his call and takes a seat. He calls out to his assistant: 'Ask them to call back as soon as they know.'

Tom: 'Who were you talking to?'

Ivan shakes his head: 'Just a small conflict.'

Hanna: 'Who with?'

Ivan: 'Some Saudis. They want to be paid more. So they threaten me. They think they can scare me.'

Samuel: 'I think I'm going to go take a rest.'

Ivan pays no attention to Samuel, turning to Hanna instead: 'My job is to be everyone's friend, but it often ends up where I'm everyone's enemy.'

Then he smiles at her, and it's such an obliging smile that Hanna blushes. She quickly reaches for her glass, to draw attention away from her face.

Samuel points at Ivan and says: 'His job is to act as an intermediary between oil companies and different governments.'

Ivan: 'Well . . .'

Samuel: 'It's a pretty smart set-up.'

Leah: 'Why's that?'

'Because you get to avoid responsibility.'

Ivan turns to Samuel – and suddenly his gaze is stern: 'What are you doing?'

Samuel and Ivan regard one another in silence.

Samuel: 'What? Am I wrong?'

'Is there something you want to say to me?'

'No.'

Ivan takes out his phone and weighs it in his hand. He says, his eyes fixed on Samuel's: 'I've got perfect pitch, don't you forget that.'

Samuel tries to smile, but it only looks strange.

Ivan slaps his knees and says: 'So, anyone hungry around here?'

22

The restaurant sits on a clifftop a few kilometres from the village. Their outdoor seating sticks out over the cliff, and from the tables you can see the lights of the village in the distance. Ivan has reserved the best table, he says, on the very edge, where the view is most striking and it's the perfect distance to the music coming from the piano bar.

Samuel is wearing a white Tom Ford suit over an unbuttoned black shirt. Tom is wearing a white shirt unbuttoned at the neck and floral-patterned silk trousers that look expensive. Leah looks like a ballet dancer, with a puffy skirt and a corset blouse, white fishnet stockings and laced shoes that look like ballet slippers, decorated with glitter.

A waiter shows them to their table.

As they're about to sit down, Ivan pulls out the chair next to his and gestures an invitation at Hanna.

She smiles and sits down beside him.

He whispers: 'Mademoiselle.'

Maybe it's her imagination, but Hanna thinks Leah shoots her a jealous glance across the table.

Ivan is in a jovial mood during dinner, relating stories from Samuel's childhood, making the group laugh again and again. Hanna has never met such a skilled teller of anecdotes. And even though he's holding court in front of the entire group, he has a remarkable ability to make her feel seen all the while. Each time his eyes meet hers she feels a current run through her, because his gaze is so clear.

Only once does the mood become strained. It happens when he asks Samuel what he's going to be when he 'grows up'.

Samuel doesn't say anything for a long time. When he speaks again, he says: 'Maybe I'm already grown up.'

Ivan looks at him and laughs. 'Nope.'

Out at sea, the big yachts are at rest, their underwater spotlights illuminating the rocky bottom through the clear water.

Ivan says: 'What happened to your coming to work for me?'

'I've already got a job.'

'But is it a *real* job?'

Hanna wants to tell him not to be afraid, not to give in.

Ivan leans over and says: 'Your mother and I both want you to.'

Samuel says: 'You don't know what she wants.'

Ivan: 'Don't say that.'

Samuel: 'Let's at least stop pretending.'

'She's the same person, deep down.'

'That's the problem.'

A pall of sadness crosses Ivan's face. He swallows. He places his hand on the linen tablecloth, close to Samuel's. He looks at their hands. It's as if he wants to pat Samuel's hand but doesn't dare.

Hanna feels called to intervene, help them connect, but she doesn't know how.

Ivan: 'Listen to me.'

Samuel: 'Stop.'

'You want to make a difference, right?'

Samuel considers this for a moment. Then he says: 'Yes.'

'Then you should be in a place where it's possible to make a difference.'

Ivan leans over the table and brings his hand even closer to Samuel's. Samuel looks at Ivan's hand without taking it.

Ivan: 'It's time to choose your path.'

At that, Samuel picks up his fork and points it at Ivan and says: 'I'm trying.'

Ivan leans back and says: 'Maybe you should try a little harder.'

23

When they get back to the house, Hanna walks out to the driveway while the others go down to the pool for an evening dip. She's exhausted from their dinner, and fairly drunk. She sits down on a bench outside the front door to collect herself.

She hears splashing and laughter in the distance and lights a cigarette.

The cicadas are singing and in the distance the bass thumps from the clubs, deep and rhythmic.

She's starting to understand where Samuel comes from. She's getting a sense of why he is the way he is. She understands his struggle better now that she's seeing it up close.

When she finishes smoking and goes back into the house, it's perfectly quiet. The others seem to have gone to bed.

It's almost a little spooky to wander alone though the dark house.

She goes up to the room she's sharing with Leah.

Leah isn't there.

She gets undressed and puts on her dressing gown. Then, as she's going to the chest to put away her clothes, she catches sight of something that makes her freeze.

On the desk by the window is the handwritten receipt from the antique dealer, right there in the middle of it. It doesn't state who the buyer and seller are, but the purchase sum is right there, clear as day.

The strange part is, not only did someone find it in her suitcase, they put it directly under the lamp.

She holds her breath and pricks her ears. It's quiet, aside from the cicadas outside.

Maybe there's an innocent explanation; did one of the maids simply unpack her suitcase? She can't quite imagine that. Would a maid really look through the interior pockets, take out the contents and place them on the desk?

Hanna pulls the curtains. Was it Tom? Maybe it was Tom; she's still not sure how much he saw when he took her phone. Maybe he's suspicious and wants to let her know he's keeping an eye on her.

Was it Ivan? Did he become curious about who his son brought home with him, and decide to dig through her bag? Or maybe it was just the maid.

She twitches the curtain aside and peers out.

Through the dim haze she sees a lighthouse, a few kilometres in the distance. Its light sweeps across the rooftops and the land, but otherwise everything is dark.

She pulls the curtain closed again and goes to the bathroom.

She sits on the floor and tears the receipt into tiny, tiny shreds, flushing it down the toilet in multiple rounds.

24

Hanna wakes up the next morning to find the room filled with sunlight. Leah's bed is empty. The white sheets glow. Outside she can hear waves breaking and children playing in the distance.

She sits up in bed, still half-asleep, and turns to face the desk. Her discovery of the receipt last night seems distant, dreamlike. In the sharp morning light, nothing seems so threatening.

Maybe she overreacted. It must have been the maid.

She gets up and catches sight of herself in the wall mirror. She approaches it and discovers that she's lost even more weight, but her sunburn is worse than she'd feared. When she presses her fingertip into her red shoulder and lets go, a white spot lingers.

She takes a shower. Her skin stings so badly that she has to enter the spray tentatively.

When she's finished, she dries off and walks naked into the bright room. The soles of her feet stick to the shiny marble floor.

She puts on her dressing gown and goes to the balcony. There's a fresh breeze. She looks down at the boardwalk.

She thinks of Samuel's fearful eyes at dinner, the way he's changed since they arrived at the house. She wonders how he'll manage to ask Ivan about the money now that he's weakened.

She gets out her phone and takes a series of selfies. So this is what it's like not to feel ugly. She opens her dressing gown and looks at her body. She runs her hand over her stomach and chest, wondering if it's normal to get turned on by your own body. She takes off her dressing gown and lies down in the bed. Her skin is brown against the white sheets. The cool comforter envelops her like a body. She closes her eyes.

A knock comes at the door.

She pulls the comforter over herself.

Another knock, louder.

She sits up in bed and calls: '*Sí?*'

'It's Ivan.'

She reaches for her shirt and pulls it on along with a pair of pants.

She gets up and looks in the mirror. She considers putting on some shorts, but then he knocks again.

She cracks the door and peers out, since she's only wearing pants and a t-shirt.

Ivan is shirtless and has a towel around his waist. The skin of his chest is aged and full of curly white strands.

They regard one another. Is this the moment he'll ask why she has a receipt for a fortune in her bag?

He says: 'Good morning.'

'Good morning.'

'You're a Goya expert, I hear.'

'I don't know about that.'

'But you work at the museum. With the anniversary celebrations?'

'Yes.'

'There's something I need help with.'

'Okay.'

'Come with me!'

Then he walks down the hallway. She would really prefer to get dressed first, but even so she follows him. He leads her into an office with paintings on the walls.

He stops in front of one of them and says: 'I need your advice.'

'Of course.'

'How long have you been there?'

'What's that?'

'How long have you been working on the anniversary committee?'

'Since April.'

He nods. He says: 'I know that gang, because I'm in on the action.'

He's standing pretty close to her. She can smell traces of alcohol on his breath.

'Cool.'

'What do you think about Xavier?'

She looks at him: 'He's fun. But intense.'

Ivan: 'You can say that again.'

'Yeah.'

He never looks away from her. He says: 'How about Jorge?'

She replies: 'He's nice.'

Ivan regards her in silence.

She adds: 'Although he can be a pain too.'

'Tell him I said hi.'

Hanna becomes aware of how quiet it is around them.

Ever since they arrived at the house, it's bustled with constant action, but all of a sudden it's perfectly tranquil.

She asks: 'Where's Samuel? And Tom and Leah?'

'They were going to the village to poke around for a bit.'

'Why didn't they tell me?'

'Maybe they didn't want to wake you up.'

They look at each other.

Hanna: 'What did you need my help with?'

Ivan: 'Picking something for the anniversary auction. I promised to donate a painting and I can't decide which one it should be. What do you think about this one?'

He points at a large painting on the wall.

It's of a naked woman standing with her back to the viewer and her face aimed at the spray of a shower. It looks like an example of naive art, with bold, strong colours, and Hanna guesses it's French, 1950s. The woman's bottom is excessively large and pink, and she's spreading her cheeks with her hands.

She approaches the painting.

She hears Ivan take a step closer. She can feel the heat of his body against her back.

She turns round and looks at him. He doesn't blink.

He says: 'What do you think?'

She turns to the painting again. The woman's arsehole is painted like an x in black strokes.

She hears Ivan breathing heavily behind her.

She observes the work.

Ivan says: 'Samuel was ashamed of that one when he was little. I told him nudity was natural. And he was so angry at me for displaying it on the wall. He was always asking me to take it down when we were expecting guests. Would you?'

'Would I what?'

'Would you take it down? If you were having guests?'

'I don't know.'

He walks past her to stand right in front of the painting. It looks as though he wants to step inside it. Hanna notices a mole on his back, big and wrinkled like a raisin.

He says, still facing the painting: 'He has so many fears. He always has.'

Then he turns to her and says: 'Especially when it comes to women.'

He's standing directly under the spotlight, which casts sharp shadows beneath the furrows of his face. He suddenly looks much older.

He goes on: 'I'm not afraid of women.'

He's breathing faster now.

Then there's a cry in the distance. It rises into a strained, primal scream.

Ivan turns to face the door.

Hanna follows suit.

Soon, it happens again – even louder this time.

With that, Ivan nods and says: 'I have to go.'

25

She's lying in the bath, thinking about that first night, when they had just met and wandered from the museum down to the city in the twilight. Their first conversation, all of Samuel's questions about the anniversary festivities and her job. And she loved how attentive he was to her responses, and how impressed he was at her knowledge of Goya and her involvement in the anniversary preparations. Even then something had awoken in her, or between them. She tries to remember how her crush on him began. She pictures him at the end of April, his face among the leaves, under the trees on the street, how he had to bend down to keep from getting whacked in the face with branches, his eyes so curious about her. They moved under the trees like a dance. Now she lies in the bathtub, smiling as she thinks of that night. She didn't know anything about him yet, but she could sense that he was available, that he made himself available to her, by asking so many questions. In true curiosity there is a certain humility. Now she remembers. They were sitting at a cafe in a park, all four of them, eating ice cream, and he told her how happy he was that they had met, since he had long wanted to arrange a collaboration between the museum and the embassy. His curiosity was obvious in his body language as well, his elbows on the table, his eyes on hers, his gestures, his searching voice, his smile beaming at her.

She can tell that the moment is approaching. It's a gut feeling.

He just has to find out about the house first, and then probably he'll be ready.

She saw how his worry, raw as pulp, came to life the moment he crossed the threshold into this house. She imagines he won't be himself again until he and Ivan have settled the money matter.

She adds more warm water.

Her breasts stick up above the surface. Salty sweat trickles into her mouth.

She shaves her underarms but is too quick about it and nicks her skin. She watches the blood swirl around in the water and is struck by a realisation. She doesn't know why it didn't occur to her before.

She can't be a passive observer of this event.

26

She takes her time getting ready. Does her make-up carefully. Blow-dries her hair, paints her nails.

Then she selects a dress she thinks Ivan will like.

Once she's ready, as she descends the grand staircase, she hears a commotion below. Samuel, Leah and Tom are heading out the front door, and Ivan calls to them that they have to hurry. He says they're in a rush.

When Ivan catches sight of her on the stairs, he stops and smiles, noticeably impressed.

Hanna smiles back. She's glad to see him properly and elegantly dressed again, with an unbuttoned white shirt and his hair slicked back. His expression is open; he looks younger. His eyes are alert and lively. He says: 'You look radiant,' and offers his arm. She takes it.

'You're not looking so bad yourself,' she says.

'Be careful,' he says, pointing at her high heels and leading her carefully down the hall, beneath the great crystal chandelier, out through the front door, across the crunching gravel, past the small fountain, over to the parking area – and his arm is strong and reassuring against her own.

He turns to her and smiles.

This is the first step, she thinks.

In the car on the way into town, Ivan is chatty and animated. He says he wants to show them 'a local attraction'.

The narrow streets are crowded; the car has to drive slowly through the throngs.

At last it stops outside a large bar, where people are standing on the street and drinking beer from plastic glasses.

Ivan leads them past the crowds and into a back courtyard, then into a smaller bar; it has low ceilings and is packed with patrons. Ivan leans over the bar and speaks into the ear of the bartender, who picks up a phone behind the counter and talks to someone. Samuel asks Ivan: 'Where are we?' and is told, 'You'll see.'

After a minute or so, a muscular man with a beard comes out and leads them through a back door. His arms are the size of a woman's thighs. He leads them down a dark staircase and into a cellar area.

The room is brightly lit and full of people. It smells like bodies and beer. Hanna notices there's not a single woman in the room, aside from her and Leah. Only Spanish men with their buzzed temples, gold earrings and tight shirts clinging to their muscles.

Hanna turns to Leah and asks: 'What is all this?' but the room is so loud that she can't hear Leah's reply. The atmosphere is electric; anticipation is in the air, as though all these men are waiting for something to discharge the tension. There's a chalkboard in one corner, and crowded around it are several men waving bills. Ivan turns to Hanna and says: 'Want to place a bet?'

And that's when Hanna realises where they are, now she can see the cages, in among the crowds, sitting on the floor. Two tall cages on a bed of sawdust, roosters inside, each throwing themselves frantically at the grille walls in a desperate attempt to escape.

Hanna replies: 'I don't know the rules.'

Tom says: 'I think I need a drink,' and goes over to a table that seems to serve as the room's bar, with a couple of bottles of spirits and some white plastic cups on it.

Ivan has moved over to the cages and is talking to a man dressed in white and wearing an odd, slouchy black hat; Hanna supposes he must be some sort of referee or emcee. Ivan gestures wildly and smiles in a way she doesn't recognise. His eyes are wide and his gums are showing. Suddenly his shirt is open to the navel.

The conversation ends with Ivan handing the man a wad of cash, at which point the man goes over to the chalkboard and writes something on it. Samuel says the smell of the birds is making him sick. Leah holds her nose. Tom comes over to them with four small plastic cups full of something that looks like urine.

Tom and Leah slug theirs immediately, but Hanna is only brave enough to take a tiny sip. The liquid is potent and smoky and swells in her throat.

Now the emcee is shouting something in Spanish and the crowd backs up to make room around the cages.

Suddenly everyone falls silent. Hanna turns to Samuel, who looks anxious. Tom and Leah crowd to the front. Hanna follows them and stands on tiptoe to peer over their shoulders.

As soon as the cages are opened, it's like the roosters are catapulted out, screeching. The men roar like fools. The roosters' feathers stand straight up. They attack each other with no hesitation. Hanna tries to see, but she's too short. She crowds her way between two men and watches the red rooster take off, flapping, and land on the white one's back, drilling its claws into flesh. The white one flaps its wings violently and eventually manages to get free. The men are shouting so loudly that it hurts her ears. She turns round and sees that Samuel's face is pale, while Tom is smiling and shaking his head.

Ivan is at the very front, bellowing things in Spanish, in English, in Swedish, his shouts hoarse and uncontrolled. The scene reminds her of Goya's *The Carnivorous Vulture*, with all the faces contorted in ecstasy.

Soon the white rooster manages to unfold its wings and fly up to land on the red one's back, and drill its claws into its opponent's wings, and no matter how hard the red one struggles, it's stuck.

The men's shouts are deafening. The red rooster throws itself from side to side in a panic but can't get loose. Hanna didn't know roosters were so bloodthirsty. The white one won't give up, won't let go; its eyes are wide as it pecks wildly at the back of the red one's head. Hanna wants to look away but can't. The white one is out to kill, hacking and tearing and yanking, and now the red one is screaming, a panicked caw, a wrenching, almost human cry for help. Red and white feathers fly.

At last the red one manages to get loose and goes on the counterattack, but with a different tactic: it attacks with its beak wide open, chomps like a mad dog at its opponent's neck and breast, all the while hopping back and forth like a boxer, and soon the white one is on its back in the sawdust and the red one stands with its claws on the white one's breast, tearing out great clumps of bloody feathers even as it pecks incessantly at the throat until the white one stops twitching and the crowd bursts into cheers and boos.

27

Afterwards, they go to a pavement café for dinner. The street they're on is lively and the tables are crowded. Samuel has retreated into himself, sitting quietly in a corner, while Ivan explains the rules and recounts every minute of the fight.

Leah's on the street nearby, talking on her phone.

Hanna recognises her body language and facial expressions by now. That concerned look, the way she's touching her hair. She's talking to the attaché.

Tom, too, seems aware of what is happening: he keeps shooting glances in Leah's direction over Ivan's shoulder. His eyes are grim.

Hanna looks down at her plate. The squid tentacle on it looks like a black intestine with suction cups. Surely it's not meant to be eaten. It's like sticking her knife into a baby's arm.

She tries to chew, but it's like gnawing on rubber. Ivan says it's exquisite, so she nods in agreement. But when she tries to swallow she gags and has to surreptitiously spit the bite out into her napkin.

Leah returns and sits down.

Tom: 'Who were you talking to?'

Leah takes a sip of her beer. Then she says: 'My agent.'

'What about?'

'A job offer.'

Tom chuckles.

Leah turns to him: 'What?'

'That would be the first one in a while, is all.'

Leah shakes her head: 'How's the book going, by the way?'

Tom's smile vanishes.

Then Ivan says: 'I showed Hanna some art today.'

Samuel: 'Oh?'

Ivan stuffs half a tentacle in his mouth. He chews for a long time. It appears that even he has trouble swallowing it. After a while, he manages.

He points his fork at Hanna and says: 'I'm going to talk to the museum. I'm going to make sure they're aware of how grateful they should be to have you there.'

Hanna: 'You don't need to do that.'

'Please, I'd be happy to. If you're doing as good a job as I think you are, you're sure to get a promotion once the anniversary is over.'

'I don't want any help. It will only make my colleagues jealous.'

'I'll call Xavier tomorrow. You have to aim high.'

Hanna tries to smile. She takes a big sip of beer but the taste of squid won't go away. Ivan has his mouth full: 'I'll talk to them.'

She notices that his silver hair is no longer properly combed back but is sticking out every which way.

Hanna says, a little too loudly: 'Don't.'

171

Ivan turns to her and fixes her with the same look as when
he showed her the painting.

He says: 'Why?'

Hanna: 'Hardly anyone knows this yet, but I'm going to quit
soon.'

Samuel turns to her. Hanna meets his gaze.

Ivan: 'Why?'

Hanna: 'I'm thinking of leaving Madrid.'

Silence.

Hanna continues: 'At least, during some parts of the year.'

Ivan: 'Where are you moving?'

Samuel and Leah exchange glances.

Hanna says: 'That isn't quite decided yet.'

Now she sees both Tom and Leah looking at her.

Ivan: 'You should move here, to the coast.'

'I'm thinking about it.'

28

The next morning, Hanna wakes up early and walks around
the house as she waits for the others to get up. There's something manic about the wild patterns and loud colours. The floral
sofas, the curlicued wallpaper, the navy-blue velvet sofa.
Suddenly she hears a low voice coming from the library.

She moves closer to the doorway and realises it's Tom.

She stands as close to the edge as she can without being
discovered.

Tom whispers: 'Now you know what will happen if you
don't take a step back. The choice is yours.'

Then there's silence for a moment.

After that he repeats himself, his voice trembling with rage:
'Now you know what will happen.'

Hanna sneaks back to the living room.

On the walls are photographs of Samuel as a child. She strokes their frames and glass to touch his history.

In one corner is a large, dark wooden desk, with thick, carved legs and drawers with copper pulls. She turns round to make sure she's still alone in the room, then approaches to try the drawers. They're locked.

She leans over the desk but doesn't find anything of interest. Some bills, an antique globe, a gold letter opener with Ivan's initials on the shaft.

On the floor behind the desk, she finds a stack of leather-bound photo albums.

She picks one up and opens it. It's full of family pictures: Samuel at five, Samuel at eight, Samuel at twelve, on trips all around the world.

She sits down on the sofa and starts to browse.

She sees the young Rakel. She looks into Ivan's eyes, thinking about the contrast between the elegant person in the pictures and the mottled red face during the cockfight. She studies his gaze.

On the last page is a photo of Samuel as a teenager. He's perhaps eighteen or nineteen, and he's standing in a field and laughing at the camera. She carefully loosens the picture from the page. It's not hard to do – the glue is old and yellowed. She looks at his open, joyful face and can't help but smile.

Then she brings the picture to her mouth. She uses the tip of her tongue, which glides across the matte surface. She closes her eyes and kisses him softly, tenderly.

When a voice interrupts her she jumps and hurriedly presses the picture to her chest.

'Miss?'

The butler is in the doorway.

'Yes?'

'Would you like some tea?'

She manages a smile: 'Yes, please.'

He approaches and sets a teacup and saucer on the coffee table. The cup looks expensive, hand-painted in a blue pattern. The butler pours the tea. It steams, smelling of lavender. He asks what she would like for breakfast.

Once he's left the room, she folds the photo and tucks it into the back pocket of her jeans. Then she goes back to browsing through the album.

After a while he returns and places a silver tray before her. Fresh berries, scones just out of the oven, various tiny jars of marmalade, and coffee with hot, foamy milk. She breaks a scone and watches the steam rise. She spreads it with butter, which melts immediately.

She goes over to the desk to grab more photo albums.

She's insatiable.

She pages and pages through them. It's a journey through Samuel's life. She notices that Samuel is always standing just a bit apart from his mother.

Suddenly a pat of butter slides off her scone and falls right onto the photo album. It slides across the paper and leaves a shiny, dark stain on the page. She tries to clean it up with her linen napkin, but the stain only gets bigger. Then she hears someone coming down the stairs. She quickly closes the album.

It's Leah, coming in from the pool. She's wearing a black kimono over a white bikini.

She asks: 'Is Tom here?'

Hanna: 'No, not that I know of.'

Hanna has never seen her skin so brown. Her dark hair falls to her navel.

Leah: 'What are you doing?'

Hanna: 'Looking at old photo albums.'

'Can I see?'

Leah sits down beside her.

Hanna hands her an album. Leah starts paging through. After a while she stops at a page with a family picture taken on a

174

beach. Samuel is maybe eight, and he's digging in the sand. Ivan stands behind him, smoking, wearing a light-coloured suit. Rakel is hugging her own waist as though she's cold.

Hanna points at Rakel: 'Did you meet her before the stroke?'

'No. Ugh.'

'What?'

'I'm afraid of her.'

'Why?'

'Because of what Samuel has told me.'

'What did he tell you?'

Leah looks at Hanna and shakes her head.

'All I know is, she wasn't well.'

'But what happened?'

Leah suddenly looks annoyed. Or surprised. Hanna can't quite tell.

She tries again: 'What was Samuel's childhood actually *like?*'

At that, Leah bends over and closes the photo album between them.

Then she says: 'We don't deal with that stuff. I thought you knew that.'

29

Hanna is sitting on a lounge chair by the pool in the warm night, listening for sounds from the driveway. She takes out her phone again to check her appearance. The blue light from the water illuminates her face from below.

She closes her eyes and lets the warm evening breeze stroke her skin. For an instant it's Samuel touching her, asking her for help. She replies that she is ready. She will show him who she is, what she is capable of.

Each time a car passes on the road, she jumps.

At one-thirty she hears voices and a door opening in the foyer. She realises it's the staff welcoming Ivan home.

After five minutes he crosses the lawn wearing a dressing gown. When he sees her, he stops and smiles.

'Oh, lovely,' he says with a wave. 'Planning to take an evening dip?'

'No, thanks,' she laughs.

He walks up to her and points at the bottle. 'Is there wine?'

'There sure is,' she says, reaching for the metal ice bucket and pulling out the bottle.

She says: 'I found it in my room. I don't know if it's any good.'

He sits on the lounge chair next to hers and points at her glass: 'It's drinkable, at least?'

'Yes, I think so.'

'As long as it's chilled.'

'Yup.'

She pours him a glass.

He says: 'Thanks.'

'Things go okay today?'

'I don't know. People ought to listen to me. Sometimes I wonder if they do, though.'

He takes a sip and goes on: 'There are lots of people who want to hurt me.'

Hanna: 'Tell me about it.'

He smiles: 'It doesn't matter, because I get there first. I hurt them before they have a chance to hurt me.'

And she sees that flash of violence in his eyes again, the one she saw at the cockfight.

He leans back in the lounge chair. His dressing gown is gaping open a bit. It looks like he's not wearing anything underneath. She turns to face the pool.

She says: 'At first I thought you and Samuel were the same, but now I know you're not.'

He says: 'Is that an insult or a compliment?'

She smiles over her glass: 'You tell me.'

He smiles and takes a sip of his wine. Then he gazes at the pool, pondering something.

He says: 'I think I'm simply more interested in other people than he is.'

She doesn't respond. She tries to think of what to say. She doesn't want to say anything negative about Samuel. At the same time, she has to reach Ivan.

Hanna: 'He's inclined to the philosophical.'

'He makes things too complicated.'

'He shouldn't be a diplomat.'

Ivan gives her a searching look. He shakes his head. 'He should work for me.'

Hanna: 'He should get a new life.'

They regard one another in silence. It's as if her and Samuel's future together is hanging, trembling in the air between them, as if it all depends on what she says next.

She says: 'He has seen through that world.'

Ivan laughs: 'Has he?'

Hanna is encouraged by Ivan's laughter, and she says that she too was sceptical the first time Samuel told her about his lack of hope, but she's come to understand how consistent he is, how inspiring he is, how he can keep a whole dinner party rapt as he regales them, and she says the reason he captivates people is that they can tell he really means what he's saying. Whether or not his predictions are accurate, he's passionate about them. She says: 'If Samuel feels that the world is about to end, it's because he's spent thousands of hours thinking about it.'

Ivan says: 'People have always believed the world was about to end. Still, here we are. I don't see any apocalypse. Do you?'

'Samuel does.'

Ivan turns to the pool again and takes a sip of wine. For the first time since arriving at the house, she sees Samuel in him. Their noses are the same in profile.

'He needs you.'

Ivan turns to her and says: 'You like him.'

'I'm impressed by his bravery.'

'Bravery?'

Ivan stares at her with his big eyes. Then he smiles. And the smile warms her. His expression is milder now. His gaze is somehow searching, in a way that is tender rather than sexual. Perhaps she has got through to him at last.

She says: 'The bravest thing you can do is admit that you've lost hope.'

He says: 'Lost hope?' and shakes his head. 'That's not brave, if it affects other people. I've seen it happen, close up.'

He suddenly looks sad. She wonders if he's cold; it's chillier now.

He says: 'Why do you think my wife is in the state she is?'

Hanna shakes her head.

He swigs his drink and goes on: 'It wasn't a stroke.'

He points at the house: 'I found her in there, on the floor. In the bathroom.'

The blue light of the pool dances across his face. Suddenly he turns to her.

'Don't you think it would have been braver of her to try a little harder?'

He takes another sip of wine and then lies back on the lounge chair.

Hanna wants to say something but doesn't know what.

Ivan stretches out one leg to get more comfortable. The movement makes his dressing gown fall to the side, and she sees more than she wants to: the thick grey hair that covers his inner thighs. His scrotum, his stomach, his groin.

178

She meets his eyes, which are shiny. She wonders if he's sad or just tired. She tries to block out the sight before her.

After a while, he moves his other leg and his dressing gown opens even more. Now she can see his penis, thick and brown, resting on the bed of hair. Then he spreads his legs a little more, and his dressing gown falls away completely.

His penis begins to move. At first it's barely noticeable, but then it moves jerkily, first to the right and then to the left, like a pool toy being blown up, and she watches unwillingly, as if she's petrified, while it rises from the hair, pointing crookedly upward.

Meanwhile, he looks at her, while she looks at his cock.

Maybe the sight would have been easier to take in if it had been either hard or soft, but this is some sort of in-between state. It doesn't stand up; it stops midway. It's like it's asking a question – without receiving an answer. Winding along its edge is a vein that looks like a worm.

It's as though they're stuck in a photograph neither of them can leave. His eyes are fixed on her; her eyes are fixed on his semi. She doesn't know how long they sit like that, but after a while his penis starts to droop again. Slowly but surely, it sinks down.

Then he pulls his dressing gown closed and gets up to tie the belt. That done, he walks off across the lawn and vanishes into the shadows.

30

She must have dozed off on the lounge chair, because she wakes with a start when her phone dings.

It's a text from Meredith. She writes: *Where are you?*

Hanna sits up, annoyed. Texting people on holiday is crossing a line, and she doesn't like the tone. She doesn't owe it to her colleague to share her whereabouts. She won't respond.

Another ding. Meredith writes: *Did you hear?*

Hanna looks at the screen. The three dots are moving.

Meredith: *Police.*

Meredith: *At the museum.*

Meredith: *Archive theft.*

Hanna reads the text again.

Then she writes: *What do you mean?*

Meredith: *I don't know. The police are there.*

Hanna: *Where was the theft?*

Meredith: *A3.*

Hanna's reaction is physical. She instinctively stands up and leaves the pool area, walking in among the palm trees and slipping into the grove between the house and the garage, in the dark, as though someone is after her right then and there. She stands frozen there for several minutes, until she finally gets a grip and goes back to her lounge chair by the pool.

She sits down in the same spot and swigs straight from the bottle. Then she does it again, until she triggers her gag reflex, but she manages to quell the wave.

Hanna takes out her phone and writes: *Who do you think it is?*

Meredith: *One of the interns?*

Hanna: *Why? It could be anyone, couldn't it?*

Meredith: *Have you worked in A?*

Hanna doesn't respond. A second later, there's another ding.

Meredith: *Aren't you and Parisa the ones who work in A?*

Hanna puts down her phone.

She looks at it, lying there on the lounge chair, and tries to think clearly.

She calls up an image of Meredith, sitting in an interrogation room at a police station, surrounded by police officers urging her to text Hanna and trick her into confessing, because they know she's guilty, because they've been studying her bank account for quite some time now and have noticed that she's blown a ton of money. She pictures an officer clapping Meredith on the shoulder and commending her for her courage.

Then her phone dings.

Meredith: *Nuts, right?*

Hanna: *What did the police say?*

Meredith: *I don't know. I'm in San Sebastian.*

Hanna: *Then how did you find out?*

Meredith: *From Sarah.*

Meredith: *The temp.*

Hanna: *What's missing?*

Meredith: *I don't know.*

Meredith: *I don't know anything.*

Meredith: *Freaky, though, right?*

Meredith: *What if it's someone we know?*

Hanna reaches for the bottle of wine but quickly sets it back down. The smell turns her stomach. How could she be so stupid, so naive, as to steal from one of her own filing cabinets, on her own shift? She hates herself. She wants to hurt herself. She can never do anything right.

She gulps down the last of the bottle and texts: *I'm sure it's nothing.*

Hanna: *Try not to think about it.*

Hanna: *Have a nice holiday.*

Hanna: *Have fun in San Sebastian.*

31

She staggers through the dark, quiet house. Uses one hand to balance and support herself against the wall and extends the other one ahead of her to keep from running into anything in the dark. She's on her way to her room to talk to Vera without being disturbed. She's well aware that she's drunk and should wait until tomorrow, but she can't handle being alone with all of this any more. Her throat feels tight and her ears are buzzing; she's even prepared to let Vera chew her out, as long as she can stop feeling like this. But when she gets to her room she sees Leah's body under the covers, like a mountain range in the moonlight, and she slowly backs into the hallway.

She closes the door again as quietly as she can manage and stands there in the dark for a while. She hears the sound of her own heavy breathing, feels her temples pound. She leans against the wall but is overcome with dizziness. She spots another door farther down the hallway, one she guesses leads to one of the empty guest rooms. She grasps the handle, presses it down gently, and pushes the door open. It's pitch black in there, the curtains drawn, the wall-to-wall carpet thick under her feet. At last she can relax. She closes the door behind her and sinks to the floor.

She takes out her phone and brings up Vera's name. As usual, it goes straight to voicemail.

She tells her everything, describes meeting the group and what she's been up to for the past two months. She gives lots of details so Vera will understand this isn't just a whim, not a plain old crush. She says it multiple times: *This is something else.* She says Samuel is 'one in a million' and Vera would like him. She describes the way he looks, his beauty, his tortured soul. She says he's a seeker, but a seeker who thirsts for the future, and that he's going to buy them a house on the coast. After that she falls silent for a moment, to gather her strength, and then she tells Vera about the theft and is careful to explain that she had no choice. She says she found herself in an impossible bind, that she couldn't afford to go along on the group's trip so she *had* to steal, because otherwise she might have lost the opportunity of a lifetime. She says she doesn't regret doing it but . . .

She stops speaking.

A voice in the darkness. It's so close that it feels like a caress.

It's like a whimper, a prayer.

Hanna sits up straight, listening. For an instant she thinks she misheard, that it was her imagination, or that maybe the sound had come from outside.

The silence is oppressive.

She turns to face into the dark room, but is blinded by her phone screen and everything is simply black. She squints to see better. Then she sees something moving in the darkness. She hears the voice again, higher this time. It sounds like the voice is trying to say her name. A hissing animal maw trying to shape its lips to pronounce her name. Soon Hanna will hear her name, and it will do her harm. Her hands fumble in the darkness, trying to find the door; she finds the handle, hauls herself up, but she slips and falls back to the floor. At last she musters her strength, gets to her knees, stands up, yanks the door open, and flees from the room.

32

The group is sitting by the pool in the morning, waiting for Ivan, who's on a Zoom call. The time has come to head home. Samuel is pacing by the pool. Again and again, he looks at his phone to check the time.

Leah's lying on a lounge chair in a bikini. She rubs suntan oil into her arms and says: 'Just sit down. Take it easy.'

Tom is already wearing his travelling clothes, and he and his laptop are hiding from the sun under an umbrella. Hanna's sitting in a wicker chair with her sunglasses on. She wants to get out of here. The creepy house, that threatening Ivan, the sick mum, the unbearable fear straining between her ribs.

Samuel: 'Where the hell is he?'

Tom: 'He'll be here soon. Maybe you should drink something?'

Samuel raises his voice: 'No!'

Tom: 'Yikes.'

Leah and Tom have spent the morning pepping Samuel up for the talk, but Hanna is ready to urge him to forget the whole thing. She has a bad feeling about everything around this place, feels reality cracking its joints. She lights a cigarette, but it tastes like fire smoke, so she stubs it out in her coffee cup after a single drag.

Samuel says: 'It's degrading, him making us wait here like this.'

Leah: 'Just relax.'

Then Ivan comes out to the balcony and calls: 'You wanted to talk to me about something?'

Samuel stops and turns to him: 'Yes.'

'Talk away, then!'

'Shall we go for a ride?'

Ivan: 'Okay.'

33

Hanna, Tom and Leah are waiting in the driveway when Ivan and Samuel return.

Ivan parks his Lamborghini right in front of them. Then he climbs out of the car and starts to say his goodbyes.

Meanwhile, Hanna tries to figure out how the conversation went, but it's difficult. Ivan is in the same cheerful mood as always, but Samuel's face is a blank.

Ivan hugs Leah first.

Ivan: 'See you at the anniversary, then.'

Leah: 'Thanks for our time here.'

He puts out his hand to Tom: 'Come back soon.'

Tom points at the house: 'Five stars.'

Ivan laughs.

Then he approaches Hanna. Maybe it's her imagination, but it feels like he hugs her longer than Leah.

He says: 'Are you sure you don't want me to call the museum?'

Hanna nods without meeting his gaze.

34

The minute Samuel pulls onto the highway, Tom turns to him: 'Well?'

Samuel: 'I don't know.'

Tom: 'What do you mean, "I don't know?"'

Samuel: 'He's hard to read.'

Leah: 'But did he say yes or no?'

Traffic is light, but Samuel is driving awfully fast. The speed creates a pull in her stomach. Hanna appreciates it. She wants to get away from that house. She wants him to drive even faster. She wants him to drive so fast they lift off from the road.

Samuel: 'He didn't say anything.'

Leah: 'What?'

'He, like, just listened.'

Tom: 'But he must have said *something!*'

Samuel: 'He said he'll let me know at the anniversary gala.'

Tom: 'Good, he'll be drunk.'

Samuel: 'Ivan doesn't get drunk.'

'Maybe he's always drunk,' Tom says, 'and that's why you don't notice that he's drunk.'

Samuel and Leah both laugh, but Hanna remains silent. She can't laugh, not this time. Ivan is something different to her now. The only question is, what? Her image is still fuzzy. It's strange; she has never experienced this before, an image that hasn't fully developed yet, like a photo that's just been fed out of a Polaroid camera. She gets the idea that this image is going to be hard to shake once it has taken shape. She can't make sense of what he did, the lack of energy in it, the languid way he exposed himself, only to walk off and leave her there on the lounge chair. Almost as if he was pointing the finger at her with his penis, only to gently lower said finger afterwards. Or was his cock a thumbs up, an encouragement of sorts? The more she thinks about it, the more confused she feels. She doesn't understand her own reaction, either. It was like she was frozen, unable to speak.

Samuel passes a truck and Hanna sees that the speedometer has edged up to 150 kilometres per hour. Samuel is singing along to the music, and when Hanna hears his voice, she finally feels calmer.

She reminds herself that no one from the museum has contacted her. That's a good sign.

The only weak link is the antique dealer. The fingerprints on their copy of the receipt and the security camera on the ceiling, which might have been on.

She takes out her phone and writes to Meredith: *Heard anything more?*

Then she looks around, gazes out at the sea. She decides to try to enjoy this last day of holiday. She turns to Samuel. This is the only thing that matters right now, the group, in the car, on the road. Whatever happens after this, they're together now. She leans back and listens to the music. She hears her friends singing. She closes her eyes, and at last Ivan is gone.

35

All afternoon, they drive north along the coast as the sun gets lower in the sky. Tiny beaches squeezed between cliffs. Giant, pointy cypress trees along stone walls. They pass Barcelona and keep heading north.

Around seven, they pull into the drive of Hotel Eden Roc and Hanna notices right away that they've arrived at a yet higher level of quality. A half-dozen bellboys stand by the valet stand, and behind them, a group of people wait for their cars, dressed in tuxedos and evening gowns. In the car park are Lamborghinis and Ferraris in shades of neon, wide black BMWs, and Rolls Royces.

They enter the huge lobby. It smells like food and bleach. A shiny marble floor, tall mirrors, sofas with gold embroidery, a group of tuxedo-clad men in front of the big fireplace who all turn to stare at Hanna and Leah as they pass by.

As they wait in line to check in, she receives a text from Meredith. She has talked to her temp friend again, she says. The police haven't been by for a few days. *Everything seems to have calmed down*, she writes.

Hanna replies: *What do you mean?*

Meredith: *I don't know. Maybe it was nothing.*

Hanna: *What do you mean?*

Meredith: *Maybe they closed the case.*

Hanna: *Yeah, after all, it's only a drawing.*

Meredith: *How do you know it's a drawing?*

Hanna feels faint. She hates herself for being so sloppy. How could she have made such a blunder, with everything that's on the line?

She writes: *Because most of A3 is drawings.*

Meredith: *Oh right.*

Hanna: *But good to hear it's calmed down.*

Hanna: *Let me know if you hear anything more.*

Meredith: *xoxo*

Hanna: *xoxoxx*

She leans against a pillar and tries to think clearly.

Maybe the museum wanted to avoid an investigation, given that the anniversary is right around the corner. It's not as if the thought hasn't occurred to her. It would be poor timing, having to deal with headlines about a theft right now.

When she gets to her hotel room, she lies back on the big, soft bed, her hands out to the sides, looking up at the ceiling and feeling the room sway.

36

Eden Roc has a bar by the pool.

Samuel talks about how he wants to decorate the house and how the garden will be arranged.

Hanna is happy – the group is back in its rightful environment.

She can already tell that Samuel is beginning to soften back into his usual self. She can see it in his body language and his smile; she can hear it in his voice.

Tom says: 'It's only right that we tie up some loose ends.'

He smiles.

Samuel: 'What is it this time?'

Tom holds up a matchbox. 'You should take two.'

Samuel shakes his head. 'No. No.'

Tom: 'Yes. Yes.'

Leah: 'You should take two, according to whom?'

Tom: 'José.'

Leah: 'Who's José?'

'My new friend.'

Samuel smiles: 'It's just sick. How you just can't help yourself.'

Tom: 'We should celebrate. Celebrate the house!'

Samuel: 'Not yet.'

But soon hands are under the table, and Tom hands the pills round.

Hanna washes them down with her dry martini.

Then Samuel leans back, and Hanna follows suit. They need this, they deserve this, after their strange days with Ivan.

Tom raises his glass. 'Cheers to the house.'

Samuel gives an uncertain smile. 'We'll see.'

Leah: 'Think positive!'

Samuel: 'Okay. Cheers to the house!'

Tom: 'And, allow me to add . . .' he pauses for a moment, smiling, and then says: '. . . that your father is super, duper shady.'

Hanna's dry martini almost gets caught in her throat when she laughs. The others laugh too.

Leah: 'Is he a pervert?'

Samuel: 'I think you can consider it highly likely.'

Hanna laughs again. She wonders how they would react if she told them about Ivan here and now. She's not sure what would happen, so she doesn't mention it. She doesn't want to risk them thinking she led Ivan on somehow.

She takes another sip of her drink, and it's not as strong now. She notices that Leah has placed her olive on the white table-cloth. She had already nibbled at it, but Hanna nabs it unnoticed and pops it in her mouth, closing her lips around what Leah just had. It's hard and salty.

Only once she has the olive pit in her mouth does she realise that maybe she's high. Gnawing on a used olive pit isn't a sober thing to do. She takes it out of her mouth and places it on her plate. She looks at it and realises that it's flickering. At the same time, she feels a drop of sweat trickling down her forehead and towards her chin.

She takes a napkin and dabs her face. When she puts it down, she sees that it's wet.

She turns to the others to see if they're feeling the change too, but they look normal. They're discussing the music. Hanna tries to listen to their conversation but has trouble understanding what they're saying. Something strange is happening inside her. She doesn't know what's the alcohol and what's the drug, but something isn't right. Warm waves wash through her, but it's not a comfortable feeling. There's something gravelly about it, as if her body is protesting something. She struggles to think about something else, but it's hard. She feels a strong urge to move around.

She excuses herself and goes to the toilets. It's hard to walk straight. She curses herself for taking two pills.

She doesn't feel better until she's sitting on the toilet. The stream of urine feels reassuring somehow, as it hits the water, warm and familiar. The sound makes her smile to herself. She exhales. Everything is going to be fine; she just has to take it easy.

As she walks through the restaurant on her way back to the table, she finally feels the warm billowing. She's floating, she's in no rush. She passes the bar, wanders slowly past the pool. The evening breeze is warm. She's protected. She's solid. And when she sits down, she can tell right away that she's not alone: the others are high now too; she can see it in their faces. Everything is mild and warm. She has longed for this moment, sitting eye to eye with them without anything to interrupt them. Being back in the bubble of the group. And now Samuel is a storyteller as he's talking about the house again, he says they should form a collective on the island, like Hydra in the sixties or Paris in the twenties, where creative, gifted people can live together, create together. She loves his voice, so full of longing. And the waiter refills their sparkling water with ice and lemon slices. Samuel suggests a game; he wants them to picture the house and asks them to close their eyes. They do as he says. He tells them about how the house came to be, about Villa Cimino, because that's what it's called, he says, after the architect who built it in the 1800s. He asks them to picture the dining room, how high the ceilings are, and Hanna pictures it, the beams so thick, the stone floor so cool, just like in Goya's villa. She can see all of it. Herself and Samuel, their life there, how they go up to the roof at night, where no one can see them, and it's warm up there, even though it's nighttime.

But suddenly her throat is thick.

She sits up.

A wave of nausea. She's frightened. Everywhere she looks, she sees faces and bodies coming closer. She feels threatened. She feels a strong need to be somewhere else.

She says: 'Shall we head to the club downstairs?'

The others turn to her. Their cheeks are red.

Tom: 'Why not?'

Samuel waves the waiter over and pays.

The decision is made so quickly that she's disoriented.

From one second to the next, they're in a dark recess and then descending into the underworld, into a windowless room with LED screens on the walls, screens pulsing with fractals, and she stands at the bar and grabs the counter like it's a railing on a ship in a storm, and she manages to order. She says: 'Whatever' and the bartender pours blue liquid into a glass of ice and hands it to her, and she looks at in in fascination, because it is so *blue*, and she takes a sip, which tastes like mint, and it's refreshing, so she lets an ice cube slip up to the roof of her mouth and realises it tastes like mint too, it's like an explosion of freshness that spreads down her arms and on into the room, as though a cleansing wave were gushing through the bar.

Then she sees Samuel. He's dancing under a spotlight.

She's been standing here like this for two months, watching him from a distance.

She is struck by the urge to walk up to him and declare that she's tired of waiting, that it's unbearable, that she has never felt like this about another person, that 'he can do whatever he wants with her,' but before she can act he's disappeared among the bodies.

She takes another sip of the blue drink.

Soon Leah comes up to her, crying, her face contorted, saying she just got the most fucked up text from the attaché, 'out of nowhere.'

She's shouting, she's devastated, she holds up her phone and says he broke up with her, never wants to see her again, she shouts, 'never, ever!' And Hanna asks: 'But didn't you break up with him?'

Leah doesn't respond, she seems to be having trouble breathing.

Then Samuel comes dancing up, he dances his way between them and smiles, but Leah's not smiling, her eyes are wide open as if she just saw a ghost, she's pointing in the air and saying something about *blood*, and Hanna doesn't get what she's talking about, but then she sees black blood under Samuel's nose, and on his chin and his white shirt, so she takes him by the arm and drags him to the toilets and stands him in front of the mirror. He stands there all apathetic, staring at himself in the mirror as she wets some paper towel and tries to wipe the blood away from his face.

When she's done it, Samuel points at her hands.

Hanna looks down at her fingers to find that they're bloody. She presses her fingertips together and the blood sticks like paste.

By the time she looks up again, Samuel is gone.

She looks for the door. She feels lost. The room smoky and cramped, and the girls' faces at the metal mirrors are strangely repugnant, their lips like swollen red slugs, their eyeshadow like black eyes. One girl is crouching in the corner and pissing on the floor, and Hanna is disgusted by the rawness of this very public pissing, and she hands the girl a piece of toilet roll but then she sees that the girl has shat on the floor. The sight makes her take a step backwards. There's something about the girl's expression, her crooked smile, that makes Hanna feel that she has to get out.

She leaves the toilets and goes back to the dance floor.

After a while, she finds Leah leaning against a wall, muttering 'This is the end, this is the end,' and Hanna doesn't know if she means the end of her relationship with the attaché or of their trip or something else.

Leah points at her hands, and Hanna looks down to discover that the fingers of her right hand are still sticky with blood. She instinctively sticks them into her drink. She watches the blood dissolve and swirl around among the cubes of ice. It feels amazing when the ice and cold liquid envelop her fingers. Instinct tells her to bring them to her lips, and she can taste the mint and iron and Samuel's blood in her mouth. She sucks harder. Then, suddenly, she catches sight of something in the mirror behind the bar. It's the creature licking her fingers clean.

'Me too please,' Leah says, taking the glass and dipping her fingers into the drink and bringing them to her lips. They look at each other and smile. After that, everything happens fast. Hanna leans over and kisses her, and the taste of iron and mint mixes with the flavour of Leah's gum, and she feels Leah's tongue, warm and wet, and her breath panting in and out, and soon Leah's chilly hand is under Hanna's shirt, and the coolness of it feels nice, and Hanna places her chilly hand on Leah's warm thigh and moves it upward, and Leah responds by deepening the kiss, and Hanna answers by opening her mouth even more, to show that she wants this, and Leah's tongue is large, and Hanna's hand moves up Leah's thigh until she reaches her pants, and she cups her hand around her pubic bone. They stop and stand still for a moment as Hanna moves the pants aside and tests it out with her index finger, and Leah indicates with a nod that she wants to do this, and Hanna presses her finger into her, and she feels like she too wants to be filled up, her whole being is one big thirst that must be quenched, so she shows Leah, takes her hand and helps her, and at last Leah is there, it doesn't matter that her nails are sharp, or that strangers are dancing around them, it doesn't matter if someone sees, as long as she—

A violent shove from the side. She falls against the wall, catches herself with one hand, and an instant later Tom's face is right up close to hers.

He shouts: 'What are you doing?'

Hanna straightens up. She sees Leah's back vanishing into the crowd.

Tom points at Hanna: 'Who *are* you?'

She responds: 'Don't tell Samuel.'

He looks at her, baffled.

She says it again: 'Don't tell Samuel.'

Then she points at the spot where she and Leah were just standing: 'It's nothing. It was nothing.'

He repeats: 'Who *are* you?'

'Stop saying that.'

'Who the fuck *are* you?'

'What do you mean?'

'I mean, something about you doesn't add up.'

He looks at her.

She replies: 'I could say the same thing about you.'

He stares at her. 'What are you talking about?'

Hanna: 'What do you think Leah would say if she knew what you'd done?'

'Huh?'

'You know what I mean.'

He looks at her.

She continues: 'You threatened her boyfriend. You were the one who messed things up for her.'

'I didn't mess up anything.'

'He broke up with her today.'

Tom looks at her: 'It was for her own good.'

Hanna says: 'Do you think she'd agree?'

Then she pushes him aside and heads to the exit.

37

She wakes with a start.

Slowly she adds shards of memory to other shards.

She tries to remember how the night ended.

She goes to the bathroom and kneels in front of the toilet, but hardly anything comes up. Spasmodic convulsions. Sticky strings of bile or mucus falling from her lip into the toilet bowl.

The morning light is white and innocent and knows nothing of the darkness that preceded it. She thinks about Tom's face in the darkness. She thinks about Leah. She thinks about Samuel, tries to remember what she's done.

She opens her mouth again and leans over the toilet. She shouts out her anguish and watches it land on the porcelain, soupy and unchewed.

Why did she kiss Leah? What did Tom say? How could she have risked it all like that?

A fresh cascade.

How could she do that?

Now all that's coming out is burps, but the cramps linger.

She flushes the toilet. She remains on her knees, her head deep in the bowl. She flushes again and feels the cold water splash her cheeks. She closes her eyes. The toilet water smells like bleach. Her head is full of voices that won't stop, that keep talking about Samuel and about betrayal. She opens her mouth as wide as she can and throws up one last time, violently and noisily. She didn't know the stomach could hold that much liquid.

When it's over, she sinks to the tile floor. She pants as if she just finished running a race. Tries to get her thoughts in order. Tries to figure out how likely it is that Tom will say something to Samuel.

Regret radiates down her arms.

She crawls into the shower and turns on the hot water. Lies on the floor and lets it wash over her. Steam quickly fills the room. It's not long before she feels a little better. She opens her mouth to the spray and lets it fill her throat and wash it clean.

Tom's face, his threatening eyes. Leah's fingers in her mouth. Samuel's blood.

Another wave of nausea. It feels freeing to vomit right into the shower spray.

Afterwards, she crawls back onto the bathroom floor and hides her face in the thick terrycloth towel. She sits there for a long time, until the voices get a little quieter and the images have faded a bit.

She takes out her phone. Fourteen messages in the group chat. Samuel says he caught the morning train back so he can work. Leah says she's going to stay in Barcelona for a few days to see her cousin. No messages from Tom.

She closes her eyes.

Her face burns with shame.

How could she be so stupid?

Tom was so upset when he approached. She had never seen him like that. And when she clapped back, there was rage in his eyes.

Now her panic is growing like a wave. The walls are closing in. And suddenly she gets an impulse, there on the floor. She bends forward until she's on her knees. Then she closes her eyes and folds her hands atop the lid of the toilet for the first time since she was little. At first she doesn't speak, just prays on the inside, a silent call for help, but then she whispers, says the words, praying that everything will work out, that Tom won't say anything, that Samuel will love her the way she loves him. She whispers that if he just accepts her, everything will be fine. She presses her forehead to her clasped hands and promises to stop lying, to stop messing up.

But there's no response.

AUGUST

1

Madrid vibrates in the heat wave. The streets are full of tourists. She keeps close to the façades as she walks, but the heat is brutal even in the shade. She read online that this is the hottest summer in centuries. Eight hundred Spaniards have died since the first of June.

She is on her way to work for the first time since her holiday. Now and then she feels a stab of fear in her gut, but she reminds herself that everything seems fine.

The bigger issue is that Tom hasn't gotten back to her, even though she's texted him more than once and begged him to call.

The park around the museum is unusually crowded. All over the surrounding neighbourhoods, the shops have decorated their windows with the number '200' and garlands and flags have already been hung from the tram wires.

Hanna thinks of everything she has to do before the gala. She really ought to be skimping, after the expensive trip, but she needs a new dress and shoes.

She walks into the museum and hangs her jacket on the hook in the locker room.

As soon as she opens the door to the staff room, she realises something is off.

The interns are standing in clusters, conversing in low voices. Soon Meredith comes up to her. She has gained weight during her time off. Hanna feels that there's something disturbing about that kind of quick weight gain, when it goes to your face, like a corpse bloated from lying in water.

Meredith says: 'Have you heard?'

'No?'

She hands Hanna a sheet of paper; it seems to be a list of all the interns' names.

'What's this?' Hanna asks.

'They're going to question everyone.'

Hanna looks down at the list to find that every name has a time next to it. Hers is 1:30.

Hanna: 'But you said everything was fine.'

'It *was* fine. Not any more, apparently.'

Hanna tries to smile. She gulps. She has prepared herself for this moment. She knows what she has to do. Just keep a cool head if anyone asks her any questions. She decided on this strategy early on.

'What did they steal, exactly?' Hanna says.

'Isn't it creepy?' Meredith says, pointing at the sheet of paper: 'Can they do this?'

'I don't know.'

'I feel accused.'

'Why?'

'Don't *you*?'

Hanna: 'But we didn't do anything.'

'It feels scary.'

Hanna glances at the wall clock: 'I have to change.'

2

At quarter past one, she follows the directions on the sheet of paper and takes the lift to the fourth floor. Rosa is waiting on a chair in the corridor outside the conference room. Hanna sits down next to her. She can tell that Rosa's lips are tense, as though she's trying not to cry.

The chairs face the large windows that look out over the park. Outside, the treetops move silently. Rosa grabs Hanna's hand and squeezes it hard. Her hand is chilly and damp.

Hanna wonders why she's never realised how beautiful those trees on the south side are before. Their trunks are thick and their leaves hang down in bunches. They look like jungle trees.

Rosa whispers: 'Who do you think it is?'

Hanna: 'I don't know. One of the Spanish girls, maybe?'

Rosa whispers: 'I feel sick.'

The door opens and a woman in her sixties calls Rosa's name. Rosa quickly fixes her hair, then stands up and goes in.

Once the door closes, everything is quiet, aside from the dull murmur of tourists in the courtyard.

Hanna closes her eyes. She tries to find a point of calm. An abyss is about to open up beneath her. She thinks about the antique shop, of the security camera above its front door. Nothing bad is allowed to happen now. She won't accept it.

Outside, the swallows soar above the trees. The windowpanes are old and distort the view, making the world outside look like one of the museum's oil paintings.

After fifteen minutes, the door opens again. Rosa walks by Hanna without a word. She looks grim and her gaze is blank. When Hanna's turn is called, she jumps in surprise. It's as though her very name is an accusation.

3

The conference room is large, with a long table in the centre.

The older woman points at a chair. Hanna takes a seat. Sitting across the table is a man with a black beard and glasses; he's shuffling papers in silence. The older woman sits down beside him and opens a binder.

Farther off, in the corner, is Andrés. She nods at him, but he doesn't return the greeting.

When the man with glasses starts speaking, it's in surprisingly good English. He introduces himself as the museum's head of security and says they find themselves in a poorly timed and sensitive situation.

She nods.

He continues: 'And that's why it's very important we get to the bottom of what's happened, and that we do so now.'

She nods again.

He says: 'You are here because you are one of the people who has had access to section A3 of the archives most recently.'

Hanna says: 'What happened?'

'I would actually prefer that you don't say anything for the time being, so I can explain. It's a very serious matter.'

Hanna nods.

He continues: 'One week ago, one of the museum's archived works turned up in Pamplona, during a police raid. The local police quickly determined that this artwork came from our museum. And this was very strange, we thought at first, because the museum hasn't discovered any thefts for some time.'

Hanna turns to Andrés, but he's staring at the floor.

The head of security goes on: 'But the nifty thing is, we know which employees have handled which filing cabinets, so it's quite easy for us to find out who might be the guilty party here.'

He reaches across the table and hands Hanna a printout; one she recognises instantly. It's her daily scheduled checklist.

'If you would be so kind as to read line seventy-two, please.'

'Now?'

'Yes.'

She looks down at the paper and reads: 'Monday, twenty-second of June. Hanna, cabinets A335–A365.'

Then he reaches across the table again and hands her another printout. He says:

'Could you read this, starting with line one-sixteen please.'

'But . . .'

'Read it.'

Hanna: 'What is this?'

'This is your report list from the twenty-second of June.'

She looks down at the paper: 'I don't understand.'

He says: 'Could you read line one-sixteen on, please.'

She turns to Andrés, but there's no response. She feels the room tilting. She turns to Andrés again:

'I didn't steal anything.'

Andrés: 'That's enough.'

Then she looks into his eyes, and that's when she realises he knows, because his eyes are furious. She turns to the head of security again to avoid Andrés' accusatory look.

'There's no point in telling more lies,' says the head of security.

And she realises they only questioned the other interns in order to mislead her. They already know. Hanna opens her mouth, but nothing comes out. She looks out the big windows that face the courtyard. The windowpanes there seem even older than those in the corridor. The world is distorted, the trees smear, the birds fall to the ground.

The head of security starts speaking in a gentle, calm tone:

'How did you sneak it out?'

Hanna searches for the right words. She has prepared answers to these questions, but in the moment she doesn't remember them. She opens her mouth, but nothing comes out. The room is silent. She feels a tear fall from one eye and trickle down her cheek. She quickly wipes it away.

The head of security says: 'We know that you, and only you, were responsible for the filing cabinets the stolen work was located in.'

She says: 'All the interns have access to all the filing cabinets.'

The head of security nearly shouts: 'What?'

'What?'

'Speak up!'

'All the interns have access to all the filing cabinets.'

Now he stands up and walks round the table and perches on its edge, right next to her. She can smell him: smoke and cologne.

'That's why we can't arrest you. But I want you to know that our investigation starts today. And we are putting all of our resources into it. We will leave no stone unturned.'

Beyond him, she sees Andrés' gaze again. It's unbearable, because not only is it angry, she sees now, but also sad.

'I understand,' she says.

'What did you say?'

'I understand,' she says again.

He regards her for a long time. Then he returns to his seat. He pages through a binder without saying anything.

'What did you do on your holiday?'

He nails her with his gaze.

'What?'

'I said: what did you do on your holiday?'

'I was down on the coast.'

'That sounds expensive.'

Hanna feels her heart skip a beat.

'How did you afford it? An intern earns . . . how much?'

He turns to Andrés, who answers:

'Twelve hundred euros per month.'

The head of security repeats: 'Twelve hundred euros. That won't get you very far, down there.'

'I stayed with a friend of a friend.'

The head of security signals to the lady next to him, who stands up and comes round the table to Hanna.

'Could you write down your friend's contact information?'

'Why?'

'Write their contact info down, please.'

Hanna picks up the pen. She presses it to the paper. She can hardly give Ivan's number. But she doesn't want them to contact

Samuel, either. For lack of a better idea, she puts down Leah's number. They already share one secret; maybe they can share another.

Hanna says: 'Can I go now?'

The head of security says: 'You can go. But you have to stay in Madrid while the investigation is ongoing.'

Andrés: 'Because we're going to have to question you again.'

She looks at him and says: 'Of course I won't be leaving Madrid. I have to work.'

'No you don't,' says Andrés, without meeting her gaze. 'You are suspended until further notice.'

4

The moment she's outside the museum she vomits behind a tree. Bitter yellow bile that trickles down the bark. As luck would have it, she still has a napkin from breakfast and uses it to wipe her mouth.

She has trouble walking straight. She tries to hail a taxi, but it passes her by. She turns down an alley, wants to throw up again and stops by a tree, but nothing will come. Oppressive heat. She calls Leah repeatedly but to no avail. The phone rings and then the voicemail picks up. She doesn't leave a message.

Then she calls Samuel. He doesn't answer. She's mostly calling because she wants to hear his voice. It's just an impulse; she doesn't know what she'll say if he picks up.

When she arrives home, the room is unusually stuffy. She takes off her clothes but still can't breathe. She stands in the middle of her flat in only her underwear. The air is sticky and her skin feels itchy. She takes a cold shower, but even afterwards she's as sweaty as if she's just stepped out of a sauna. She doesn't feel hungry or thirsty at all.

Then she sits down naked in her easy chair and stares into the distance.

Time is warped; she doesn't know how long she sits there, but she notices the light fading.

At last the sun has set. At that point she puts on clothes and leaves the flat. She wanders aimlessly, with no idea where she's going. It's still hot. Her lungs can't get air. The stench of the fish market's trash is unbearable. Big, shiny, dead fish in transparent bags. She speeds up, doesn't stop walking. She wants to walk away from herself. She thinks about the head of security's face, about Andrés' face. She plays the scene in her mind over and over.

After an hour or so, she comes to Roma Park and turns onto a gravel path there. She sits down on a bench in the dark to collect herself. The park is colourless and dry. The grass is scorched from summer. She remembers how green it was in April. Now it's as thin as the hair on an old person's head. The crickets chirp anxiously, as though they're as nervous as she is.

She takes out her phone. She's so exhausted that she's prepared to tell Samuel everything. The thought is liberating, but she doesn't dare to actually dial his number. She can't trust herself. She doesn't know what's what any more.

Then, suddenly, she sees someone on the gravel path nearby. It's the old man from the antique shop.

He's walking slowly along under the streetlights, a cane in one hand and a leather portfolio in the other.

Her first impulse is to run up to him and kick his cane away. He looks so cocky strolling along there, supported by that bamboo stick. He's fooling those around him into thinking he's an upstanding citizen, but she knows the truth. She remembers his vacant gaze as he threatened her. He is so fat that his body sways. She looks at him, hating the injustice of his knowing things about her that no one else knows, of the fact that he can hurt her if he wants to. A man who has himself devoted his entire life to fencing stolen goods. She watches him go. He constitutes a risk she wants to eliminate. Somewhere in his shitty little antique shop, her fingerprints are on a receipt, and there might be an image of her on a hard drive. It's only a matter of time before the police pay him a visit and start asking questions.

Then she hears a girl's voice: 'Are we there yet?'

And now Hanna sees: trailing a few metres behind the antique dealer is a six- or seven-year-old girl with a net in her hand.

The girl asks again: 'Are we there yet?'

The antiques dealer replies: 'Soon.'

Hanna takes out her phone and pretends to be looking at it. Once they've passed her bench, she gets up and follows them.

Each time he puffs on his cigar, it makes a blue cloud of smoke that she has to walk through.

She hears the girl say: 'I want two,' and she hears his response: 'Quit your whining.'

Hanna wishes she had a plan, something to offer him or some way to threaten him.

The antique dealer takes the little girl's hand and turns left, towards the fountain. When he does, Hanna leaves the path and ducks between the trees, following them from the darkness there.

As they approach the fountain, the path becomes more and more crowded.

At one point they stop next to a streetlight. Hanna stops too, and leans against a trunk. She sees the antique dealer raise a finger towards the girl: 'One!'

The girl retorts: 'Two!'

The antiques dealer: 'I said one!'

'Two!'

He responds with a laugh: 'Fine then. As long as you don't tell your dad.'

The girl sticks out her hand and the antique dealer shakes it. Then they start walking again, hand in hand.

A moment later they reach the fountain plaza, where there's a café and an ice cream stand. The outdoor seating and lawn buzz with voices; people are on blankets all over, drinking wine in small groups.

Now Hanna dares to emerge from the woods and walk onto the big gravelled area. She stops behind a group of teens to spy. The antique dealer and the girl have found a bench.

The girl sits down while the antiques dealer goes to get in line for ice cream. The girl stays on the bench.

Hanna pulls her hood up to hide her face. She crosses the gravelled area, approaches the bench and sits down beside the girl.

She says: 'Hi.'

The girl looks at her: 'Hi.'

Hanna glances over at the ice-cream line. The antique dealer will soon be at the counter.

The girl asks: 'Who are you?'

'I'm a friend of your grandpa's.'

The girl looks puzzled.

Her face is as white as porcelain. Her skin is so exquisitely delicate that Hanna has the sudden urge to stroke it. She thinks for an instant that maybe it was a mistake to close the door on childhood so definitively. There were nice things there too, like picking out a dress, wandering around a city on a summer evening, eating ice cream. On days her mother was well. She sees the tiny white hairs at the girl's temple. Her red lips. The yellow fabric rosette in her hair.

Hanna continues: 'I have a present for him.'

The girl smiles. 'A present?'

Hanna nods.

'If I give it to you, can you give it to him?'

'Yes.'

Hanna takes out the folded watercolour from her purse, the self-portrait made with the blood from her fingernails, and hands it to the girl. Here and there, the blood has leaked through, as if the paper itself is inflamed.

Hanna says: 'Thanks.'

She stands up and leaves the girl, walking through the crowds, away from the pavement seating, taking the gravel path that leads into the woods.

After a moment she hears the girl's scream behind her, shrill as a train whistle. She turns off the path and vanishes among the tree trunks.

5

On Wednesday morning, a fresh and flooding rain hits the city. She sits on her sofa, smoking, surrounded by the sound of the rain pelting outside, her windows open to let the cool, damp air fill the room. It's been two days since she was questioned. The uncertainty is taking a toll. She lights another cigarette. She wants to make herself numb. She looks around for alcohol, but all she finds is the bottle of wine Samuel gave her for her birthday, which she's been saving for a special occasion. She opens it and settles on the sofa again. Tasting the wine, she imagines Samuel is sitting beside her. She takes small, thoughtful sips as she listens to the rain pattering on the steel roof above. She walks out into the downpour. She doesn't care if she gets wet. The water surges through the gutters. Litter and leaves along for the ride. People are hunkered under umbrellas. She walks and walks. Her hair sticks to her face. After a while, the rain gets lighter and lighter and eventually stops completely. When it does, she sits down on a bench in El Retiro Park. Puddles and mud everywhere. Some time later, the sun comes out. The weather turns on a dime, and the park becomes a steamy sauna. She has to leave. She walks into the network of alleys, looking for a café or a bar. She walks into

Parque de la Elipa, but the air is stagnant there too. The park stinks of dog shit and heavy florals. Everything dies, everything rots. She speeds up and crosses the road to the shady side, but under the trees the air is swarming with mosquitoes and gnats, forcing her back into the sunshine. A homeless man is lying on a bench; his nose is bleeding. She considers asking him if he needs help but decides against it: she imagines he probably wouldn't help her if their situations were reversed. Under another bench is a wet stray dog, panting in the heat. She leaves the park again, intending to get a taxi home, but no cars are in sight. She takes out her phone but doesn't know who to call. She looks up at the vast treetops and hears their rustling and all of a sudden she can't take it any longer. She collapses onto a bench and pulls her jacket over her head and closes her eyes. She doesn't care what people think.

6

It's dark, and she's standing outside his flat. The lights are on up there. She stands under a tree, gathering her courage.

It's hard to think clearly, but her plan is to open up to him. There is no reason to tell him everything, but she's prepared to reveal select parts. She wants to show him that she is devoted, that she trusts him. And make him understand what she's been willing to risk in order to be close to him.

It's sink or swim. Maybe this – being more honest with him – is what she should have done from the start.

She remembers the first time he shared his big secret with her, about how unhappy he was at his job. It was the moment in which he was the most beautiful, and they bonded over it. Now it's her turn to be vulnerable. Now it's his turn not to judge her, just as she didn't judge him. Now he will listen the way she listened. Now he will go grab a towel. She's been walking in the rain, and her hair is wet, and she's crying like she's never cried before. Now here he comes with the towel, now he's placing it over her head and tenderly drying her hair with his big hands. Then he kisses her, and it's a kiss that hits her deep down. They don't hold back. It's like they're kissing the secrets they hold, kissing their future. And she cries again when they do it, and she's crying now, as she stands on the street thinking about that kiss, hot tears running down her face, as she thinks of the towel over their faces. She cries because she knows she isn't going to ring his doorbell. She cries because she can't take those steps across the street and up to his door, even though she so badly wants to.

7

The next morning, she gets a text from Andrés: 'Come in.'

She stares at her phone for a long time, trying to interpret the message.

Come in?

Why had it come from Andrés, and not the head of security? Did someone ask Andrés to text her, to lure her in?

She has no energy left to think. She's so tired she almost feels ready to tell them everything. She's defenceless. There's no way she'll make it through another interview. She's so shaky that she has trouble getting dressed. She chooses something white, since she's read that defendants in trials often wear white, the colour of innocence. The mascara smudges around her eyes, she's trembling so hard. When she's finally ready, and checks her appearance in the mirror, she feels like she's on her way to an execution.

It's absurd, watching the city get ready for the big gala while she's so isolated in her fear. In the streets around the museum, shop windows are done up for the anniversary and garlands and decorations are hung from all the façades. Eventually she manages to hail a taxi and can sink into the back seat. The only thought that brings her comfort: it will be over soon. Whatever happens, it will all be over soon.

8

Andrés' office is tidier than she remembers. He's standing by his little coffeemaker by the window and offers her coffee. She shakes her head. Just the thought of drinking anything makes her feel nauseated.

Then he says: 'He went kind of hard, didn't he?'

Hanna: 'Who?'

'Luis.'

'Who?'

'On Monday. He was playing a bit of cat and mouse with you. That's how they roll.'

She watches him, trying to understand what's going on. He pours himself some coffee and slurps at it, as if to gauge its strength.

Then he sits down and runs his hand through his beard: 'The police investigation has been closed.'

For some reason, he's smiling. He goes on: 'Yesterday a witness recanted.'

She's not familiar with the Spanish term: 'Recanted?'

Andrés laughs. 'Someone who was involved in the sale. Suddenly he doesn't remember a thing.'

Hanna doesn't say anything. Outside she can hear the clamour of people waiting to enter the museum.

Andrés sets his cup on the desk and says: 'But it doesn't matter. He wouldn't have been any help anyway.'

She stares at him. Her mind is a blank; she's completely unable to grasp what he's saying.

He continues: 'There's no way to know how the work left the museum.'

'What?'

'So, I suppose I want to apologise.'

'What for?'

'For dragging you into this.'

Once again he takes a deliberate sip of his coffee: 'It's our own fault too, for not keeping better track of our documentation.'

Then he falls silent, leaning back in his chair.

She says: 'I don't understand.'

'A few days ago, we found a piece with the same number as the stolen one.'

And he recounts the details: 'Someone must have assigned the same inventory number to two different works.'

He throws up his hands: 'Which means we're talking about a duplicate. Mislabelled fifteen to twenty years ago.'

Hanna: 'So no one stole anything?'

'Who knows?' he says. 'It's possible someone marked them with the same number in order to steal one of them. A pretty clever little crime, if so. But it was so long ago.'

'Do you know who it was?'

'Impossible to say. There's no documentation left from the aughts, of who worked with what.'

'I see.'

He breaks into a big smile: 'But one thing is clear: *I* didn't work here then.'

And he laughs out loud and Hanna hears her own laughter, shrill and hoarse; it doesn't sound like it belongs to her.

9

After she takes the lift down to the archive and punches in with the guard, she heads straight for the toilets, where she collapses onto the lid and bursts into tears.

She tries to breathe normally.

It feels wrong, going back to work as if nothing happened. At the same time, she has no choice. She can't do anything that would seem odd.

It's a tough afternoon in the archive, and when she gets home that evening she falls into bed without undressing. She lies face down, eyes closed. She figures maybe it makes sense, what happened, the interrogation and the suspicions against her. Maybe it was some sort of test. The universe subjected her to a trial. Only now can she and Samuel come together.

She sits up in bed and writes to tell him she's missed him. Then she stares down at her phone, waiting for an answer.

As darkness falls outside, the room grows cooler.

After a while, she hears a tune from a street musician echoing between the buildings. The music trickles in and fills the room with a sweet sorrow. The wandering notes of the accordion, the wistful mandolin. It's a song that says *no one will be spared*. Hanna listens to the weeping voice and the lyrics. 'Everyone carries a sack full of stones,' he sings. Hanna thinks: I suppose that's true, but not everyone carries their sack with dignity. The singer's voice is full of sorrow but it doesn't break. He converts the darkness into something lovely. Like Goya, when he withdrew to his house and finally dared to let his dark fantasies out, when he covered the walls floor to ceiling.

That's how she wants to live too, how she has tried to live. It hasn't been easy. She has made some tough decisions, ones that involved a certain amount of risk, but the danger will soon pass.

When her phone dings, she nearly drops it on the floor. She squints at the screen, glowing in the dark. It's Samuel, inviting her to Leah's birthday party.

Hanna lies back and smiles. Her muscles slacken and her body grows heavy on the mattress.

10

On the way to the restaurant she feels nervous, but as soon as she sits down on the pavement seating she becomes calm. To be sure, Tom is avoiding eye contact, but he doesn't seem to have said anything about the kiss, because Samuel is in a good mood, ordering oysters on beds of ice, and champagne.

Once they've sung and cheered for Leah, Hanna takes out a box and hands it to her: 'Here you are.'

Leah opens it and removes a bracelet. It sparkles in the sun.

Leah is speechless. She runs her fingers over it and says: 'Oh my god.'

Hanna helps her put it on.

Leah holds up her slender arm to admire it. Her eyes are moist. She turns to Hanna and shakes her head: 'You shouldn't have.'

Hanna is overcome by Leah's strong reaction and doesn't know what to say. She's prepared a speech but can't remember it. The only thing she can manage to say is: 'I just wanted to show you. Somehow show—'

Then her voice breaks, and she stops talking.

Leah points at the bracelet and says: 'I'm going to wear this to the gala.'

Tom turns to Samuel:

'Have you been in touch with Ivan?'

Samuel: 'No, I didn't want to push him.'

Leah: 'When are you going to see him?'

'At the gala. He won't be in town until then.'

Samuel says he's spoken with a contractor and shows them pictures of the construction plans. He says he's been thinking of building a greenhouse with a view of the sea, where they can have dinners.

Hanna watches him, notes how cheerful he is when he's talking about the house, how happy Tom and Leah are, listening to him.

They order an enormous meal. Hanna isn't thinking and eats an appetiser, a ton of bread, and two mains. During dessert she notices Samuel's eyes on her, just as she's stuffed a huge bite of banana split into her mouth, and realises what she's done. She puts down her spoon.

11

After dinner they walk down Gran Via, and Hanna has never seen the street so crowded. In the park behind the museum, construction workers are standing on ladders and assembling enormous iron skeletons covered in white sailcloth. Behind the museum itself a stage is being built and lanterns are being hung in the trees. It's getting dark. Smoke rises from the kebab stands; street musicians are playing under the trees.

Tom and Samuel go up to an accordion player to listen, while Leah and Hanna head to the fountain.

They sit on the edge, the water burbling and gushing behind them.

Hanna asks: 'We're fine, right?'

Leah looks at her: 'What do you mean?'

'After what happened.'

'What? What are you talking about?'

'At Eden Roc.'

Before Leah can respond, her phone dings. Leah stops to look down at the screen. Her face is lit by the blue glow.

Hanna asks: 'Who is it?'

Leah looks up at her in fear, as though she's just been discovered doing something forbidden. She says: 'Don't say anything to Tom and Samuel. They'll just get mad.'

Hanna looks at her. Leah takes out a cigarette and lights it.

Leah: 'He's serious this time.'

Hanna can tell that her fingers are trembling.

Leah continues: 'I know how it sounds, but it's true. He's going to leave his wife once and for all.'

And Leah tells her that she didn't trust this news at first, obviously, but they've been texting back and forth for days and he's saying things he's never said before. 'It's something about his tone,' she says, 'he's changed.'

Hanna says: 'Are you going to meet up?'

Leah shakes her head and says: 'The day after tomorrow. He's going to tell her everything. We'll see each other after that.'

Tom and Samuel are waving at them, saying it's time to go, and they walk down to the Alfonso XII monument, all four.

Tom and Leah are walking a few metres ahead of Hanna and Samuel when Hanna hears Tom raise his voice. He says: 'No way!' and stops on the gravel path and points at Leah. He goes on: 'This is self-harming behaviour,' and Leah responds, 'Stop judging me,' and walks away from him, but he runs after her and grabs her arm.

Hanna and Samuel stop and watch their argument.

All around them, tourists and families with little kids stroll along the gravel paths. There's action and movement every-where, but Hanna senses an island of calm where she and Samuel are.

Then, suddenly, it happens.

Samuel places his hand on Hanna's back. He moves his hand up and down. He might just as well have hit her, the way her body reacts. She melts beneath his touch. There's such tenderness in the place he's chosen to touch her, too – just above the small of her back. It hits her right deep down. She feels the warmth of his hand radiating down between her legs.

219

12

The atmosphere at the museum is unusually playful in the days leading up to the gala. Andrés is in high spirits, full of energy. Maybe he too is elated that the investigation has been closed.

She has lunch with Rosa and Meredith and is able to engage with them around a new topic: the interrogations, the vulnerability they felt, the creepy head of security, being made to feel guilty even though you're innocent. They talk over each other and laugh.

'I thought I was going to shit my pants,' Rosa says, telling them how the head of security had sat down on the edge of the table in front of her, in the same threatening manner as he did with Hanna.

'He was so fucking nasty,' Meredith says.

'It should be illegal to threaten people like that,' Hanna says.

What's more, both Meredith and Rosa have a ton of questions about Hanna's new guy. She's finally told them about him, without giving his name, and she loves to watch their eyes widen as she talks about the hotels, the Bentley, Ivan's house. It's like she's seeing her life from the outside, through their eyes, and being reminded how blessed she is. She loves to thrill them with details about this mysterious guy, his father's wealth, the house they're going to buy. They want to know everything, but she's cautious. She says he's something of a public figure and that she can't get into too many details.

Rosa: 'But you're a couple?'

Hanna offers a secretive smile: 'It's complicated.'

Meredith says: 'Welcome to the club.'

13

On Thursday, it's cloudy and cool. Hanna watches the city change with the shift in weather and takes it as a sign that her relationship with Samuel will soon enter a new phase.

They're approaching the moment of truth, when the feverish nature of the summer will transform into a calmer, more mature life.

As the two of them are sitting outside the university that evening, waiting for Leah and Tom, she notices his legs are full of goosebumps from the cold. She wants to place a hand on his leg and warm him, or get him a blanket. Maybe he can tell what she's thinking, because he asks if she's chilly. She shakes her head with a smile. They don't need to say much. They have their own codes now. At the start of the summer, they didn't have a history together, but now they've got tons of memories and in-jokes they can return to in conversation. Maybe that's why their togetherness has a different sort of calm to it now. Their summer together offers them a weight, a security. Which means they can sit under the big oaks at the university café and read side by side without saying much. Everything began in silence and everything will end in silence. Everything is still. The leaves move across the gravel as though an invisible hand were shepherding them cautiously along. The ash from Samuel's cigarette doesn't fall to the ground; instead it drifts across the table and vanishes sideways.

When the waiter arrives to fill Samuel's mug with lavender tea, she finally asks for a blanket. When the waiter brings it, she spreads it over both her own legs and Samuel's.

He smiles at her. She smiles back.

Then she pretends to read, but all she can think about is the warmth of his legs under the blanket.

She thinks: it was greedy of her to want to start a relationship early in the summer. Neither she nor he was ready for it then.

14

On Saturday, she buys a Valentino dress and a new pair of shoes. She feels sick all the while, anxious about the evening to come. She even considers staying home, out of fear that the group will run into her colleagues, but she knows she has to be there when Ivan announces his decision about the house.

At six o'clock, they meet at Samuel's for a pre-drink.

Leah's wearing a white dress with a wide band of smocking at the waist that emphasises her breasts and curves.

Samuel is nervous. He's agitated as he drinks. He says: 'It all depends on what kind of mood he's in.'

Leah places her hands on his shoulders and says: 'It's going to be fine.'

He looks at her without responding and drains his glass.

Hanna wants to tell him she understands, that she's at least as nervous as he is, but she knows she has to hold out. Only a few hours to go.

Tom pours chilled champagne into foggy glasses and Hanna and Leah help each other do their make-up. Tom rubs wax into his hands and runs them through Samuel's hair.

Hanna goes out to the balcony for a smoke to calm her nerves. When she blows out the match, she can see her hands shaking.

She reminds herself of the plan: keep as much distance as possible between herself and the group this evening, so she can flee in case a museum colleague approaches.

She's also worried about what Ivan's going to say about the house.

She watches the group through the glass doors. Leah's sparkling dress. Samuel in front of the mirror, his fragility. Tom, trying to adjust the handkerchief in his breast pocket so it's perfectly jaunty. In the distance she hears fireworks and firecrackers. The evening air is heavy with gunpowder.

Hanna joins them inside and asks them to line up next to her. Then she holds up her phone. They all toast the camera.

The flash goes off.

On the street, as they wait for their Uber, Hanna looks at the picture they took and realises she's even skinnier. No wonder, really. She's hardly eaten since they got back from their trip, on account of all the weirdness that's been going on. She zooms in on the picture and thinks: it took two months, but now she could be mistaken for one of them. Soon she will be one of them. She just has to make it through the night.

15

In the Uber, Tom and Leah are insufferable. They try to link their phones to the stereo but it doesn't work and they argue with the driver. Hanna and Samuel sit quietly in the back seat.

Hanna rolls down the window and lets the warm evening air fill the car. She tries to get hold of herself, but it's hard. She looks at the crowds making their way to the museum. Children with mylar balloons and young people carrying bags heavy with wine bottles and big families in groups. Laughter and screeching everywhere.

As they reach the museum park and she sees the entrance, she feels a stab in her gut.

Outside the car window, it's chaos. Hundreds of people in tuxedos and evening gowns behind the riot fences. Crowding and shouting. At last they find the VIP entrance. After passing through metal detectors and having their bags inspected, they're finally let into the building.

The foyer is full of people standing in groups and mingling. The floor looks shinier than usual and chandeliers are hanging from the high ceiling. They each take a glass of champagne from a waiter and share a toast.

All the while, Hanna is scanning the room for familiar faces, preparing to slip away. She suggests to the group that they go out the back, out to the park, in the hope she'll have a better overview from there. Before they go out, Samuel grabs another glass of champagne from the waiter's tray.

The park looks like a totally different place from usual. Under the trees are big white tents with bars and dance floors. A band is playing on a stage, and hanging along the façade are banners featuring motifs from the museum's past.

They stand by a bar that's been erected between the big oaks. Soon Ivan approaches them.

He raises a glass in their direction: 'Madrid's hottest gang!'

He looks younger and more vivacious than in Alicante.

When he embraces Hanna, he says into her ear that he loves her dress.

Then he turns to Samuel: 'Your mother wanted me to tell you she wishes she could be here.'

Samuel forces a smile.

Soon Ivan catches sight of someone nearby and excuses himself.

Hanna turns to Samuel and says: 'How does it feel?'

Samuel gazes in Ivan's direction.

'We'll see,' he says.

She can tell that his eyes are changed. She has trouble determining whether it's the alcohol or his anxiety. Ivan is standing with a semicircle of men around him and shaking hands, gesturing and laughing.

Samuel points at him and says: 'Life of the party.'

224

Tom says: 'You can always talk about it tomorrow, too, in peace and quiet.'

'Won't work,' says Samuel. 'He's going to Berlin tomorrow.'

Hanna notices he's slurring his words.

Suddenly Leah places a hand on Hanna's arm. She's about to lose her balance, and she leans on Hanna with all her weight. Their glasses fall to the ground. Leah looks like she's about to faint. Hanna puts an arm around her and leads her over to a chair, sits her down and kneels before her.

Leah whispers: 'He's here.'

Hanna: 'Who?'

Leah points.

Not far away, a balding, stocky little man is chatting with a woman.

Leah says: 'He's here with his wife.'

Hanna studies the man. She has a hard time coming to terms with the fact that this is the person Leah has talked so much about, the man who has caused her so much suffering. He's in his fifties, his face puffy and red. Hanna is shaken. It's an insult to Leah's beauty that such an unattractive man has been leading her on all this time.

When she turns round again, Leah is gone.

Hanna walks through the throng but can't find her. On her way out of the toilets, she ends up in a corridor so stuffed with people that she can hardly move. She spots Andrés far off in the crowd. She turns to flee but is wedged between all the bodies. She lowers her gaze, but it's too late. When he reaches her, he says: 'Aren't you glad to see me?'

'Yes, of course I am.'

'Are you having a good time?'

'Yes.'

He's standing close to her, way too close, and telling her in great detail about all the Spanish celebrities he's seen here and what he said to make them laugh. She pretends to listen but is having a hard time focusing. She's worried someone from the group will walk by, but she can't get away. She smells his foul champagne breath.

He changes the subject: 'What a fucking couple of weeks.'

'Yeah.'

'You know what? When this is all over, I think you and I should hang out just the two of us sometime. Maybe a drink after work.'

She can't help but laugh, because it's such a cheesy line, and he seems to recognise his mistake. He smiles like an abashed little boy and shakes his head: 'Sorry, I've had too much to drink,' and then he gives a girlish giggle she's never heard him make before.

She says: 'It's fine,' and is about to excuse herself when she hears someone say her name.

Suddenly Tom is right there in front of them.

It's a mistake, it's not supposed to be this way, he shouldn't be there.

'Aren't you going to introduce us?' Tom says.

Hanna is startled. 'Sorry. Tom, Andrés. Andrés, Tom,' she says, and they shake hands.

Andrés says: 'Have we met before?'

Tom: 'Maybe.'

Andrés: 'Where, when, how?'

She takes Tom's hand. 'Shall we go?'

But Tom stays put. He says: 'My friends and I came up to you at the museum last spring and asked you about tickets for tonight.'

'Did I give you some?'

'No.'

Andrés laughs. 'Well, seems like it worked out in the end.'

Tom points at Hanna: 'Thanks to Hanna.'

Andrés puts a hand on her shoulder and says: 'Hanna is one of the best interns we've got.'

Hanna stares down at her glass.

'Is she?' Tom says, looking at her.

Hanna is frozen in place.

Andrés says: 'Yes. It might not be the most fun job, toiling down in the archives, but it's a start.'

Tom says: 'It's a start, indeed.'

Hanna can't take it any more. She grabs Tom's hand and pulls him away.

Behind them, she hears Andrés call: 'Nice to meet you.'

There are even more people in the foyer now, so she pushes her way through the bodies, hand in hand with Tom, and doesn't stop until they reach the bar by the entrance.

They stand by the counter. The buzz of voices is deafening. Above them, the chandeliers glow.

Tom looks at her; she looks at him.

Hanna: 'Don't tell Samuel.'

Tom doesn't say anything.

Hanna: 'Please.'

Tom smiles. He takes a sip from his glass. 'Why did you lie? Are you trying to get at the money?'

Hanna shakes her head: 'Please.'

'But why?'

She doesn't respond, just tries to read his expression, but it's difficult. His eyes radiate a mixture of contempt and pity.

He nods and walks away. She is left behind with a pounding heart and a blazing face.

16

Hanna forces her way through the crowd. She hopes Samuel has talked to Ivan by now so it can all be over. Her high heels are hard to walk in, and just as she reaches the exit out to the park she stumbles and has to catch herself against the wall.

Just then, Samuel appears. He asks: 'Are you okay?'

She's so relieved to see him that tears spring to her eyes.

She nods and smiles: 'Thanks.'

He points out of the door; Ivan is nearby in the park, talking to two laughing women.

Samuel says: 'I'm going to do it now.'

Hanna: 'Are you sure?'

'Might as well get it over with.'

Suddenly Leah comes their way, walking briskly through the trees. She looks shaken. Her face is blotchy red and her eyes are wild. When she reaches them, she says: 'We have to go.'

Samuel: 'What?'

Leah: 'Now!'

Samuel: 'Why?'

Leah: 'I did it.'

Hanna and Samuel gape at her.

Leah: 'I went up to his wife.'

Hanna and Samuel exchange glances.

Leah: 'I went up to her while he was in the toilets. I told her everything.'

Samuel says: 'Oh my God.'

Leah: 'He can't do this to me. Right?'

Tom walks up. He can tell right away that something's wrong: 'What's going on?'

Leah says: 'We have to go. Now!'

Tom: 'Why?'

Now Ivan has spotted the group and approaches them.

Samuel turns to him and says: 'We have to take off.'

Ivan: 'Fine by me. I'm sick of cheek-kissing.'

He drains the rest of his champagne and says: 'Follow me,' and then he takes the lead. They follow him. Hanna has her hand on Samuel's shoulder to keep from stumbling, and Leah has her hand on Hanna's. They make their way out and pass the smoking tent, then the crowd around the entrance. They come to the car park, where Ivan's SUV is parked.

Hanna, Ivan, Samuel and Leah hop into the roomy back seat. It smells like leather and vanilla. Hanna is glad that Tom gets into the front seat so she doesn't have to make eye contact with him.

Samuel undoes his bow tie and Ivan takes off his jacket. Leah stares out the window, fear in her eyes.

Ivan calls to the driver: *'Vamos!'*

Then he taps Tom on the shoulder and says: 'Where to?'

Tom replies from the front seat: 'Where do you want to go?'

Ivan: 'I want to see dancing.'

Tom asks: 'What kind of dancing?'

Ivan: 'What do you think?'

Tom laughs: 'Okay,' and turns to the driver.

Samuel doesn't say anything as he stares out the dirty car window.

17

Ten minutes later, the car stops outside a metal gate in a deserted alley. When the bouncers see Ivan, they lift the velvet rope. On the other side of the door is a till, and Ivan swipes his card. Soon a hostess in a headset shows up and leads them down a steep staircase.

The room looks like a hotel lobby, with groups of furniture and mirrors on the walls. It smells like eucalyptus and marijuana. Everything is bathed in a red light. There are quite a few people there, but Tom says: 'It's pretty empty now, but it'll fill up.'

The hostess leads them past the seating areas and across the dance floor. They pass a round stage where a woman in a mask and a thong is dancing around a pole. At the other end of the room is an archway guarded by two men in black suits. There the hostess asks Ivan to swipe his card again. Then she pulls the black curtain aside and lets them in.

The next room has a lower ceiling and it's darker, more crowded. In the corner are transparent plastic cylinders that run from floor to ceiling. In each cylinder, a nude woman is dancing. Their bodies are illuminated from below with a bright red light. Around each cylinder is a crowd of people. A bar runs along the wall; it too is lit from below. The music is loud. The hostess leads them to an empty table near the dancefloor and sets out glasses, cans of soda and buckets of ice containing bottles of liquor and carafes of juice.

When Hanna takes a seat, she notices that only she and Leah and Tom are in the booth. She turns round but sees no sign of Samuel and Ivan.

Hanna: 'Where are they?'

Leah: 'Who?'

'Samuel and Ivan.'

Tom: 'Who cares?'

Leah: 'I need something strong.'

Tom takes her glass and says: 'On it.'

While Tom mixes her a drink, Leah says to Hanna: 'It was awful, seeing her reaction. All the air went out of her. She got so pale. It was like I had stabbed her.'

Behind Leah, Hanna watches one of the nude dancing women. She's got pretty lacklustre moves. Hanna wonders why she isn't making an effort, when there are so many people watching.

Tom says: 'Want to take a look around?'

Leah: 'Yeah.'

He helps her up.

Hanna stands up too, but Tom shakes his head: 'Someone has to keep an eye on the table.'

They leave.

It's awkward, sitting by herself at such a large table. Hanna looks at the women in the cylinders again and wonders if she would ever be brave enough to do that.

A waitress approaches, dressed in a lingerie set, and asks if they need anything else for the table. Her lips have so many fillers that it looks like someone punched her. Hanna says she would like a gin and tonic.

Once the waitress leaves, she feels lonely again. She thinks of Tom's expression when Andrés said she was an intern. She looks around, trying to spot the group. Soon the waitress brings her drink. The liquid looks fluorescent in the blue light. The waitress holds out the card reader. Hanna says: 'I'm with Ivan.'

'Who's Ivan?'

'He already paid.'

'That was for the table, then. You have to pay for the extra drink.'

Hanna says: 'Can I put it on the tab?'

The waitress shakes her head and explains in rapid-fire Spanish why that's not possible, but Hanna doesn't follow.

The waitress says: 'Do we have a problem?'

Hanna: 'No, no.'

Reluctantly Hanna takes out her wallet, runs her card through the reader and holds her breath. The screen notifies her that it's connecting. The waitress snaps her gum. Both of them stare at the reader's screen. Hanna curses herself for not depositing the last of her cash in her account. The connection circle spins on the screen. At last it goes through: *Pago aceptado.* Hanna exhales. As soon as the waitress is gone, Hanna takes a big gulp of her drink. It's so strong that it's like drinking straight gin.

At last Tom and Leah return. Their faces are sweaty as they sit down in the booth. A few seconds later, Samuel arrives and sits down next to them.

Tom: 'Where's Ivan?'

Samuel: 'He left.'

Leah shrieks: 'Did you talk to him?'

'Yes.'

Tom: 'What did he say?'

Samuel shakes his head: 'It didn't go so well.'

'What do you mean?'

'He said he wanted to think about it, but he didn't look happy.'

'Think about it for how long?'

Leah: 'What?'

Samuel: 'He wants to meet up tomorrow before he leaves.'

Leah: 'Where?'

Samuel: 'I'm supposed to go to his hotel. He said he'll let me know then.'

Leah: 'That seems like a good sign.'

Samuel: 'No, it all sounded bad.'

Tom: 'I think it sounds promising.'

Samuel: 'How so?'

Leah: 'Because he didn't say no.'

Tom: 'For real.'

Hanna wishes she could be as optimistic as Leah and Tom, but she has a bad feeling in the pit of her stomach. Nothing is going as planned this evening. Everything is creaking at the joints. She feels disoriented. She doesn't recognise her friends; their eyes are transformed. Especially Samuel's.

It's so crowded. The women in the cylinders are dancing more and more wildly. She is overcome by what feels like claustrophobia, turns round to find the exit. Behind a drape of glittery pink garlands she sees a woman straddling a man in a suit on a velvet chair. She's rubbing against him desperately, increasingly ferociously, in front of a mosaic of mirrors that scatter the image into bits. Hanna watches their bodies split in the glass. She takes another sip, and it doesn't taste as strong. She takes another. She watches Samuel and Leah embrace.

Hanna rests a hand on Samuel's leg and says: 'Should we go back to your place?'

He doesn't respond. Instead, he leans towards Leah again and says something in her ear. Hanna cranes to hear what he's saying but the music is too loud.

Hanna says: 'I want to hear too.'

But Samuel isn't listening; he seems too engrossed in his conversation with Leah.

She feels like she's suffocating, she has to get out.

She forces her way through the crowd but can't find an exit. She pulls a heavy curtain aside and enters a smaller, darker room. It takes a moment for her eyes to adjust, but then she sees the naked men. Here and there, women are on their knees, lending helping hands. The faces look twisted in the dim light, grim but smiling. Farther off is another circle of men, all touching themselves while something happens on the floor below them. She takes a step closer to get a better look. It's dark, but what she can make out looks like a wrestling match, two naked male bodies moving in the darkness. Hanna can't see what they're doing, doesn't want to see, but she watches the men in the circle around them, tugging at their genitals. It smells rotten, and no matter where she turns she sees men with oiled cocks in their hands. She doesn't want to be part of this scene any longer and tries to find a way out. Suddenly she feels a tap on her back. It's Tom, standing beside her and saying: 'The intern!'

Hanna doesn't recognise his expression. He's wearing a broad smile but looks threatening. She shakes her head at him, leaves him to pull curtain after curtain aside; she finds the door at last and escapes back to the other room, crosses the dance floor, makes her way back to Samuel's table.

She sits down.

Leah and Samuel are still where she left them, still wrapped up in their conversation. They're talking about Ivan, and Samuel says something about how he's a sadist.

Tom has followed her, it turns out, and he sits down beside her.

'The intern,' he hisses, tugging at her arm.

She snaps back: 'Stop it!'

'The intern!' he repeats.

She leans over and says into his ear: 'Quiet. Please. Quiet.'

He says: 'I knew it. I had a feeling.'

Then she grabs his arm. 'If you say anything to Samuel, I will tell Leah everything.'

'Tell her what?'

'That you secretly ruined her relationship.'

But he's still smiling: 'That doesn't matter any more.'

Hanna stares at him.

He says: 'Did you forget? Their relationship is over.'

She reaches for her gin and tonic and takes a sip.

Tom leans towards her again and says: 'But you can rest easy.'

He takes her glass from her and drinks. He grimaces, baring his teeth.

Then he continues: '. . . on one condition.'

He narrows his eyes. He's making a face she's never seen on him. He looks cruel.

She says: 'What?'

'I want to see you *gone*.'

'What?'

'I want to see you *fucked up*.'

She laughs. But his expression doesn't change. She says: 'What do you mean?'

'I want to see you lose control.'

'How so?'

'Lose it all.'

'I'm pretty drunk.'

'No you aren't.'

Hanna says: 'Yes, I am,' and reaches for her glass, and takes a sip. She says: 'Cheers.' But Tom shakes his head. He says: 'It's time. For you to *show* yourself, once and for all.'

She tries to smile, but she can tell it looks unnatural.

Tom: 'And I don't just mean the lies.'

'What do you mean?'

'You're hiding something.'

Hanna tries to smile again and says: 'What would that be?'

'That's my condition.'

'What?'

'My condition for keeping my mouth shut.'

'What do you mean?'

'That you have to fuck up. Okay?'

She turns to Samuel and Leah in order to make sure they're not listening. They're still talking.

Tom says: 'Agreed?'

'I don't get what you mean.'

Tom replies: 'This is what I mean,' and he takes her hand under the table. His hand is sweaty and it's touching hers and pressing a little baggie into her palm.

Hanna says: 'No, no,' and shakes her head and tries to give the baggie back, but he presses it into her hand. Then he stands up before she can say anything and vanishes onto the dance floor.

Now the bartender is setting a tray of shots on the table. Samuel hands them round. Leah says she doesn't want any, but Samuel says he won't take no for an answer. He raises his glass and says: 'We have to, because soon it will all be over,' and Hanna wonders if he's referring to Ivan's apparent disapproval of the house idea. Leah throws back the shot and gags; it looks like she vomits into her mouth but manages to swallow it back down. Samuel watches Hanna with eyes at half-mast and pushes the shot glass across the table. Behind him, the dancers are moving in their cylinders. The walls are closing in. The music is sharp and spiky. Hanna tries to calm her breathing, but it's difficult, it feels like the oxygen in this place is running out. Samuel takes another shot. Then he presses a lemon to his teeth, his face contorted. He looks like he's sucking venom from a snakebite. He shouts at Hanna to do it too. His eyes are drooping.

Hanna does as he says but makes a mistake – she takes the lemon first, then the shot, and the salt last of all, and Samuel and Leah laugh. Their laughter sounds like shattering porcelain. Then she spots Tom across the room, on the other side of the dance floor. He's standing stock still and staring at her. She wonders how long he's been standing there. He gestures at her with his index and middle fingers to signal that he's watching her, as if he wants to say *I'm making sure you keep your end of the bargain*. He mimes silently: *I see you*.

It feels like everything is swaying, changing shape. She looks at Samuel and Leah. Their faces melt. She doesn't know if it's the light, but she doesn't recognise them.

Behind them, Tom is pointing at her urgently. She nods at him and stands up.

Soon she's in the toilet cubicle, trying to figure out how this is done. The wall is black with graffiti. She scatters some of the white powder on the lid of the toilet. It's not the fine dust she was expecting, but grains that have stuck together until they resemble something like white gravel. But even so she manages to shape it into two lines with her Visa card, the way she's seen people do in movies. But she has no tool to snort it into her nostril, so she leans forward to suck it directly into her nose. The pungent odour of urine hits her. The floor is covered in grit and dirty bits of paper. She presses her index finger to one nostril and inhales the white gravel with the other. The bridge of her nose immediately goes numb. Then she sits down on the toilet and waits for it to hit, without really knowing how it's going to feel.

After a while she gives up and leaves the cubicle to look in the mirror. That's when something happens. She's surprised at the strength of it, like a violent hug from behind. The pressure makes her ears close off. She looks at herself in the mirror to find that her upper lip and nose are white, and she quickly rinses off under the tap.

Then she stands still and feels her energy rise.

At first the intensity is worrying. It's getting stronger and stronger and she doesn't know when it will plateau, but after a while she gets used to the acceleration. Suddenly the euphoria comes bubbling up. A tickle flutters in her stomach and rises to her head, where it crackles.

She thinks: so this is how people do it. She thinks: they cheat.

She goes back to the stall. When she scatters the white stuff on the lid, she accidentally pours out half the baggie. She snorts it up.

Something breaks. There's a crunch in the bridge of her nose, and here it comes, a trickle, the hot blood flowing over her lips and onto her chin.

She leaves the cubicle and goes to the mirror. The sight reassures her. It's not blood, just mucus, like clear water. She takes a wad of paper towel from the wall and blows her nose, but it keeps running. She blows her nose again. It keeps coming. She dabs her nose and blows it again and again. When the flood finally stops, she goes back out to the throng.

The room has changed. It has no depth now. It's a two-dimensional image, full of details that are hard to tell apart because the perspective is all messed up. And somewhere in that image, Vera comes walking by, diagonally through the frame, in a white dress, with a drink in one hand.

She catches sight of Hanna and stops.

Then she changes direction and comes for her. The image is distorted like in a funhouse mirror. And Hanna finds, without having many feelings about it, that Vera looks better than she remembered, young and dewy, her hair in a ponytail, her heart necklace at her throat.

Without hesitation, Hanna turns round and goes back to the toilets to hide. Shining from the ceiling is a spitting fluorescent tube light, and something isn't right. The walls of the toilets are no longer black; they're red. She tries to figure out why. All over the place are shiny metal panels that are meant to be

237

mirrors. In front of these mirrors are men. Men everywhere. Men pissing into metal bowls full of ice cubes, men standing around in groups and muttering, men staring at her.

Suddenly Tom is in front of her. He's smiling, but his gaze is grim. He asks how she's feeling. She doesn't know how to describe it. Tom takes her by the arm and steers her into one of the cubicles. He's standing very close, breathing on her. His eyes are black. There's no life in them.

He says: 'How much did you take?'

She wants to answer him, but she doesn't know what 'a lot' is in this context. She's having trouble getting the words out.

She shakes her head and says: 'I don't know.'

'What do you mean?'

'I've never taken cocaine before.'

He grins: 'It's not cocaine.'

'What?'

'It's K.'

She manages: 'K?'

She wants to ask him what that is, but before she can formulate the words he's gone.

The door of the cubicle slams and she's alone. She looks around. For some reason, she's no longer in the cubicle. She's in front of the mirrors. Her mouth tastes bitter and toxic. She tries to swallow, but it's like there's something swollen and blocking the way. Vera comes in. But it's not really Vera. It's Vera but not Vera. Her voice is different. It's asking how she feels. It's asking about her life. It has a stern tone and a certain lag. Each time her mouth moves, it takes a moment to hear her voice.

Vera's mouth says: *We have to talk.*

Then comes the sound: 'We have to talk.'

Hanna takes a step back.

Vera takes a step forward. Her mouth says: *Say something.*

Then comes the sound: 'Say something.'

And soon thereafter: 'You can't get rid of me.'

Hanna wants to say she can too, but nothing comes out. Vera takes a step forward, and then another, while Hanna backs away. Eventually her back is against the wall.

Hanna says: 'I don't want to.'

Vera says: 'So I gathered.'

'Stop it.'

'I just want to understand.'

Again Hanna says: 'Stop it.'

But Vera keeps going: 'Tell me why you disappeared!'

Hanna closes her eyes, she wants to disappear inside herself, but Vera won't give up, she raises her voice: 'Say something! Just say something!'

Hanna says: 'Stop it!'

That makes Vera angry, and she says: 'You have to tell me!'

Hanna screws her eyes shut. Everything goes black. Until a tiny flame appears. Then it grows into a white light, which blinds her. And when she opens her eyes, she is transformed. She lowers her head and looks down at her wings. The feathers gleam in the fluorescent light. She unfurls her claws and sees how sharp they are. She observes them in the light, admiring them. She paws at the sawdust with them. Hanna says: 'Do you want to know?'

Vera doesn't answer. She looks frightened.

Hanna raises her voice: 'Do you *really* want to know?'

And in her peripheral vision she sees that men have gathered around them, muttering and whispering, wondering which cock is going to win.

And Hanna says: 'This is on you, then,' and launches into an attack, so Vera will understand who she's dealing with. She claws wildly. Only one will exit this ring alive. She doesn't stop even when Vera starts to cry. She strikes again and again, and she tells her why she left, she spares no detail, she doesn't hold back, and at the same time she spreads her giant wings until they fill the room. She tells Vera how tragic she is and how empty she is and how no one wants to be with her, and at last Vera is backed into a corner, her hand over her mouth. And the men stand around them in a circle, cheering and pointing. And when she sees Vera's tears, sees her sag into the sawdust at last, she deals the fatal blow. She fixes her gaze on her and tells her that everyone knows she's sick and it's common knowledge that she's as crazy as her mother, that she's a chameleon, a cringy suck-up who tells lies to make people like her, she says that she's had enough, that she is breaking things off here and now, that she's moving on, that her new life starts now – and she explains about her new boyfriend, about their island, about his father who will finance all of it, and she ends by saying: 'This is the last time we will see each other.'

Then she spreads her wings and flies out of the room.

18

Her face is dripping with sweat. Her mouth is dry. She can't walk in a straight line. She searches for the table. She wants to sit down. The floor is undulating. She finds Samuel in the booth. He's in the same spot, slouched down. Tom and Leah are nowhere to be seen.

Hanna sits down next to him. She's dizzy. She doesn't quite know what just happened and isn't sure she wants to know, either. The ceiling tilts. She places a hand on Samuel's back to get her balance.

She fills a glass with ice and water to quench her thirst. But when she takes a big drink, she realises it's vodka. She gags. But even so, she takes another sip. She imagines it's good for her. Then she takes yet another sip. She tries to breathe deeply.

She turns to Samuel. She realises he isn't moving. She shakes him, but he doesn't wake up. She says his name, over and over:

'Samuel. Samuel!' At last he opens his eyes, but only halfway.
He says: 'I want to kill Ivan.'

Hanna: 'Are you okay?'

'He's going to say no.'

'Don't say that.'

He repeats: 'I want to kill him.'

'Maybe we should go home.'

At that he laughs, and it makes her happy, but his laughter
changes, it's strange, it's like crying. He shakes in her arms, but
she doesn't know why. As she holds him, she is struck by the
urge to tell him everything, why she left Sweden, that her
mother isn't dead. She's even prepared to tell him about Vera.
But suddenly Samuel stands up and says: 'I don't feel so good.'

19

When they get to his front door, she has to shake him there in
the back seat to wake him up. Once they've climbed out of
the Uber, he darts behind a dumpster.

He hunches over for a moment, perfectly still, his mouth
open, and she walks up to hold him from behind.

'Are you okay?' she says.

'Go away!' he says.

She backs off a step to give him space. She can tell the drug
is still in her blood, because the world is still distorted. The rusty
spots on the dumpster move, detaching themselves from the
metal and slipping to the ground. She wants to lie down. She
wants to sink down beside Samuel's feet and catch her breath.

After a while, Samuel emerges from the shadows, his face
pale. She gives him her jacket and he uses it to wipe his face.
Then he tosses it on the ground. Maybe he's forgotten it's a
jacket. She leads him through the door of his building.

In the lift, she looks at her face and is surprised. She likes what she sees. Those eyes radiate strength. She knows who she is. She knows what's going to happen now.

Samuel lies at her feet, curled up on the lift floor. When they reach his level she helps him up. He's heavy, but she manages to lead him to the door.

She unlocks it and gets him into his front hall. He staggers to the bathroom and bends down to drink directly from the tap. Then he squeezes a few centimetres' worth of toothpaste straight into his mouth, gargles, and spits.

She helps him into the bedroom. There he falls backwards, landing on his back. He starts to pull off his trousers. She helps. His legs get tangled in the trousers. His belt is hard to undo, and she asks him to help, but he's drunk and floundering.

She tries again.

Samuel laughs, and she smiles at him. Once again the drug makes itself known, because when she loses her balance, she falls to the ceiling rather than the bed. As luck would have it, she lands on the bed again, right next to Samuel, and that's when it happens. It feels natural. She brings her lips to his and presses her tongue into his mouth. It tastes like toothpaste. At first he doesn't respond, but then she feels his tongue start to move and soon he's as greedy as she is. He sucks in her lips, licks her throat, her neck, and she leans her face back and he pulls her close, and she knows that from now on nothing will be enough, and he feels the same way, she can tell, he's so eager he's fumbling his hands all over her body, and she pulls off her dress, bra, tights, so she will be completely bare before him, and when she's finally naked he stops and looks her in the eye.

Everything stands still.

They face one another in silence.

She feels the cool evening breeze on her skin.

Then she leans forward, and he leans back, so she can take off his briefs. She sees his flat stomach quake. And soon his cock is in her mouth, and it's soft, but that doesn't matter, because she knows this is the first time of many, this cock is her future, and soon it's growing, and her sucking makes a smacking noise, and she feels her saliva down her hand, and she lies on her back and pulls up her knees and he doesn't hesitate, he moves above her and she pulls him close and brings him inside. He pushes in gently and she holds her breath while his silhouette expands and shrinks in the dark, from little Samuel to big strong Samuel, and then back again, and she rests her hands on his hips and runs her fingers along his sides and it's like she's carving out his shape with her fingers, from his hipbones to his chest, carving out his nakedness, which has always been there, which she's dreamed of, and he's carving out hers, and it's a shape she likes because Samuel is the one creating it with his fingertips across her skin, from the back of her neck down to the spot between her breasts, and then to her nipple, and it keeps going, wherever he moves his hands her shape emerges, and now and then a gust of wind tugs at the curtain and the glow of the streetlight outside bursts in for a second, and she sees his eyes flash, like someone is taking a picture, and she sees her own body, and then she sees what her shape creates, what they're making together, she's the girl in the stone, the statue at the Norwegian embassy venue, finally about to leave the stone, his hand squeezes hers hard and lifts her out of the darkness, and she's close now, on her way up, she can feel it, his mouth is agape, and she grabs his arse and moves harder against him, and with each thrust he pushes her up, closer to the surface, so she can find her way out, and soon she feels the familiar squeeze from her tailbone up to that incandescent point, she feels it, she rises into the light.

20

She wakes at dawn. She kisses his back. Tentatively nuzzles his neck. He lets out a snore. He's so cute. She wants to laugh but doesn't dare. She doesn't want to wake him. She doesn't want this moment to end. It finally happened – he touched her, stroked her, kissed her, sucked on her nipples, like a man obsessed, she saw it in his eyes, the wildness as he lost himself. And when he finally came she saw his whole being pause, as though he were in freefall. First he made some strange noises, but the rest happened in silence. It was the most beautiful thing she's ever seen. She will never forget his eyes, his expression of surprise and tenderness.

Now he's lying next to her, fast asleep.

She rests her head on his chest and her legs over his thighs, to fall asleep again, skin to skin with Samuel. The first of many mornings. She shifts closer to his body and closes her eyes. Tom can try to take it away from her, but now she's got Samuel. This is her new life, their intertwined bodies, going back to sleep in the dawn light while the birds in the trees outside start to chirp. This is how their days in the house will begin. The house that will be theirs in only a few hours. She will make sure of it.

He can depend on her.

21

She arrives at Ivan's hotel at nine and takes a seat at a table in the lobby café. She picks a spot that gives her a view of both the lifts and the front entrance. She only got two hours of sleep, but she's so full of adrenaline that it's keeping her hangover at bay. Once this idea occurred to her, it was impossible to go back to sleep.

After half an hour, she begins to doubt he'll show up.

She looks at the clock. She knows she needs to leave soon or risk running into Samuel. But at quarter to eleven, the big glass doors facing the street open and Ivan walks in.

Behind him is a woman in her forties, wearing a black suit and white shirt. She's carrying two binders and a leather portfolio. They stop at the check-in desk and Ivan says something to her. Hanna gets the sense that this woman is an assistant of some sort, because he seems to be giving her instructions, including lots of gestures and a serious gaze.

When he's finished, the woman heads for the lifts while Ivan stays put, his eyes on his phone.

That's when Hanna approaches him.

'Hi,' she says.

He looks up from his phone. 'Why, hello there.'

'Thanks for yesterday.'

'Thank *you*,' he says. 'Things got a little crazy, huh?'

She's not sure what he's referring to, but she says: 'Yes.'

'I'm sorry,' he says: 'I just have to answer this one thing.'

He types on his phone while she waits in silence. When he's done, she points at her table and says: 'Can we talk for a minute?'

He says: 'I'm afraid I don't have time.'

She says: 'It's important.'

'I'm meeting Samuel.'

'I know. That's what I want to talk about.'

He looks at her quizzically. Then he throws up his hands and says: 'I'm all yours.'

They go over to the table and take a seat.

They don't say anything for a moment, until he says: 'Well?'

She says: 'Have you decided whether you're going to say yes?'

'To what?'

'To Samuel's question. About the money. The house.'

He looks at her in silence: 'What does that have to do with you?'

'As you know, Samuel and I are pretty close.'

He doesn't respond.

She continues: 'And I need to know.'

'I'm meeting him at noon, and we'll talk then.'

'And what are you going to say?'

'That's between me and Samuel.'

'Not really.'

'What do you mean?'

'I don't think Samuel is able to be himself with you.'

'Okay?'

'That's why I'm here.'

He looks at his gold watch. Then he glances out at the street. He heaves a sigh and turns back to her.

He says: 'What are you talking about?'

'You are going to give him everything he asks for.'

Ivan's gaze deepens, but his expression doesn't change.

He says: 'Oh, really?'

She continues: 'You will say yes to what he wants. And you will not tell him I was here.

'Or else I'll tell him about the assault.'

Hanna had expected he would be frightened, but there's no fear in his gaze.

Finally: a shift in his expression.

He says: 'What did you say?'

'Or else I will tell Samuel about what you did by the pool. I'll tell anyone who will listen. And I think lots of people will.'

He stares at her, his face impassive.

For the first time, she feels worried. She was prepared for him to deny it, or argue, or go along with her demands – but she wasn't expecting silence.

It's painful to look into his scowling eyes, but at the same time she doesn't want to look away. At last, when she realises he's not going to say anything, she stands up.

She says: 'Now you know what will happen if you don't do as I say.'

Then she leaves him at the table and heads for the exit.

22

She doesn't get out of bed for the rest of the day. She has a stomach ache, but no matter how hard she racks her brains, she can't see how she did anything wrong. Ivan is fickle and needed a nudge in the right direction.

To give herself a sense of security, she inhales Samuel's scent. She sits on the edge of the bed and brings her fingers to her nose. She doesn't shower. She wants their night to remain in her skin. She longs for later that evening when they'll see each other again.

Samuel has invited the group to the same pavement café where they ate dinner that first night, where he'll tell them about Ivan's decision.

She wishes time would go faster.

When the sun finally starts to go down, she gets ready and heads out on the town. Here and there, street sweepers glide along, cleaning up after the festivities. It smells like spilled beer and cleaning products. Broken plastic glasses are scattered along the façades and get sucked up by the machines. She wanders along slowly. She likes to watch the cleaners work. Where the machines have already gone by, the streets are shiny and washed clean, gleaming in an otherworldly sort of way in the evening sun. She feels more at ease now, as she gets closer and closer to their meeting. There's nothing more she can do.

As she crosses the small square behind the embassy, a church bell rings out. She stops, and all around her she sees other people doing the same thing, stopping short on the pavement and looking up at the sky while the clang echoes through the buildings and makes the cobblestones vibrate, finding its way into her body. It feels like a sign.

23

When Hanna arrives at the pavement café, she notices right away that something is wrong. Leah and Tom are staring at nothing, without speaking. Samuel is leaning back in his chair, smoking. He greets her with a curt nod.

Hanna sits down. 'Hi.'

Samuel stubs out his cigarette in the ashtray and says: 'He said no.'

Then he looks at her. She has never seen him look so grim.

Hanna: 'What?'

'Ivan said no.'

Hanna turns to Tom. He nods gravely.

Samuel shakes his head: 'And not just that. He said he's putting all payouts on hold.'

'What?'

Samuel lights another cigarette.

Hanna turns to look at Leah and Tom again, but their faces are blank.

Tom pours her a glass of red wine. She takes the glass and brings it to her lips, but the scent repulses her. It smells smoky and heavy. She wonders why Tom has to drink right now. It's like nothing is holy. She sets the glass down on the table.

'It's all over,' Samuel repeats.

Tom stares at nothing. Leah smokes in silence.

Samuel tells them about the meeting. He had overslept and arrived late, so Ivan had been annoyed from the start. They had sat in the café in the hotel lobby. Ivan had been snappish and stressed out, because he had a flight to catch. It was all just an opportunity for Ivan to chew him out. Ivan had told him no flat out, and not only that. He had called Samuel 'frivolous' and said he no longer understood him. He had said Samuel was cut off until further notice.

Hanna tries to absorb this information.

Samuel says: 'He said it was time for me to make it on my own.'

Hanna looks at Samuel's face and finds that it looks older than usual. Faces are so strange, she thinks, the way they can look different from one moment to the next. One day they're so lovely, and the next they're unattractive. You can deny it by looking away, waiting it out, but it's still creepy when it happens. His skin looks all worn out, his face is a little swollen, and his stubble is uneven.

Samuel speculates about what caused Ivan to say no, but he's not making any sense, isn't thinking as clearly as he usually does. He lights another cigarette and takes frantic drags of it, scratches his head. He tells them about all the cruel things Ivan said. He called Samuel spoiled and asked him how much partying the group does and said it was his job as a parent to teach Samuel a lesson.

Hanna: 'But why?'

He shakes his head.

Hanna: 'Maybe it's possible to change his mind.'

'How so?'

She doesn't have an answer. She feels confused and ashamed. Her mind goes to Ivan's face during their talk, his aggressive glare. What made her think she could scare him? She's hardly the first woman he will have exposed himself to, he doesn't give a shit how she felt about it. She's worth nothing in his eyes; he didn't even mention their encounter to Samuel, that's how insignificant she is.

Leah wipes her eyes under her sunglasses: 'It's fucked. Shit.'

Hanna is ashamed for her. They need to show Samuel strength right now. Classic Leah, expecting Samuel to fix everything. And Tom is just sitting there, not saying a word, accusing her with his eyes. If only he knew what she and Samuel had experienced last night. Hanna turns to Tom: 'What do you think? Can't we do something?'

'Just be quiet,' Tom replies. 'Just shut up.'

'What?'

'You're all, "Can't *we* do something?" but it should be "you all".'

Hanna looks at him, sensing his sudden aggression.

His eyes drill into her: 'Because you don't have any money, do you?'

She has the urge to break the wine bottle against the table and slice his face with it. Stab and stab, his eyes, his forehead, his mouth, until nothing but shreds is left. But she sits there quietly.

Samuel stands up. He looks pale.

He says: 'I'm going home.'

Hanna: 'Hold on.'

She stands up, but he pays no attention to her, just places a hundred-euro bill on the table and walks off. Tom follows him.

Once they're gone, Hanna and Leah sit in silence.

Hanna tries to think of something to say. The wind is picking up. Leah's hair flutters wildly in the breeze, and she tries to keep it away from her face. Hanna hands her an elastic. Leah accepts it without saying thanks and puts her hair up, then places her sunglasses on the table. Her mascara has run, and her cheeks are red. Hanna leans over and strokes her arm, but Leah doesn't react. A flock of swallows soars above them. The sky is so clear. This is the first time Hanna has seen Leah look ugly.

'It's going to be okay,' Hanna says, but she can tell how hollow it sounds.

'I don't give a shit about the house. It's Samuel.'

'What do you mean?'

'He needed this.'

'But he's got his job. He'll be okay.'

Leah stares at Hanna, shaking her head.

Then she takes out a cigarette and tries to light it, but it's too windy. Hanna takes the lighter from her to help. At last the flame catches and Leah takes a deep drag.

'Everything is just such fucking shit,' she says.

Hanna: 'But we have each other.'

Leah doesn't respond. Her eyes are fixed on the horizon and her face is devoid of expression.

24

Hanna is lying in bed at dawn. She's back in the silence. It ought to scare her, but Samuel's saliva and heat is still under her skin. She thinks of his mouth in the faint light. His lips were as soft as a woman's. She sits up and looks out the window. There were times during that night when Samuel gave himself to her, moments when she could see that he, too, realised that they were experiencing something great. A combination of reverence and bashfulness in his eyes. At some point she straddled him, and it was a fraught moment because, for once, she had been in control of him. Now she thinks of that moment, now it's exciting to think about it. She saw in his eyes that he was surprised at the things she did. When she thinks about it now she feels both embarrassed and proud. She takes out her phone and texts Samuel to say she misses him. He doesn't respond.

25

At work that afternoon, she writes to him again, a few brief messages about their night. Fleeting moments that have burned themselves into her brain. He doesn't respond, but she knows he feels the same way. She could tell from his touch, could hear it in his voice.

That evening, she texts him again. About how it felt when he was inside her. He doesn't respond. Then she writes that they'll just have to solve the money problem some other way. He doesn't respond to that one either.

26

She wakes up early the next morning but falls back to sleep.

She floats in dreamlike images of their life together. He's pottering in the garden again, while she organises the library. They have an impressive collection of art books. In idle moments she rearranges them. At first she arranged all the volumes by era, but now she's changed her mind and is alphabetising them by artist. The Goya books take up a whole shelf. Sometimes she goes to the studio they built for her. Now she can finally paint wildly, truthfully. Sometimes she makes a big pitcher of iced tea and brings it out to Samuel. He wipes the sweat from his brow and kisses her. Then they drink the fresh, lemony drink in the shade, before she goes back inside to resume her painting.

Then she wakes up and her dream fades. Frustration takes its place. She shouldn't be lying here on her own. Right now, they should be down at the market together, picking out fruit, or eating breakfast on a square somewhere, or walking around the cool galleries of the Reina Sofia.

She takes out her phone to text him again.

Just then, she gets a message in the group chat. It's Samuel, who writes: 'Come to my place at nine tonight.'

27

She's back in Samuel's flat for the first time since their night together. It's wonderful to step into his front hall and smell the familiar smells and hear jazz coming from the living room.

When she walks into the living room, she sees that Leah and Tom are already there. They're sitting side by side on the sofa. Samuel walks in from the kitchen, carrying a tray of drinks.

'Welcome,' he says cheerfully as he passes her.

It fills her with warmth to see him in a good mood again.

He sets down the tray on the table and goes back to the kitchen. As he passes her, she strokes his back.

She notices that Tom has noticed. She doesn't care. He'll know soon enough.

Samuel returns with a cheese tray and some lit candles. Leah takes a cracker and dips it in a bowl of melted cheese and says, with her mouth full: 'This is so fancy.'

Samuel sits down in the leather chair and lights a cigarette.

Tom says: 'Is it a special occasion or something?'

Samuel doesn't respond. He just smokes in silence.

When he starts talking, he sounds serious. 'Thanks for coming.'

Tom: 'Okay?'

Samuel: 'I don't know how to say this.'

Tom laughs, and says: 'You're scaring me.'

Leah: 'Say what?'

Samuel looks nervous. Hanna imagines he's about to tell Leah and Tom about their night.

He says: 'I'm so happy we had this summer. It's been wonderful.'

Leah says: 'Okay?'

Samuel: 'And I thought our trip was great too, even if it didn't lead where I hoped it would.'

Leah: 'Why do you sound so weird?'

Samuel: 'But autumn is almost here.'

Tom: 'What are you talking about?'

Hanna, too, tries to understand where Samuel is going with this.

Samuel takes a sip of his drink. Then he leans forward and hugs his own middle, as though he's freezing.

Leah nearly shouts: 'Say something!'

Samuel: 'This is the last time we'll be here.'

Complete silence.

Leah is the first to speak: 'What?'

Samuel: 'I'm renting out the flat starting the tenth of September.'

Tom and Leah gape at him.

Samuel continues: 'I've decided to move to Berlin.'

Silence.

Samuel: 'I have to move on.'

Leah: 'What?'

Samuel: 'I've been here for almost three years.'

Leah: 'What are you saying?'

Tom says: 'Was this Ivan's idea?'

Samuel doesn't answer.

Leah: 'When are you moving?'

Samuel: 'In two weeks.'

'But . . .' Tom says.

'Admit it, you all feel it too, deep down. Madrid is kind of *over*.'

'What do you mean?' Hanna says.

He replies without looking at her. 'That everything comes to an end.'

She repeats her question: 'What do you mean?' And Samuel explains. He says it's been a long time since he enjoyed his job. If he can't get any respect at the embassy he might as well start working for Ivan.

Hanna can't believe her ears. She has to ask: 'What about the island? What happened with the house?'

Samuel: 'I can't afford it.'

Tom turns to her: 'Can *you?*'

He almost snaps at her. It feels like a slap. Hanna brings her hand to her cheek to double check. Samuel gets up and goes over to the balcony door, gazing out. Hanna tries to figure out where she is. The furniture and décor in this room are familiar, but the atmosphere is new.

'Well, there are worse places than Berlin,' Tom says.

Samuel turns to Tom and smiles: 'I knew *you'd* be happy.'

'Berghain 2016,' Tom says.

Samuel smiles, and says: 'I was actually thinking about asking if you wanted to move there too.'

Tom looks at him.

Samuel says: 'You could finish writing your book there, in peace and quiet.'

Tom nods.

Then Samuel turns to Leah: 'The modelling industry here is dead. You should be in Berlin too.'

Leah nods: 'I know.'

Samuel raises his glass and says: 'I'm going to go check out housing tomorrow.'

Tom: 'Tomorrow?'

'My flight leaves at eleven.'

'Cheers.'

'Cheers!'

Hanna can't believe her ears. Not only has he made up his mind, he's also leaving the very next day.

Leah says: 'I know more people in Berlin than in Madrid.'

Samuel: 'I know.'

Tom turns to Leah: 'Berlin suits you.'

Leah: 'People do tell me that.'

Then he points at Hanna: 'But you, you're good in Madrid.'

Hanna is so blown away that she doesn't know what to say.

Tom: 'I get it.'

She doesn't respond. He stares at her with a sneer: 'Being a higher-up at the museum and so on.'

She excuses herself and gets up to go to the toilet.

Once she's locked the door behind her, she grabs hold of the sink with both hands and looks in the mirror. It's no surprise that Tom doesn't want her to come to Berlin, but she doesn't understand why Samuel doesn't say something, either about their future or about their night together.

By the time she returns to the living room, the conversation has moved on. Now they're talking about which pubs in Berlin they like, and which clubs are best these days.

Outside the large windows, darkness envelops the city.

She wants to fall to her knees and cry out, ask what is going on, but suddenly Tom and Leah are in the front hall, putting on their things.

Hanna turns to Samuel, but he looks down at the floor and won't meet her gaze.

28

She's sitting on the sofa, staring into the distance. The balcony door is banging. She's cold. It's raining outside. Nothing can protect her. She closes the balcony door. For the first time in a long time, she's chilly. A change in the air, a damp rawness. Suddenly there's a jab of pain in her stomach and she goes to the toilet. She sits doubled over and lets go. It's like throwing up, the same feeling of purification. When she's done, she stays put, surrounded by the stench, trying and failing to come up with a solution.

She gets dressed and heads out on her own. The rain patters against her umbrella. It's midnight.

She sets off for Tom's flat.

She doesn't quite know what her plan is, she just knows she has to put her foot down. Enough is enough. She is tired of the way he always tries to thwart her, how he mistrusts her. She should have done this a long time ago. A memory comes to her mind. One morning at Ivan's house, she got up early and found Tom on the edge of the balcony. He was writing, dangling his legs nonchalantly, high above the jagged rocks. She stood behind him, studying his back. A tiny shove would have been enough. She wishes she'd had the courage to do it. She wouldn't have had to endure being disgraced today.

She looks around, then turns off at the courtyard of his building and opens the gate. She walks up the stairs and knocks on the door.

No answer.

She can hear music playing inside, so she opens the door.

She calls: 'Hello?'

No answer.

The front hall is small and smells like old cigarettes. Unlike Samuel's flat, Tom's place is modern and soulless, with blank white walls and grey stone floors. On the floor is a stack of books, and the bureau next to the front door is full of beer bottles, ashtrays and glasses.

The music that's playing is Samuel's favourite song. She is disgusted by Tom's parasitism. So he's already started celebrating the move to Berlin.

She calls out again, but he doesn't hear her.

She closes the door behind her and goes to the kitchen. Dirty plates and half-empty wine glasses clutter the counter. She goes to the table and looks around, picking up a pile of bills, and finds something she recognises: Ivan's gold letter opener, with his initials on the shaft.

There you have it. The great author is a petty thief.

She picks it up and looks at it.

She can't help but be impressed by the audacity. She may have stolen too, but never from a friend's family.

She weighs it in her hand. Her fingertip fiddles with the sharp point.

She closes her hand around the shaft and goes to the living room. It's empty and dark. A couple of tealights are burning on the coffee table.

She follows the music down a dark hallway until she comes to a doorway.

She approaches the threshold.

It takes a moment, in the darkness, to understand what she's seeing. Someone who looks like Tom is on his back in the bed, and someone who looks like Samuel is kneeling over him. Tom is naked while Samuel is wearing the black-and-white striped shirt he bought on the Alicante trip. His long hair falls over Tom's legs, which are white where his shorts have covered. The music is loud, but she hears Tom saying his name over and over. He says it in a tone Hanna has heard once before, through the hotel wall on their trip, when he was having sex with Leah. She is frozen, watching as Samuel's head bobs up and down over Tom's crotch. One of Tom's hands is in his hair, the other at the small of his back. But the whole thing is bizarre, because Samuel's hair is longer than usual, and his back looks like a woman's, and as Hanna's eyes adjust to the darkness she sees that those legs are sleek and that neck is skinny, and when she finally realises what's going on a chill washes over her. So this is Tom's secret. This is the sad answer to his riddle. She doesn't know whether to laugh or cry as she witnesses this human trainwreck, as Tom moans Samuel's name while Leah plays along, her motions sure. Tom pulls her arse into place above him and presses his face between her cheeks while Hanna watches and the pieces of the puzzle fall into place, when she realises why Leah kept wearing Samuel's shirts to breakfast on their trip, why Tom has treated Hanna as a threat, why he's following Samuel to Berlin, why he doesn't want Hanna to come too. She brings her hand to her mouth. This is all so stupid and trite. Tom wants to sabotage Samuel's and her future for an impossible dream. If only he knew what they had done that night, swimming in one another's waters, when they doing all the stuff Tom fantasises about but will never experience. She feels hatred welling up. She squeezes the shaft of the letter opener so hard that it feels like the gold will melt. She stands in the darkness, surrounded by music, and is so shaken by what she's witnessing that at first she doesn't realise she has pressed the tip of the letter opener into her palm, but soon the pain radiates into her fingertips and up along her wrist, but it's a good pain because it's freeing, so she doesn't stop, and the louder Tom gasps and groans, the deeper she presses the tip into her flesh, and she keeps going as he cries out *I'm coming, I'm coming now Samuel, I'm coming, Samuel, Samuel, now, Samuel,* until she turns round and walks out.

29

She reels along through the downpour. The rain rushes through the gutters like a river. She tries to hail a cab but it's no use. At last she finds a bar that has opened its wall of windows to the street. She sits at the bar and orders a glass of wine. She drinks it fast. Then she orders another.

After yet another glass, she finally feels calmer. Her hatred has subsided a bit. She thinks about Tom's moans in the darkness. He seems less threatening now that she's seen how trapped he is. Let him pretend, he'll never get to experience what she and Samuel have.

Once she's ordered her fourth glass, the bartender turns on the TV above the bar. A reporter is summarising the day's bullfights.

She drinks her wine and watches the matador move in the sunshine. His pink cape gleams. The bull glares at him. The audience murmurs anxiously. The sawdust is neatly raked, soft. She takes note that the image looks like Goya's *Bullfight*, with the black bull standing still and magnificent in the centre of the ring, surrounded by the audience. After a while, it begins to move towards the matador.

Hanna puts down her glass. The drama is hypnotic. First the bull's steps are slow, then quick, until without warning it charges, and it all happens so fast that the matador can't get away but is tossed into the boards. He falls to the ground and lies motionless.

The bull backs away and glares at him.

But soon the matador wakes up and tries to get to his feet. The bull attacks again. It knocks the matador to the ground and lowers its head to thrust its horns under his body and tosses him into the air. The matador lands on his back, hard. The audience gives a collective gasp. Then the bull slams right into him again. The sequins flash in the sun as the matador is tossed here and there like a rag doll. The bull is wild now, goring him again and again, as if obsessed. The audience screams. But suddenly the bull stops and backs off a few metres, pausing to observe its victim. Hanna thinks at first that the matador is dead, but then he moves a little. It's clear to see he's in great pain; it takes some time for him to get to his feet. But at last he stands, brushes off the sawdust, and takes out his rapier. The audience cheers. Then the matador slowly approaches the bull, and he's regained a bit of his graceful gait and pulls the rapier through his cape as if to polish it. Then he stops, eye to eye with the bull, and takes his aim. Everything is so still that the image looks like a photograph. Then he heaves himself up over the bull and sinks the rapier silently between its shoulder blades. The bull mostly just looks surprised. The black orbs of its eyes are wide in the silence. The handle of the rapier sticks out of its back like a cross, and here comes the blood welling up, thick as tar, flowing into the sawdust in heavy swathes. The bull's purple tongue protrudes from its jaw like an eel, and then its heavy body falls to the sawdust. The audience shouts.

Hanna turns to the bartender to order another glass of wine. That's when she catches sight of something in the mirror behind the bottles. It's the creature, smiling at her. She looks into its eyes. Its gaze is dark and its hair wild, its lips black when they speak to her. The words strike her with such violence that she's suddenly sober. The exhortation is clear and obvious, and it doesn't frighten her. When the creature is done, she nods in response, and the creature nods back.

30

She reaches the diplomat district just after two.

The city has a fresh, post-rain sort of smell. It's the middle of the night, and the streets are deserted. She waits in the park across the street for a moment to be sure all the windows truly are dark and that no one is coming or going.

She looks around, then crosses the small park and walks straight to the entrance. She slips on her white museum gloves. Then she takes out the access badge and enters the code.

She goes upstairs without turning on any lights; she opens the door and is filled with a sudden calm, because she knows the girl is waiting for her in there.

When the light from her phone hits the girl's face, she catches a brief glimpse of her frightened eyes. The first time Hanna saw this statue, she thought it depicted her own battle, but now she can see: the girl is also Samuel, longing for freedom.

31

When she wakes up the next day, the room is bright. She can tell from the sounds on the street outside that it's a weekend. The buzz of the crowds and the troubadours' music. The sound of pigeons cooing extra loudly under the rafters. She closes her eyes and sees Samuel's skinny chest when he was on top of her. His dark nipples and that little path of hair under his navel. His hard cock burning in her hand. Everything Tom wants but will never get to have.

She goes down to the corner café and eats a peaceful, quiet breakfast. The air is brisk and the sky clear.

She sits there for a long time, watching the crowds. Everything feels simpler and purer again.

Samuel is in Berlin until Monday, so she knows there's no rush, but even so she elects to go to his flat. She can't bear to wait.

She walks down the street carrying the little statue in a red canvas bag. In some ways, it's too bad he's in Berlin, because she would like to see his face when he finds out.

She smiles as she thinks of how he'll react when he realises he doesn't need Ivan's money.

She feels a remarkable lack of guilt. If anyone's guilty, it's the Norwegian, who failed to keep a close eye on his access badge, or the embassy, who skimped on surveillance cameras. She's not ashamed. She did what she did out of necessity, and it didn't hurt anyone. She isn't like Tom, actively trying to sabotage someone else's life, or like Ivan, with a need to oppress everyone around him.

Besides, the statue was forgotten, tucked as it was in an out-of-the-way corner of a shitty party venue.

She walks in the sunshine, her steps light, and smiles to herself. It was remarkably easy. Maybe that's the way it goes when things are obvious, when things are preordained – it's like they're chained to the future. All she'd had to do was grab the chain and follow it ahead, just as she did when she met the group.

32

She unlocks Samuel's office. The room is full of his belongings. It's like being inside him. The bulletin board with all its tacked-up post-its and photographs and newspaper clippings. Everywhere, traces of his thoughts and words, scattered books and notepads.

She sits down at the desk and thinks about what to write in the letter, letting her gaze linger on the Goya poster above the bureau. The enormous goat with a wreath of foliage around its horns, the gaunt women with their arms stretched out to him, pleading.

After a while she tears a sheet of paper from a notebook, takes a ballpoint pen from the pen holder and starts to write.

She explains that she has solved their problem. She writes that she believes the statue can be sold for at least five hundred thousand euros, and that it will be enough to both buy and renovate the house. She urges him not to ask her any questions about how she came to be in possession of the statue; rather, he should simply trust that she knows what she's doing.

She stops and reads through the letter, and she's quite pleased with the result. She leans back in the chair and ponders how to close it.

Then she sees it. A red, leather-bound volume on a chair by the wall. She picks it up and leafs through it.

Samuel's diary.

She weighs it in her hand. Now's the time to keep a clear head and think fast.

If she goes down to the post office on the corner and copies the diary, she can put it back within the hour.

She tucks both the letter and the diary in her handbag and goes out to the hallway.

Just as she's locking the door, she hears a familiar voice. Muffled, as if through a wall. She holds her breath and pricks her ears. It sounds like Samuel's voice, but she knows it must be her imagination. He's in Berlin. But then she hears it again. She approaches his flat door, across the corridor, and listens. Yes, it's him. She places her hand on the door handle. The door is unlocked. She sticks her head in and calls: 'Hello?'

Samuel replies: 'Hello?'

She's overjoyed. Now she can show him the statue and see his reaction. She hangs the canvas bag on a hook in the front hall, pulls off her shoes and dashes into the flat. But he's not alone. Leah and Tom are in the easy chairs, each with a glass of red wine in hand.

She almost bursts out laughing when she sees them sitting there, looking so proper and mature. Last time she saw them, they weren't acting quite so well-bred.

Then she turns to Samuel. He's standing in the centre of the room, glaring at her as though he's been waiting for her.

Hanna says: 'I figured it out!'

No one says anything.

Hanna repeats: 'I figured it out!'

Samuel says: 'Sit down.'

She looks at him, at his rolled-up sleeves, his tanned chest, his blond hair, his face – and it occurs to her that in every person's appearance, there is one focal point, one spot that emits or reflects everything else about them. In Samuel's case it's his Adam's apple, she realises now. It's large and pronounced.

He says: 'I said, sit down.'

She sits down on the sofa across from Tom and Leah.

Samuel points at her without a word. He looks upset. His eyes are transformed. It strikes her that she doesn't think she's ever seen him angry. He tells her that she is mentally ill. He repeats his words: 'Mentally ill.'

Her first impulse is to laugh, because the words are so out of the blue.

He asks her if she is aware she's sick. Hanna tries to laugh again but fails. Then he says, once more, that she is sick. That she is 'sick in the head'. He won't stop saying it. He shouts it, even: 'Sick in the head!'

She looks at him while he shouts.

'It's all your fault.'

She tries to work out what he means.

'I saw Ivan in Berlin yesterday. He finally told me why he said no. Can you guess?'

'No.'

'He also told me why he cut me off.'

'Don't shout,' Hanna says.

'I will shout as much as I want,' he shouts.

He shapes his lips to say something else, but nothing comes out. It's like he's too angry to express himself.

Hanna: 'What is it?'

Samuel is shaking with rage: 'You just keep running your mouth.'

She says: 'What?'

'You just spout bullshit, you walk around saying all sorts of shit,' Samuel shouts.

'I never said anything!'

'So now you're lying on top of it?'

Then he comes over and brings his face close to hers, and he's not making any sense, he's so upset that he's slurring his words.

He bellows: 'He told me everything!'

She says: 'What is going on?'

'You said we were going to take his money.'

He goes over to the windowsill and takes a cigarette from his pack. He tries to light it, but he's shaking so hard he fails.

He tries again, and once it's lit he takes a deep drag. The smoke pours from his nose and mouth. 'You said you and I are together. And that we're going to steal his money. What the hell kind of thing is that to say?'

And when she understands what's happened, a chill descends on her. It spreads from her stomach out to the rest of her body.

She stops to think. She says: 'When was this?'

Samuel goes on: 'Last Saturday. At the club!'

She regards him in silence.

Samuel takes a step closer, and now he's pointing at her again. 'You were in the men's room. The *men's room*, for some fucking reason, and you were broadcasting far and wide that we were going to fool him out of his money. *While he was standing right there!*'

The chill flutters in Hanna's chest. It wants to expand. It wants to shut her down and protect her. But she has to focus. She tries to remember what she said to Vera in the toilets. She tries to call up the two-dimensional image of her and Vera standing in the fluorescent light in front of the mirrors. She tries to remember if there was anyone else in the room.

Samuel says: 'Why?'

She says: 'It's not true,' but even she can hear that she doesn't sound very convincing.

'So he's lying?'

'He must have misunderstood.'

Samuel: 'I don't think so, because he said you spouted a bunch of shit in Alicante too. You sat around by the pool with him at night, babbling on, didn't you?'

The tears start to fall. She doesn't want to cry, but she can't help it.

She says: 'We talked *one time*.'

Samuel: 'Stop it.'

She says: 'Maybe you shouldn't trust everything he has to say.'

'What?'

'There are other sides to him you might not know about.'

'Were you trying to get close to him?'

'What?'

'Did you flirt with him?'

'What?'

'Try to seduce him?'

'He's lying!'

'Jesus Christ.'

'He's lying!'

'Just shut up.'

'But . . .'

'Christ, there's truly no limit to how far you will go.'

And then he laughs, and it's a terrible laugh because it doesn't sound like it belongs to him, but to someone else. Hanna tries to recall who. Then his expression changes and he looks disgusted, as if he just took a gulp of a strong drink; his eyes squint, and he says horrible things. That she whores herself out – 'to *everyone*' – that she tried to have sex with Leah, that she used him too, that she *seduced* him after the anniversary gala when he was under the influence, and that she also tried to go after his father, his *father*, that she has no limits, everything is about sex with her, always sex, sex, sex. And as he shouts, he flaps his hands like a wounded bird.

Hanna turns to Leah again, but Leah casts her eyes down, and it's too much, the tears spring out again, because she has no defence. She turns to Samuel to explain but doesn't know where to start, because the events he's describing did happen, to some extent, although they didn't exactly happen the way he said, and in some ways she can imagine how this looks from the outside, if you pluck those particular puzzle pieces out of the whole and put them in a pile of their own – but she wants to say that everything she's done has been for his sake, because she loves him, because she was trying to help him. It's just that she doesn't know how to put that into words now, to make it sound true. All she can manage to say is: 'There's no pattern,' but her voice has no strength, and now Samuel is shouting again and he's so loud that what she's saying in her faint voice can't be heard. She wishes he wasn't shouting so much, so that she could have the space to say she never wanted Leah or Ivan, it was always Samuel, only Samuel, she's not even attracted to women, but she can't get a word in edgewise because Samuel keeps shouting: 'my father', again and again. 'My *father?*' as if he's trying to convince himself it didn't happen.

Then, suddenly, he falls silent. It's like something new has occurred to him. He gazes at the floor, thinking. He says: 'What else were you lying about?'

They stare at one another.

Hanna: 'Nothing.'

'Do you work for the anniversary committee?'

She gazes at him for a moment. Then she replies: 'Yes.'

Samuel turns to Tom – and then back to her. 'So you're not an intern?'

Hanna turns to Tom, who is staring at her with a crooked smile. She should have pushed him off the balcony when she had the chance. Then that face would have shattered on the rocks and she wouldn't have to look at that nasty sneer.

Hanna turns to Samuel again. 'I'm getting a promotion.'

Samuel throws up his hands. 'You see, I can't trust anything you say.'

Hanna turns to Leah and Tom, who are shrouded in smoke. It's like they're dissolving into the white swirls. Hanna feels naive for not seeing their true nature from the start. Now she knows. They're as formless as everyone else, when the chips are down: Clouds of smoke, no substantive core, soon to be gone with the wind.

Samuel sits down beside her on the couch and shouts: 'What have you done? What have you done?'

And now his face is so close. She squeezes the shaft of the letter opener in her pocket.

He shouts again: 'Why can't you just stop?'

She looks at his bare neck, the tiny mole above his collarbone. She looks at the place under his Adam's apple where the skin is thinnest. She thinks about how she could pull out the letter opener and end this all in the span of a second.

But suddenly he transforms.

It's as if all the energy drains out of him. The change happens in an instant, and he sinks back against the cushions.

He says softly: 'I'm so stupid,' and rubs his eyes.

He leans back, his face turned to the ceiling.

She sees that his eyes are moist, and that does something to her. He's not threatening. He's not dangerous. That's *Samuel* sitting there.

She lets go of the letter opener and pulls her hand from her pocket and places it on his shoulder.

She rubs him there and says: 'I didn't mean any harm.'

He says quietly: 'It doesn't matter what you meant to do.'

She looks at him. He looks at her.

She says: 'I'm sorry.'

He smiles faintly. 'It's too late.'

She says it again: 'I'm sorry.'

'It doesn't matter.'

'Can you forgive me?'

He looks at her. He says: 'Why did you say we were together?'

She tries and fails to laugh. All that comes out is a weird noise. She says: 'Of course we're not together.'

'No?'

'But of course it's not like it didn't mean anything to me, either.'

Silence.

'Our night together.' Hanna goes on: 'I just mean, sure, maybe we're not *together*. But we're not just friends either.'

She turns to Tom and Leah: 'Which is something you two know a thing or two about too, don't you?'

They look at her but don't respond.

She points at them and raises her voice. 'Want to talk about your relationship for a bit?'

Tom: 'Huh?'

Then she turns to Samuel and continues: 'It's pretty interesting, I must say.'

Samuel looks at her, and now he seems more resigned than angry. He says: 'I think you should go now.'

She looks at him. She strokes his shoulder again.

He repeats: 'Just go.'

'Please, Samuel. Please.'

'Go.'

'I said I'm sorry.'

He raises his voice: 'Go before I say something stupid.'

She realises he's in a deadlock of some sort, and she needs to break through it. She leans over and tries to embrace him. He leans back, away from her, but she gets one arm behind his back and pulls him close. For a few seconds her face is in his neck, and she's drinking in his scent, so familiar. But he twists out of her grasp and pushes her away. She tries again, putting her arms around him once more, but then he shoves her away so hard that she falls off the sofa and ends up on the floor.

She sits there looking up at him. She leans in to hug him again, but he shoves her harder and she lands on the floor again, and this time her knees take the brunt. A stab of pain in her right knee. When she tries to stand, her leg folds beneath her. She falls back to the floor. Her tears are hot when they reach her lips. She tries to get up but can't do it. The pain is sharp and radiates from her knee, up her leg, to her back. She realises there's a gash just below her knee. The blood is trickling down her calf.

Samuel stands up and points at the front door and shouts: 'I said, get out of here!'

270

At last she manages to stand up and limp towards the door; she grabs her handbag and puts the canvas bag over her shoulder, but she tips on the threshold and falls headlong, hitting her elbow on the floor.

She's lying in the hallway, on her side, pulling up her elbow to inspect the wound. Black blood is flowing down her arm. She reaches for her handbag, which has sailed across the floor. She realises too late that her fingers are bloody, leaving sticky red fingerprints on the white strap of the bag. She studies the stains and recalls reading somewhere that blood is particularly difficult to clean off leather.

'Give me my key,' Samuel says, putting out his hand.

She searches through her bag, but it's full of stuff. At last she finds the key and holds it out to him. He yanks it from her hand and goes back into the flat and slams the door. She hears him lock it from inside.

When she reaches the street, she discovers that it's raining.

33

She stands under a big tree in the park and cries. Above her, raindrops patter the leaves. She stands close to the trunk so no one will see. She covers her mouth with her hand. Her lips are cold. She tries to make sense of what happened. She tries to recall what she said in the nightclub toilets when she was arguing with Vera. She racks her brains to remember what she said to Ivan by the pool. She tries to figure out if she should have formulated her words differently when she tracked down Ivan at his hotel. She knows she has only ever had good intentions, that all she wanted was to make Samuel happy. She wants to blow her nose but has no tissue. She picks up leaves from the ground and tries to wipe her nose but it only leaves a smear of soil and grime. She takes out her phone and starts to compose a text. Her fingers are muddy. She can hardly see what she's typing for all the tears.

'My beloved,' she writes first. Then she changes it to 'My dear', but that sounds too formal as well. Again and again she erases her words and starts over.

She starts with an apology. She says she didn't know Ivan was in that toilet. She writes that she has never approached Ivan in a sexual manner, that this part is a lie. But the words float around and change meaning; she's not sure about their values. At last she decides to finish composing this text at home, in peace and quiet.

She tucks her phone into her bag and starts walking.

When she comes to the river, she stops in the middle of the bridge and leans against the railing. She gazes down at the black water that churns and foams. It's getting dark. The sky is full of dark grey clouds. She shivers in the cool breeze. Her elbow seems to have stopped bleeding, but the cut on her knee is deeper than she thought. She inspects it. Jutting from the centre of it is a sliver of wood the size of half a toothpick. She pulls it out. A warm trickle of blood runs down her leg. In some strange way, this seems fitting. She touched something in her heart of hearts, and that means a deep wound, and now her skin is split open.

She takes a pad from her handbag and presses it to the cut. After a while, she has stanched the blood and starts walking again. When she reaches the southern bank she spots a taxi and hails it. In the back seat of the cab, she closes her eyes, but that's when it hits her: the image of his face as he shoved her to the ground.

34

The first thing she does when she gets home is try to scrub the bloodstains out of her handbag. It doesn't work very well. No matter how hard she rubs the leather with towels, a pink spot remains. At last she gives up and throws it on the bed. The contents fall out. Keys, receipts, lipstick, all the random rubbish she's accumulated – and Samuel's diary.

She opens it. The pages are full of his neat handwriting. She sits down on the edge of the bed and begins to read.

She starts by turning to their first day and night, which he describes in fairly positive terms. The same night he returns home from dinner at Plaza Mayor, he calls her 'shy but sweet and a quick thinker'. He writes that he's glad to finally meet someone who's working on the anniversary planning, because he wants the embassy to collaborate on it somehow. He writes that Hanna 'could be the key I'm looking for' and even describes her as 'pretty cute'.

He's also impressed by her knowledge of art.

But most of the entries that follow have to do with his job.

What she reads surprises her. She quickly realises his role at work is not what she thought.

He's not employed by the embassy; rather, he's a member of some sort of private think tank, made up of a crop of young writers. Apparently they've struggled to convince anyone to pay attention to the texts they produce. Time and again he tries to get people at the embassy to read the think tank's reports and agree to a meeting, but it never works. That's why he needs Hanna's help. If he can get the embassy to participate in the anniversary, 'maybe someone up there will be impressed' (3 May), and his meeting her might lead to a position at the embassy.

The more Hanna reads, the more she realises that the reason he spoke so negatively about a diplomatic career seems to have more to do with bitterness than his lack of belief in the work itself. He isn't accepted into those circles, he writes, which makes him increasingly frustrated. In entry after entry, he airs his grievances: 10 March, 'It's degrading to be shut out'; 4 May,

'I can't keep doing this. Standing there with my cap in hand, begging.'

Nor has Leah been entirely truthful. In the diary it comes to light that it's been five years since she got any modelling jobs. According to Samuel, she frittered away her career because she was lazy. He's annoyed about it: 'It's all her own fault and now she's too old' (7 May).

He's also annoyed about Tom's novel project, which he describes as 'an ongoing self-deception'. On 12 May, he writes: 'Sometimes I wonder if Tom himself even believes there's a book.'

Hanna keeps reading. She feels dizzy.

Each time she sees her own name, she stops to read through the entry several times.

On 8 May, Samuel writes that she's 'something of a catalyst' in the sense that she makes Leah and Tom 'wake up and dig down deeper inside themselves, thanks to all the questions she asks'.

On 9 May, he writes that she 'must be gifted to have climbed through the museum's hierarchy so quickly' and on 10 May that she promised to help him get in touch with the museum leadership, and that this was 'generous' of her.

But on 20 May, she senses a shift in tone.

When Hanna gives the group roses, Samuel says the gesture is 'a little obtrusive' and writes that she is 'starting to seem clingy' and it bothers him that sometimes she's waiting outside his door when he gets home at night.

Nor does he like the way she shows up at their usual restaurant of her own accord and sits down at their table. He writes that she frequently watches him 'across the table, at the cafés, at the clubs' and that he's worried she's developing a crush on him. He writes: 'The last thing I need is another Tom.'

On 23 May, he writes that he doubts she's actually going to make good on her promise to put him in touch with the museum.

Little by little, he grows increasingly hesitant about Hanna's presence in the group.

On 25 May, he writes that he's starting to wonder if she's even really on the anniversary committee.

He seems more and more sceptical and is considering breaking ties with her, but he writes that he doesn't 'have the heart to ask her to go, when she's obviously so lonely'. And on 27 May: 'She seems to be burdened with sorrow. The only question is, where did it come from? Today I asked her when she started painting. She said, "When I was little, when I was hiding in my room." Then, when I asked what she was hiding from, she turned beet red and changed the subject. She's so closed off, and I feel sorry for her.'

As she reads, tears run down her face.

On 28 May, he writes: 'She has to be the loneliest soul I ever met.' More than once he makes up his mind to break off ties with her, but each time he changes his mind out of pity. On 30 May: 'She's empty, and all she does is imitate other people to fill that void. When Tom talks about writing, she always has to bring up her interest in art. When Leah talks about some brand, she immediately has to say she loves that one too.'

It hurts to read, but she can't stop.

Then his tone becomes gentler again.

She has just told them about her mother's drowning accident, and he writes it was 'sad but beautiful' to see her open up. He writes that now he 'better understands her trauma' and is 'reluctantly fascinated' by her, that she's 'complex', that she has 'an abyss inside her' which he has to admit is 'hypnotic'. He writes that he's decided she should come along on their trip to Alicante, because 'after all, she does contribute something to the group dynamic'.

On 9 June, he writes about her weight, that she 'looks emaciated. Maybe sick,' and he's thinking about suggesting she get help, but he doesn't want to raise the topic because he's afraid it might hurt her feelings. The next day, he mentions he's starting to doubt the tale of her mother's death: 'We were talking about mental illness today, and she said some things that make me think she's got some experience with it, like with someone close to her. Maybe her mother was sick before she died. If she's even dead. Sometimes I get this eerie feeling that that drowning accident is completely made up. There's something evasive and anxious about H's reaction when you ask about it.'

On 12 June, something dramatic happens; Samuel gets a call from an attaché and is chewed out for lying to a delegation from China, for telling them he's a diplomat. After that, he's banned from anything to do with the Ministry for Foreign Affairs.

Now Hanna understands why, in mid-June, he stopped asking her about the embassy's participation in the anniversary celebrations. They simply wanted nothing to do with him any more.

She reads on, as if in a trance. It's like binge-eating, page after page, on and on and on, to keep from feeling anything.

During their trip, he only writes about his relationship with Ivan. Nothing about how he feels about his mother, nothing about Hanna. Just a bunch of entries about how anxious he is about asking Ivan for the money, and about how annoyed he is at Ivan's behaviour.

She reads on; it's like falling through the pages. The closer she gets to the end, the more she skims, because she wants to get to their night of lovemaking. That's when she'll finally get some answers.

But the diary ends before that.

After 3 August, the pages are empty.

35

Afterwards, she lies curled up on the bedspread. She wants to cry, but there are no tears left. She has been scraped clean.

The glow between the curtains tells her it's getting lighter out. The dawn is dim and grey.

When the sun finally forces its way in, she sits up. She pulls the curtains to block out the light. Then she takes out her phone to check train departures.

36

When she wakes up, the compartment is flooded with sunlight and she can no longer see mountains outside – it's all vast fields. She gazes out at the landscape. It's transformed; the foliage is richer and more lush.

She takes out her baguette and tries to eat it, but it doesn't appeal. She puts it down and gazes at the landscape outside.

Nothing is ever what you think. Everything changes shape. She learned this lesson early on in life, and yet she forgot it when she met the group.

She bought into their self-deception and their lies, and now she's alone again.

Certain sentences still echo inside her, extra painful ones. How could Samuel have the gall to call her clingy? She simply accepted it when they let her into their lives, laughed with her, ate and drank and danced with her, showed her their Madrid, kissed her, made love to her, travelled with her.

She looks out the train window. The sunlight is so bright there are no shadows over the land.

Who was Samuel, really?

Maybe she got too close to him too fast. That would explain the rage in his eyes when he blew up at her. Maybe he was afraid of all the feelings their night of lovemaking had awoken in him.

She cracks the window just a little and the compartment fills with the fresh scent of soil and hay.

She closes her eyes, trying to find peace, but what immediately pops into her mind is Samuel's contorted face shouting at her. He was so furious that he looked as old as Ivan.

But soon he changes shape and softens into the Samuel she knows. He's not angry any more. Now he's smiling at her, across the table at a pavement café, and she's smiling back. And now he's standing on the roof of his dream house, telling her about their future together, about all his plans for interior decorating, for the garden. And now he's lying close to her in the dark. Their eyes meet. And there's her confirmation: in his gaze is genuine tenderness.

37

She arrives in Marseille at lunchtime and catches a taxi outside the station. Her trip to the village outside the city only takes half an hour.

From the car she can see the bright blue sea and the little French fishing villages, and suddenly she bursts into tears. It's all just so unfair. Just a few days ago, they were the closest two people in the world. Now she's in a taxi in a strange country, miles and miles away from him.

The taxi parks on a small square in the village.

She rolls her suitcase along the cobblestone street and is struck by how different the atmosphere is. Different smells, different colours from in Spain. There's a fresh breeze from the sea. The big clouds look like cotton candy. A pier extends into the water at the harbour. People lie on the beach, sunning themselves and eating ice cream.

She picks up the envelope with the key from a corner shop and then tracks down the right building. She unlocks the front door and carries her bag to the third floor.

This flat is even smaller than the one in Madrid. A hard bed, a small tube TV, a camp stove. Woven beige curtains, full of snags. But there's a fantastic view of the sea from the balcony.

She changes clothes and goes out again, sits down on a bench near the harbour and watches the soaring gulls and the passing people. In the distance is the sound of a metal cable striking a mast. The sound reminds her of something, but she can't think of what.

Once again she considers calling Samuel but decides against it.

She takes in the waves, gentle low rises that break and wash up onto the sand.

Not far down the boardwalk she spots a pavement café. Maybe she'll eat there later.

The exhaustion is bone deep.

She decides to go back to her room and sleep for a while.

SEPTEMBER

SEPTEMBER

1

She hardly leaves the room for a week. Sleep is a shield. Now and then she wakes up to find she's slept late into the afternoon, but when that happens she simply decides to doze off again.

Now and again she goes out to eat. She chooses cheap places to keep from wasting money. She returns to the flat as soon as she's finished the meal. The weather is autumnal and cool, but it's warm under the blankets in her room. She tells herself that it's good for her to sleep so much, that it's smart to charge her batteries. Sooner or later she'll have to return to real life.

Now and then she dreams about him, and each time she turns on her phone, her heart skips a beat. But he doesn't get in touch.

She makes every effort not to think about him. She can't even bring herself to open the suitcase from Madrid; instead she leaves it in the cupboard, wears only the clothes she had shoved into her backpack. Sometimes she takes out her phone and very nearly calls him. Then she reminds herself about the diary, all the things he wrote in it, and what a mirage it all was. Tom's so-called novel, Leah's modelling career, Samuel's crushed diplomat dreams.

His soul was more tortured than she knew. Besides, his reaction revealed that he had strong feelings for her. It's not like he would have chewed her out like that if he didn't care. Also, there are several diary entries where he describes her with tenderness.

Sometimes she wakes up at night to find it's storming. The high winds and the smack of rain on the window tell her that

she's no longer in Madrid. She pulls the covers over her head
and tries to go back to sleep.

2

When she's been in France for two weeks, the clouds break.
The villagers take to the streets again. She spends more time
outdoors. The September air is clear and fresh. She starts to get
to know her little village. She knows when the tides will be
high and low. She knows that the clock on the church tower
is wrong, that it chimes five minutes early. And in the morning,
she wakes to the scent of freshly baked bread wafting up from
the bakery downstairs. In the evenings she goes down to her
bench on the boardwalk to do some people watching. She's
starting to feel rested.

3

One evening, she is finally ready to open the suitcase.

She places it on the white bedspread and considers it for a
while, as if to gather her strength. Then she pulls it close and
opens the zipper.

It's stuffed.

At the top is the cardigan she bought before their trip to
Alicante. She brings it to her face and can smell Samuel's flat.
Also in the bag are her make-up bag and the two Goya books
Samuel gave her back in May. She also finds the Gucci sunglasses
Leah gave her in Barcelona.

She takes each object out reverently, one at a time, as though
they are shards of a broken vase that must be glued back together.

She finds her planner from the museum, full of receipts and tickets and notes. In addition, it contains restaurant receipts and bills from their trip to Alicante, a couple of Polaroids of her and Leah at Eden Roc and the ticket from the flamenco club where she saw the group a few tables over. What she finds most touching is the sketchbook, especially the first few pages, the portraits she drew of Samuel when they first met.

He smiles at her from the pages. She recognises that smile from their first weeks together, before they were subjected to all the trials and he lost his footing.

Once again, he changes shape.

She can't help but smile back.

She reaches into the suitcase again and takes out the red canvas bag, rolled up in a ball. She unfolds it and takes out the statue.

It's as heavy as a little bowling ball.

She picks up the statue and hugs it close. She feels its weight, the weight of their meeting, of joy and sorrow, the dream of merging together, of everything that came between them and made it impossible.

Embracing it is like embracing him.

4

That evening, she wanders out on the pier. It smells like salt-water and seaweed. When the waves crash into its walls, a fine mist falls in her path.

Forgotten umbrellas on the shore flap in the breeze. Above her soars a flock of gulls, motionless in the wind.

When she reaches the end of the pier, she stands at the railing and gazes out to sea. A sailboat passes nearby. Its shiny prow cleaves the water. Its big white sails look like shields. She thinks of their boat trip to the island, when Samuel showed them the house for the first time.

Once again, his presence looms over her.

In the distance is the sound of a motorboat, getting louder and then softer again until it fades completely. She gets a whiff of cooking food, and she realises she's pretty hungry. But first she wants to cool her feet. She climbs out onto the rocks that surround the pier, takes off her sandals and sits down.

The waves break beneath her.

The cold water splashes her feet. She can see Vera's scar on the top of her right foot – and she quickly moves her other foot to cover it. She can't deal with her right now.

Down on the shore, a couple of fishermen are lugging a big rowboat into the water. The sand is dotted here and there with fresh seaweed.

It occurs to her that Vera hasn't shown up for a while now. That's nice. It's about time.

Hanna has spent far too much time being angry at her and her self-pitying ways.

Vera, little Vera.

Poor, bitter little Vera, chained to the old ways, always glancing over her shoulder, always whining about her mother's illness. Eventually, the break was inevitable. She drove Vera from her body and left Sweden.

Samuel, too, was trying to reinvent himself, and he was successful – partway, at least. It was obvious from his diary. The diplomat who hung out at the pavement cafés of Madrid was an enhanced version of the person who had written the entries, with an equally strong desire to make a break with the past as she had.

Presumably that was why they were drawn to one another. They recognised each other's longing for a different life.

And this is where the next chapter begins, where she will look neither backwards nor forwards, where the only thing that matters is the present moment, where the creature lives.

When she turns round to head back to the beach, she leaves Hanna on the pier.

5

The first thing she sees when she gets back to her room is the statue, in its spot on the windowsill.

She sits down on the edge of the bed, in front of it.

The curtains sway gently and outside she can see the vast sea, the white fringes of the waves, and, farther out, the great sails of the boats that lean into the wind. On the horizon she can make out a few pale islands through the haze. She hears the sound of children playing on the beach alongside the clatter of silverware and laughter from the restaurants.

She places her hand on the cool statue and exhales. The granite sparkles. She leans closer and studies it. This is the first time she has seen it up close in daylight.

That's when she realises she misinterpreted it.

The girl isn't afraid; her eyes aren't unhappy. Her time in the underworld has sharpened her gaze. She looks up at the light, and playing over her lips is a secretive smile.

APRIL

She looks in the mirror one last time and goes up on the roof to scout.

The view is good; she can see all the way to the mainland. Alicante to the right, Cartagena to the left. She squints into the sun, keeping an eye out for the boat.

Below her is the garden, leafy and thriving in the spring sun. She looks out at her work, relieved that she managed to finish it all. It was a sign when the cherry tree unfurled its first blossoms yesterday.

Just as she's starting to doubt whether he's really coming, she sees a boat on the bay, one that looks like the fishing boat they arrived on in July, the first time they visited the island.

Perhaps she should be nervous, but she feels remarkably calm. She's proud of herself for returning here, letting him find his own way back to her.

She relied on this new life philosophy when she sold the statue as well. She knew she was sitting on a valuable piece and didn't accept the first offer. And she got lucky – the house was still for sale when she finally received the money.

The renovations took longer than expected, but Samuel's plans were fresh in her mind, and she managed to make almost all of them a reality. Before Christmas she'd hired a local builder to lay a quartz cement foundation on one side of the house, and in February she planted roses and lupins alongside it and had a carpenter build an oak patio table there. Then she hung lanterns and grapevines from a pergola, just like in Samuel's sketches.

She even managed to finish the little reading nook on the cliff overhang, and in one corner of the garden she planted two lemon trees. One for Vera and one for Hanna.

Now she's standing on the roof in the sunshine, watching the boat moor at the pier. One person steps off, a tiny fly down there, and at first she's not convinced it's him, but then she recognises his walk.

She leans down and gazes out at the property one last time to make sure everything is as it should be. The table settings are lovely. She has picked fresh flowers and placed them on the table. Everything looks as it did when they fantasised about it last summer. There's the lounge area, where they decided they would sit together on warm nights once the dinner guests had gone home, gazing at the stars.

He's coming up the slope, his strides quick as always. He must be a hundred metres away, but she can tell from his body language that he's eager.

The real estate agent was so cooperative when she asked him to contact Samuel and let him know the house was newly renovated and available to rent for cheap. It had only taken Samuel ten minutes to respond.

Now she stands in the sunshine, watching him approach, and behind him is the wild sea, dark blue and foaming white, fading into a pale silhouette of mountains on the horizon.

She goes inside and turns on the spotlights.

The beams of light illuminate the living room, all black, red, orange and brown.

It's a magnificent sight. The murals on the wall, from floor to ceiling. She looks up at her art. She freed the creature at last and recreated the witches, Saturn, the goats, the old folks, the devils. The paint hasn't quite finished drying yet, but Samuel will understand. She closes her eyes and drinks in the odours of oils and turpentine.

Outside she can hear the great crowns of trees rustling, and the gentle clinking of the dreamcatcher on the veranda. She knows he is close, she can feel it with all her being. Time slows. The present moment is heightened, concentrated, and as he approaches, all her speculation about how he might react falls away. Soon he will see what she has done for him. Soon he will see the big picture.

———

Notes:

1. The archive of the Prado is not underground.
2. There is no Munch sculpture depicting a girl emerging from a stone.